The Strickland Sisters Series: Book 3

Alexandria House

Pink Cashmere Publishing, LLC

Arkansas, USA

Pink Cashmere Publishing, LLC
pinkcashmerepub@gmail.com
http://pinkcashmerepublishing.webs.com/

Be with Me

Former career student, Nicole Strickland, is smart, spoiled, loud, irreverent, and flagrantly promiscuous. Her greatest desire is to live a life of leisure, and Attorney Travis McClure is just the man to make her dreams come true.

Entrepreneur Damon Davis is Nicole's best friend, has been since they crossed paths in second grade, and has loved her for as long as he's known her. And the truth of the matter is, Nicole cares for him, too. There's not much Damon doesn't know about Nicole and he accepts her, all of her, as is. The only thing keeping these two apart is a past hurt Nicole can't seem to let go of. Oh, and her engagement to Travis.

Damon wants his rightful place in her heart.

Nicole wants to protect her heart from the only man with the power to break it.

In the end, will Nicole give Damon what he's craved his whole life, the chance to be with her?

For all the friends who should've been lovers.

1

Nicole

I took a deep breath, unlocked the door, then stepped inside to find him sitting on the sofa, laptop balanced on his thighs. He glanced up at me and smiled, muttered, "Hey, how was work?"

"Tiring. Had a long day. Sooo glad it's Friday," I said, as I plopped down beside him. "How was yours?"

"Tiring, had a long day. Still working," he mumbled, his eyes glued to his laptop.

"Hmm…" I hopped up and headed to the kitchen, found one of my wine coolers near the back of the fridge, dug in a kitchen drawer for a bottle opener, and was guzzling it down when I felt his big hands on my hips and his lips on my neck. I grinned and brought the bottle back to my lips, finishing the cooler as he moved his hands to my breasts and squeezed them through my blouse.

"I need to throw this away, baby," I murmured, as he slid his mouth from the side of my neck to the back of it.

He responded by moving one of his hands from my breast and taking the bottle from me, making use of his long arms to pitch it in the trash can. Then he wrapped his arms around my waist and led me to a counter. I leaned over it as he pulled my pencil skirt up around my waist. He pushed my blouse up my back and over my head, dragging his tongue from just above my ass to my neck before moving my panties to the side and gliding inside of me.

I released a low moan as I clawed at the countertop, glanced over my shoulder at him as he slid out of my wetness and back inside with his eyes closed.

"Ooooo, baby!" I whined, as he delivered slow, languorous thrusts, rubbing one hand up and down my back, while gripping my hip at the same time.

"Shit..." he replied.

I closed my eyes, leaning forward and pushing my ass out at him, knowing that would make him deliver harder, deeper thrusts. Soon, he was driving into me so hard that the kitchen was filled with the sounds of our moans, our labored breathing, and the glorious squishy sound of his shaft sliding in and out of my wetness. Faster and faster he thrusted, causing throngs of pressure to gather inside of me, making me drag my nails over the countertop as an incendiary orgasm ignited deep within my core. My knees buckled, and he slid out of me, turned me around, and lifted me from the floor, wrapping my legs around him and swiftly entering me again. His mouth found mine, and our tongues tangled as we kissed each other greedily. Gripping my ass, he pushed my pelvis into his, thrusting so deeply that I yelped into his mouth. It hurt in the most delicious way, and I was soon on the edge of another orgasm. I gripped his shoulders tightly as he circled the flesh of my neck with his tongue, and moments later, we were both roaring as we climaxed together.

*****

We were in bed now, having enjoyed another round of sex and both fallen asleep. I was lying on my back while he slept with his head on my chest and his hand between my legs, his fingers inside of me. I didn't want to move, but I had to pee and I needed to shower because I smelled like sweat and his cologne, both scents that, along with the awareness of his fingers inside of me, made me want more of him. Nevertheless, I eased from under him and tip-toed to the bathroom. I'd barely stepped into the shower when he joined me.

He backed me up against the shower wall, and said, "Why didn't you tell me you wanted to clean up? I would've done it for you."

I smiled as he dropped to his knees, lifted my leg, and covered my yoni with his mouth, licking and sucking until my legs quivered, then once again, he lifted me, this time using the wall as leverage as he thrusted inside me.

Finally, an hour later, I slipped out of Damon's apartment, locking the door behind myself. It was time to go home to Travis.

2

Nicole

This thing between me and Damon Davis, whatever it was, started eons ago in junior high school after we'd spent years as a couple of geeky, video game and anime-loving best friends. I was the one who brought up sex.

We were both fourteen, both virgins, and since we'd been friends forever, our parents trusted us enough to leave us alone quite often, all the time, really. I was tired of reading all those sex articles in my mother's *Cosmo* magazines and not really knowing what they were talking about. Damon, who was painfully thin and gangly and didn't possess even a remote amount of swag or charm when it came to girls—he'd never even had a girlfriend when I had a new boyfriend every month, although I didn't deem any of them worthy of taking my virginity—was sure he'd never find someone to have sex with. So my idea for us to take each other's virginity was a sound one.

We fumbled through it the first time, and it hurt me so bad I started crying. So did Damon, who apologized every day for a solid week afterwards. And there was the bleeding. Not regular period bleeding, but extended two-week bleeding that concerned me to the point that I told my sister, Angie, about it, afraid I'd never *stop* bleeding. By then, she and her boyfriend, Benny, had done it tons of times, and she assured me the bleeding would eventually stop, schooled me on using protection, which Damon and I already knew to do, and that was it. She didn't ask me who it was, and I never told her. I never told anyone.

A week after the bleeding stopped, we tried again...and again...and again, until the pain was replaced with pleasure and we went from fumbling to experimenting. And over the years, our sex transformed from slow and unsure to urgent and raw and downright nasty. Eventually, sex became a regular part of our routine—doing homework at Damon's house, then sex. Dinner at my house, then up to my room to do homework, then sex. A game of *Final Fantasy* or *Grand Theft Auto* in Damon's basement, then sex. As the years passed, we'd had so much sex and knew each other's bodies so well, being with Damon in that way became something I craved all the time. I never stopped having boyfriends, and he eventually started having girlfriends, but our sex continued and just got better and better. Believe it or not, Damon was the only boy I gave myself to until after he left for the Navy, because I knew no one else would satisfy me like he did.

The beautiful thing about it all is that the sex didn't put a dent in the strength of our friendship, and as twisted as it sounds, I still held this brotherly love for him as long as we were out in public or at school or around other people. But when we were alone? Something would come over me. I almost always initiated and he was always a willing participant, but toward the end of our senior year, that all came to a grinding halt. I don't like to think about that. It makes me cry and if I abhor anything, it's crying.

So anyway, I slept with lots of guys after he went off to the Navy and we lost touch, but none of them felt like he felt. There was something about sex with Damon that I never found again, a sort of innocent passion that only we shared, and we just knew each other so well. I knew what he liked; he knew what made me scream. We were the very definition of being in tune with each other. And when he came home for that short visit three years ago, it didn't matter that he had a live-in girlfriend in South Korea, or that I was seeing several people, or that we had parted on bad terms all those years before. It didn't even matter that it was never my intention to go down that road with him ever again. As soon as we were alone, it was on, and it was on every day that week until he left.

And it was wonderful.

Now, he was in Romey to stay, and our situation was what it was. I lived with Travis McClure, wore his ring, shared his bed at night, but had a key to Damon's apartment, came and went as I pleased, and no matter the time—day or night—if I wanted him, I could have him. He never refused me.

And I *always* wanted him.

*****

"Babe, your hair is wet," Travis said, as he pulled me into a hug. I'd just made it home and already wished I was back at Damon's place.

"Yeah…I took a shower at the gym. Didn't wanna come home to

you all sweaty. I'll fix it later. How was your day, sweetie?"

He smiled and kissed me lightly on the lips. "Rough, that voter suppression case I'm working on…"

As per usual, I tuned him out, nodding and widening my eyes when it felt appropriate, giving him the illusion of me giving half a fuck about what he was saying when I honestly didn't. Travis was tall and handsome in a Michael Ealy sort of way, a pretty boy with a slight edge to his looks. Super intelligent, articulate, a lawyer from a family of lawyers, judges, and politicians, and had a gorgeously veined penis that curved upward. That would've been an asset on most men, but Travis had no clue how to work it. Sex with him was completely and utterly frustrating. But he loved me; that, I was almost sure of. And he was kind and patient, virtually to a fault. He'd proposed nearly a year ago and didn't push the whole setting-a-date thing that I was avoiding like an STD. I cared about him, and the idea of marrying him pleased me. I just wished he was someone else.

Damon, maybe?

No, that wasn't it. I could never marry Damon. That ship had sailed long ago.

"…a wedding planner."

Shit, what was he saying?

"What?" I said, as I walked into the kitchen to find he'd ordered us dinner from Naba, a fusion place with the best curry fried chicken in the world.

"I said, my mom has made us an appointment with a wedding planner."

I frowned. "But we don't even have a date set."

He took my hand and led me out of the kitchen to the living room, sat down on the sofa, and pulled me into his lap.

I sighed.

"Don't be like that," he said. "We need to set a date. Right now. No more playing around, Nicky. I mean, you *do* wanna marry me, right?"

"Of course I do!"

"Then we've got to pick a date. I'd love a fall wedding. How about September?"

"Um…but that's so soon. It's July now and I have my job, and—"

"You can quit your job. You don't need it."

Ding! Ding! Ding!

He said the magic words. *Finally!*

About. Damn. Time! Took his ass long enough!

"Really, babe?" I asked, with wide eyes.

"Yeah, Nicky. Really. I'll take care of you. I *want* to take care of you."

I grinned, bit my bottom lip, and laid a kiss on him that had him gasping for air. "Okay, when in September?"

"Uh…the sixteenth? That's a Saturday."

"Sounds perfect!"

3

Damon

Nicky Strickland was an addiction for me. Her pussy would call to me on the night wind at like three in the morning and I'd find myself waking up in cold sweats and shit. I didn't want to be this person, this guy who sat around and waited for her to show up, was happy for the stolen moments, didn't mind being the side dude, but I *was* this guy. Because, shit, I couldn't help it.

I knew every inch of her body, had memorized it back in junior high—all five feet, five inches, one hundred and thirty pounds of her, from that jet-black hair that she always kept straightened, parted on the side, and hanging just below her shoulders, to those little feet. I knew where to touch her, how to touch her, when to be gentle, when to pile-drive her ass (her preferred method of sex and mine, too) and when to just hold her and let her cry. She could walk through the door and the look on her face would tell me whether she was happy, sad, horny, or bored, all reasons for her to visit, and I knew what to do for every occasion. Because I knew Nicky Strickland like you know a video game you've played since you were a kid. She was *Super Mario Brothers* to me. I knew all her levels. Had all the cheats, and the crazy thing is: she knew all of that about me, too. She knew me probably better than my own mother. We spent so much time together, years as friends before we became lovers. We knew everything about each other. *Everything*. And the sex? Once we knew what we were doing, the sex just brought us closer together, added a layer to our relationship neither of us knew how to peel off.

I loved Nicole Strickland, loved her before we ever made love. Loved her before I understood what it meant to be in love. Loved her despite the fact that she didn't love me the way I wanted her to. And Travis, her fiancé? He was inconsequential to me just like all those boys she dated in high school. She could wear his ring, sleep in his bed, have sex with him, but they'd never be us. She knew that, and so did I. I also knew she'd never marry him, not as long as I was in town. That was one of the reasons I moved back. Well, that and the fact that my ex-girlfriend threw me out some months after I returned to South Korea from Romey since I'd basically stopped sleeping with her. All because of Nicky Strickland.

No, Nicky couldn't marry him, *wouldn't* marry him, because he wasn't me. I was sure of that. So I would just remain available, give her what she needed, what only I knew how to give her, and wait patiently for her to leave him and come to me, because one thing I knew about her was that she didn't like being pushed. If I pushed, I would push her away, and I definitely didn't want that.

*****

Thanks to the Navy, I no longer possessed the body of a stick figure. I had bulk to go along with my height. I got over my fear of touching my eyes and started wearing contacts about five years ago, lost the afro and still maintained a low haircut, shed the self-consciousness that was signature of me throughout my childhood and adolescence, and acquired a slick potty mouth while in the service. When I returned to Romey to visit three years ago, I was a different man. If it wasn't for the fact that I still lived in jeans, t-shirts, and Chucks, I might've been unrecognizable even to Nicky when I showed up at her mother's house. During that visit, she clung to me like a wet shirt, something she did in the past anyway, but this time, we were adults with money for hotel rooms, the freedom to do whatever the fuck we wanted, and a cognizance of that freedom. I had a girlfriend waiting for me in South Korea, but I screwed Nicky in every way imaginable that week with no feelings of guilt or remorse, because if I was honest about things, Missy, my girlfriend at the time, was just a temporary replacement for Nicky.

Missy was a gorgeous half-Haitian, half-Columbian woman who was raised in Florida. She was running a successful YouTube channel centered around South Korean pop music and culture when she decided to move there to live. Missy Mae was her YouTube name. Her real name was Fabiola Rodriguez, and I met her at a market in Daegu City, South Korea, after I moved there to teach English following my time in the service. At the time, I was trying to stay as far away from Romey and Nicky as I could, and with good reason. It wasn't even my intention to hook up with her when I came home to visit; it was just what always happened when we got together. Sex between us was almost involuntary, automatic, and so damn good.

As I sat in my apartment, working as usual, my body reacted to the thought of her. I checked the time—1:00 AM. I smiled as I grabbed my phone and snapped a picture for her. Since I knew she kept her phone on lockdown, I wasn't worried about her man seeing the pic. Shit, I wasn't worried about that anyway.

After that, I closed my laptop, deciding to put my workaholic tendencies to rest and take a quick shower. I'd just dried off and slipped on some underwear when I heard the key turn in the door. She was in my bedroom in a second flat, hair tied up in a scarf, wearing jogging pants and a tank top.

"Hey," I said, with a grin. "What you doing out this late?"

She gave me a smirk as she pulled her pants off, letting them drop to the floor. She wasn't wearing any panties. "Someone sent me a dick pic."

I lifted my eyebrows. "And…"

She pulled her tank top over her head. No bra. "And I assumed it was an invitation for me to come get some of said dick." Stepping into my personal space, she rubbed her hand over my chest. "Dame, you are so motherfucking fine."

I smiled. "Thank you, Nick. So are you, baby."

As she tugged on the waist of my underwear, pulling them down over my ass, I asked, "How'd you get away from your man?"

She grasped my dick and rolled her eyes. "Why you gotta bring him up?"

"Because I'd like to know how you managed to get out of the house so late." I bent over and kissed her neck.

As she stroked me, she said, "He's asleep. Knocked him out with some pussy—celebratory sex. He's none the wiser."

I sucked in a breath and grabbed one of her nipples, twisting it as I said, "What'd y'all celebrate?"

She winced, stopped stroking me, and looked up at me as if deciding whether or not to say what she said next. "He told me I could quit my job, and we set a wedding date."

That was the beauty and the curse of being in love with your best friend. She told me everything, but stuff that wouldn't hurt me under normal circumstances stung like a motherfucker. Still, I raised my eyebrows, and said, "Oh, really? Congrats, Nick."

She rose on her toes and kissed me. "Thanks, Damon. Oh, and he mentioned wanting you to be a groomsman since me and you are so close."

What?! I nodded. "Word? That's cool." I released her nipple and reached around, grasping a handful of her ass. "So, wait…you screwed me, what, three times this afternoon? Then you went home and screwed him, and now you're back to screw me again?"

She fell to her knees in front of me. "What I did with Travis doesn't count. Believe me."

As she took me in her mouth, I said, "Oooooh, shit! Uh-um-um…did you wash your ass after he tried to screw you? You know I don't like swapping dick germs."

She slid me out of her mouth. "Yes, I washed my ass, Damon, and I make Travis use condoms, anyway. You're the only man I've ever given the luxury of going raw. Now, you wanna talk or have sex?" she asked, sliding her tongue up and down my erection.

"I wanna…I wanna…shit!"

4

Nicole

After Damon screwed me like he had a point to prove or something, I went back home to Travis, who was still in a pussy coma, and took a bath in his guest bathroom so I wouldn't wake him up. As I sunk beneath the peppermint-scented bubbles, I thought about Damon, about how hard it had been for me to climb out of his bed, how he'd lain there and watched me dress with this look on his face that no other man had ever given me. Then, when I leaned over to kiss him goodbye, he'd reached up and pulled me on top of him, kissing me so passionately that I had to drive home with a wet, throbbing yoni. I'd screwed a lot of men, but no one else made my body react like that.

And that scared the shit out of me.

Back in the day, our sex was kind of like a routine thing. We did it because it was fun and we could get away with it. Kind of like smoking weed. Damon's dick was like a nice blunt on a boring, I-ain't-got-shit-to-do day. It was undeniably pleasurable and made me feel all relaxed and mellow afterwards. I wanted it all the time, but I didn't have to have it to function. Now that he was a grown man and sexed me like a grown man? Damon's penis was crack to me, had been since he came home for that little visit three years ago. I literally couldn't be in the same room with him and not want to have sex with him, and I was going to have to do something about that, because I was marrying Travis.

I *had* to marry Travis, because he was…Travis. Only son of Samuel and Grace McClure—a federal judge and his semi-retired law professor wife. Successful and popular, with a bank account full of trust fund money. Plus, he'd given me the go-ahead to quit my job, and I'd accepted his ring and proposal ages ago. And as wonderful as Damon's dick was and as gorgeous a man as he'd morphed into in the ten years he was away, Damon was still finding himself. He'd left the Navy, traveled Europe for a bit, moved to South Korea to teach English, and was now back in Tennessee running not one, not two, but three fledgling Internet businesses while paying his rent out of his savings and buying groceries with credit cards. The smart thing to do would've been for him to move in with his mom until one of his businesses took off, but he said he got the apartment for me, for us, because I was living with Travis. That, plus he and his mom didn't exactly get along.

I mean, I believed in what Damon was doing, but I was past struggle mode. Damon was deep in struggle mode. And besides his financial status, he'd fucked us up years earlier and I still couldn't see past that. So, Travis it was. And if I was going to make this work, if I was really going to be able to marry Travis, I was going to have to stop screwing Damon. But shit, how?

I slid all the way down in the water, wetting my permed hair again. Closing my eyes and holding my breath, I thought about how Damon was the reason I'd refused to set a date for so long, because…hell, I really don't know why other than I lost my ability to think around him.

When I felt a hand touch my knee, I bolted out of the water, sending some of it sloshing out of the tub. I gasped for air as I opened my eyes to see a naked Travis smiling down at me.

Please don't wanna have sex again. Please.

"Hey, I missed you in bed. Did I scare you?"

I swiped my hand down my wet face. "Yeah, you did."

"What are you doing in here so late? Did you start your period? Cramping?"

I nodded and lied in agreement, because I simply could not take a chance on him trying to screw me again. That was the one thing I was going to have to learn to deal with. Sleeping with Travis had been almost bearable before Damon moved back. Now, it was just horribly bad in comparison. Hell, half the time I didn't think he enjoyed it either.

"Come back to bed. I'll make you some tea," he said.

"Thanks, babe."

Travis and I had a great weekend together. He decided to take me on an impromptu trip to New York City—shopping, dining, and we even caught a showing of that new hipster musical, *Polaroids, Starbucks, and Vapes*, that everyone had been raving about. We stayed in a five-star hotel, and in the absence of Damon, the sex was pretty decent (I told Travis the cramps had never materialized into a period).

I was feeling good, mentally making plans to wear one of my new outfits to work, strut into my supervisor, Delois-the-bitch-mistress's, office, and hand her my notice. I really wanted to just walk in there and quit without notice, but Travis talked me into doing what he termed the "responsible" thing.

When I made the mistake of looking up from my freshly-manicured nails and out the windshield, I saw Travis had decided, for some unknown reason, to take a route home that would put us on Damon's street. So I pulled out my phone, tapped on the Instagram icon, and tried to pretend I gave a damn about the latest picture Halle Berry had posted—I honestly did like her photos; they were so beautiful and ethereal—but somehow managed to look up again just as we were passing Damon's apartment complex. I didn't turn my head, but let my eyes take in the fact that his car was on the lot right in front of his apartment, and my insides began to shift. My core began to deliquesce, and my heart rate rocketed.

After we made it home, I had to fight not to come up with some asinine reason to leave at 10:00 PM. But I wanted to so badly, I started feeling anxious and irritable. So I took a bath like I always did when I didn't want to be in Travis's presence but was trying not to do the wrong thing, something I'd struggled with long before Damon returned to town. The only difference now was that I'd only messed around with Maurice maybe a dozen times over a period of months during my relationship with Travis, just to take the edge off from having to be around him all the time. But Damon? Shit, I'd lost count of how many times we'd done it in the past ten or so months. We could hit a dozen in a few days, less than a week. And my coochie was on five-alarm fire for him after a whole weekend without him.

So I sank deeper into the tub, closed my eyes, and willed the desire to climb my BFF like a tree away.

*****

Three days later, I found myself in Damon's lap, grinding and moaning during my lunch break.

Our eyes were locked as Damon's huge hands slid up and down my back. I watched him lick his luscious lips before asking me, "So, where did he take you last weekend?"

I closed my eyes as I continued grinding. "New York...shopping...Broadwa—oh, shit! Shit, Damon!"

He leaned in and gently suckled my neck. "Celebratory trip?"

"Mm-hmmmm..."

"Yeah, I figured he took you somewhere out of town when I didn't see you all weekend. I know how you gotta have it."

I opened my eyes and frowned at him. "Whatchu mean 'I gotta have it?'"

He reached between us and slid a finger over my clit, causing me to bite my lip. "Just what I said. *You gotta have it.*"

As he thrusted upward, I said, "Ohhhh, damn, baby! Wait, are you saying I can't be in town with you and not have sex with you?"

"Yeah, that's exactly what I'm saying, and you damn sure can't be in the same room with me. It'll really be on then."

I stopped moving and stared at him. "You think I'm sprung on you or something?"

He stood from the sofa, taking me with him. Almost involuntarily, I wrapped my legs around his waist as he walked us to his bedroom. Once there, he laid me on the bed and settled between my legs, gliding back inside me so deeply that I released a gasp. "You *are* sprung...and so am I," he finally answered me.

"Ohhhhhhh! No...I'm...not."

He thrusted deeper. "Yes, you are."

"Damon...do you think I'm still gonna be screwing you after I marry Travis?"

"I think if we stop screwing, you and Travis are going to break up, because me and my dick are the only things making being with him bearable for you."

"For your...shit! For your information, we were in a relationship and got engaged without you even being in the country."

He started plunging faster and faster inside of me, his voice vibrating from the impact of his pelvis hitting mine. "Yeah...but—damn, Nick! Shit! But-but, you were screwing someone else then. Remember? You told me you dismissed his ass after I moved back."

Shit, I did tell him that. "I...I...I can stop fucking you whenever I want tooooooooooo," I wailed, as an orgasm so intense hit me, tears sprung to my eyes.

He thrusted a few more times, grabbed my face, plunged his tongue into my mouth, and yelled my name. Then, through labored breaths, he said, "Prove it."

I kissed him as my heart pounded in my chest. "Fine. No more sex."

"So, that means I'll never see you again, huh?" he asked, with this big, dumb grin on his face.

"I can be around you and not have sex with you, Damon."

"So, I'm still in the wedding?"

"If you want to be."

He smiled, slid down my body, and flicked his tongue across my clit one time before hopping out the bed. "Oh, I want to. Gonna take a shower. I'll be in there all wet and naked if you need me."

I rolled my eyes and sat on the side of the bed, fighting like a ninja to stay put, but I managed to do it. I took a shower by myself and was actually a little disappointed when he didn't join me. When I left, I said, "Bye, Damon."

Without looking up from his laptop, he said, "Bye, Nick."

5

Nicole

I can't stand Damon Davis's stupid ass, I thought as I sat in Travis's living room. He was watching a damn *Matlock* DVD, and I was stuck there sitting next to him like I gave half a shit about what was happening on the TV screen.

Damon knew me too well, knew which buttons to push, and the other day, the last time I had some of him, he pushed the you-can't-tell-me-how-I-feel button along with the I-can't-stand-to-be-wrong button, knowing I'd take the bait. He did it on purpose, too, and I hated him for it. Mainly, because he was right. I couldn't stand to be on the same continent as him and not touch him, and knowing that, I'd kept myself away from him. Four days had passed, and I was about to climb the walls because I hadn't seen him.

Asshole.

Fine, sexy, irresistible asshole.

I was considering jumping off the roof of the condo when Travis turned to me with this serious look on his face, and said, "I really feel like Conrad McMasters is a highly underrated character."

The fuck? "Who?"

"The black guy, babe."

"Oh, yeah. Totally. Hey, sweetie, I've gotta go potty. Be right back."

"Hurry. You don't wanna miss the end."

"Of course I don't. Won't take but a second."

I locked myself in the bathroom, sat on the closed toilet lid, and dialed his number. After two rings, he answered with, "Hey, Nick."

It was the same greeting he'd been giving me since elementary school, and it shouldn't have made me feel the way it made me feel. I laid a hand between my open legs and sighed quietly. I missed his stupid ass so much.

"Hey, Dame. What you up to?"

"Not shit, really. Sitting here trying to decide if I wanna play *Call of Duty*. Theo's been worrying the hell out of me about playing it with him."

Oh, good. His cousin was there. Theo was a complete turn-off for me. "Hey, let me say hi to him."

"Oh, he's not here. His girl is due any day now, so he's sticking close to the house. We were gonna play online."

Shit, don't tell me you're alone.

"I'm alone right now."

I groaned inwardly as I slipped my hand inside my jeans and then my panties. Maybe if he kept talking... "Oh," I said softly.

"What are you doing?"

"Watching some bullshit with Travis. *Matlock*."

"Seriously?"

"Yeah."

"That nigga stay watching some court shit, don't he?"

I closed my eyes as I stroked myself. "Mm-hmm."

"You've got to be bored as hell. I know *Project Runway* is more your speed. Or old-school *Star Trek*."

That he knew that about me and Travis didn't *really* turned me on. "Yeah…"

"Why haven't you been over?"

"Uh…been…busy."

"You sure that's the only reason and not because you're scared you'll wanna screw me if you see me?"

"No…just been…busy."

"Nick," he said, in this husky voice.

"Yeah?" I almost whined, because I was right there, about to—

"Are you touching yourself right now?"

I sucked in a breath, fell against the back of the toilet, then panted into the phone. "No, why do you think that?"

"Because, unlike Travis's unskilled ass, I know what it sounds like when you're about to come."

I closed my legs and shook my shoulders a bit. I felt so much better. "Well, you heard wrong."

"You know, there's no reason for you to be over there touching yourself, baby. I'm here for you. Just hearing your voice has got me all hard. Damn, Nick. You know what I would love to do right now?"

I glanced at the bathroom door. "What?"

"Oops, gotta go."

And then his stupid ass hung up. And I was hot all over again from the thought of what he was possibly going to say. I despised him for playing with me.

So I texted him: *I can't stand u. U play 2 much.*

Damon: *I love u 2.*

I sent him a picture of Michelle Obama giving side-eye.

He sent me a dick pic, then quickly followed it up with a picture of his smiling face—gorgeous pecan shell-colored skin, slightly slanted eyes that were so dark they were almost hypnotic and swathed in thick eyelashes, gorgeous nose, juicy lips, closely-trimmed beard and mustache, a faint vertical scar on the right side of his forehead from when a bully pushed him into a tree on the playground when we were kids (I kicked that bully's ass for it, too), his thick hair cut so low it was almost imperceptible. Damon was extremely handsome, something I'd recognized about him long before he did. He might've been awkward, had a bad acne problem, and worn glasses back in the day, but I always saw his beauty. And that body of his? That was a hashtag Transformation Tuesday for the record books! He was six-two with chiseled muscles covered in tats. So strong, he could toss me around if he wanted to, and I loved it.

Damon was finer than a motherfucker.

Hell, he was finer than *ten* motherfuckers.

And the confidence he exuded as an adult? Shit! There were times when his confidence bordered on arrogance or pure assholery, and that *really* turned me on!

Next, he sent a video of him licking and slurping on an apple that had a wedge cut out of it. He was licking the part of the inside that was exposed while closing his eyes and moaning loudly as Ro James's *Burn Slow* played in the background. The caption of the video read: *This could be you, but you over there watching Matlock.*

I fired another text to him: *Fuck u, Damon.*

Damon: *Anytime, Nick. Anytime.*

Me: *I can't express how much I despise u right now!*

Damon: *No, u can't express how much u want this D!*

At the end of his text, was an eggplant emoji.

"Ugh!" I yelled, as I shut my phone off.

"Hey, you okay in there?" Travis called through the door.

"Yeah, constipated!" I replied.

"Oh, need anything?"

"No, be out as soon as I can."

"All right, babe. I'm just gonna start the *Perry Mason* DVD now."

I rolled my eyes. "Okay, sweetie."

Against my better judgment, I turned my phone back on to find Damon had sent another video. In this one, he had Joe's *All the Things (Your Man Won't Do)* playing while he stood in front of his dresser mirror licking his lips and giving me a full view of that beautiful body of his in his boxer briefs and nothing else. I smiled, watched the video ten times, and then finally rejoined Travis just as some man confessed to committing murder right there on the witness stand.

6

Damon

The first time I kissed Nicky Strickland, we were in sixth grade. We were on the huge playground at our school, hidden behind a tree. By then, we'd been friends since second grade and spent most of our time in our own little world. Me, the smart, awkward, super geeky video game addict who loved anime and all things Asian. Her, the tiny, pretty, smart, too mature for her age, geeky video game addict who loved anime and also loved fashion. I was too lame for the other boys, and Nicky was too complicated for the other girls. We were outcasts, but we had each other. And I can't remember a time when I didn't worship her.

The kiss was her idea like just about everything else we did together. She'd always loved to read, but never read age-appropriate books. In the fifth grade, she was into Stephen King. In sixth grade, she became obsessed with romance novels, and at twelve, said she wanted to know exactly what it felt like for tongues to dance or mate or tangle. Of course, I said okay. I was already experiencing random erections, especially when I was around her, so I wasn't going to object.

"You ready?" she asked, as she sat in the grass in front of me. "You know what to do, right?"

I nodded. "Yeah. I'm supposed to close my eyes and move my

face close to yours real slow and put my mouth on top of yours and then put my tongue in your mouth. I've seen it done in movies, Nick."

"I know. Are you nervous?" she asked.

"No," I lied. "Let's just do it."

She nodded and smiled. "Okay, because I'm so ready to see if it makes me moan like Lilly DuPont did in *Croissants of Love*."

"Where do you get those books, anyway?"

"The public library. Come on, Dame. Let's do this."

"Okay."

She was sitting crossed legged, and so was I. I scooted so close to her that I was damn near sitting on top of her, and leaned in slowly. Her eyes were already closed, and her mouth hung slightly open. I stared at her for a second, thinking to myself that it was right to share my first kiss with her, because at twelve, she was already the love of my life.

Our mouths finally met and I closed my eyes, opened my mouth, and soon, we were both moaning. It was...no words can describe what it was or what it felt like. But we both liked it so much that we kissed right there behind that big oak tree every day for weeks until a teacher almost caught us.

That kiss and all the ones that followed it were on my mind as I headed to Theo's house. I missed the hell out of Nicky, but I knew this little challenge was necessary. She'd actually set a date, something I never thought she'd do. I was making it too easy for her to stay with dude. So I had to do this, even if it was driving me nuts. When I closed my eyes at night, all I could see was her dark, almond-shaped, wide-set eyes that revealed themselves to be brown in the right lighting, her high cheekbones, pillowy soft lips that were somewhere in between thick and thin, and brown sugar cinnamon skin. And her body, she was so tiny but somehow still possessed the curves of a woman with thick thighs that I loved.

I missed the slope of her back and the hollow of her neck, and shit, of course her pussy. I really, really missed her pussy. But I needed her to miss me like she did when we were apart all those years. I needed her to give her time only to me like she did when I came home for that visit. I needed her to want me so bad, she'd forget about what happened in the past and be willing to make a future with me and me alone. So if I had to suffer to make that happen, I would.

I pulled my car into my cousin, Theo's, driveway. Well, it was actually my aunt's driveway since he and his girl, Onika, lived with her. I pushed Nicky out of my head as I knocked on the front door of the yellow frame house.

"Who is it?!" Theo yelled.

"Nigga, really?!" I yelled back.

Theo opened the door wearing what was his daily uniform: a faded black tee, raggedy black jogging pants, white socks, and black Adidas sandals. He was short and stocky with a messy beard and an afro that hadn't been trimmed in years. He grinned, took a pull from a blunt—another part of his uniform—and handed it to me.

"Shit, I forgot you was coming, cuz," he said, as he backed out of the doorway, letting me into the house.

"How, when I just called and told you I was on my way like

twenty minutes ago? You need to stop smoking, man."

He shrugged, and I handed the blunt back to him, letting the smoke seep through my lips. I smiled when I saw my aunt sitting on the sofa. "Hey, Auntie."

She grinned. "Well, if it isn't the best thing my sister, Wanda, ever made! You better come give me my hug!"

I saw Aunt Monda at least once a week since me and Theo were in business together, but she always acted like she hadn't seen me in years. That was probably because she was always high. Aunt Monda smoked weed every day like other women her age took daily multivitamins. She was the cool aunt, the one who always let us curse and smoke weed around her, and I loved her for that because my mom was so straight-laced, she was painful to be around. They were identical twins, but nothing alike.

My aunt had been having an affair with some married guy forever, but they were so stealthy, no one in the family had ever seen him or even knew who he was. Well, Theo knew, but Aunt Monda had apparently sworn him to secrecy, probably because whoever it was, was his father. We'd always been tight, but he still wouldn't tell me anything. What we did know was he took good care of her. She hadn't worked in years and was doing well enough to still be supporting Theo's grown, lazy ass. Nicky called Aunt Monda her she-ro.

After Aunt Monda smothered me with a hug, I followed Theo down the hall, past his bedroom where an extremely pregnant Onika was in bed snoring, to the small room he called his office. Theo and I were collaborators on an online comic book/strip. He created the digital artwork; I wrote the story. We had twenty subscribers who paid ten dollars a month to read *Foreign Son*, which followed the adventures of Jules Marks, a quick-witted, angsty, snarky African American teenage boy who moves to South Korea with his parents. A real fish out of water story loosely based on my experiences while living there and what I observed of some of the expat students who attended the school I taught at, highlighting my love for Asian culture along with what it means to be a black man who's secure about who he is but is living in a place where the only positive representation of you seems to be Will Smith. How it feels to be the only one of you in the vicinity, the desire for sameness in a place that is ninety-plus percent Asian, which was one of the reasons I hooked up with Missy Mae—familiarity.

No, we weren't making a bunch of money off of it, but it was a labor of love for me, and Theo had ridiculous talent and a lot of time on his hands, so it was a partnership made in Heaven. He showed me the line art for the next chapter, and after we talked business, we shared a beer, smoked another blunt, and I left, sufficiently numb to an aching need to touch Nicky Strickland.

7

Nicole

It only took three days of being voluntarily unemployed for me to go out of my mind with boredom. Not that I wanted another job. Hell no to that. It was just that before I started working, I was in school forever, and when I wasn't in class or at work, I was screwing someone. Now I had no one to screw to my satisfaction because of Damon-Motherfucking-Davis. I couldn't let myself lose this bet, and there was no one else I wanted. So, to combat my boredom, I decided to visit my sister, Renee, and get a Baby Zo fix.

My sister lived in a mansion with a painfully handsome husband, and their chubby little two-month old son was so cute, he made my ovaries pulsate and I didn't even want kids. Of course I planned to give Travis a couple via surrogate or something—I wasn't about to carry the man's offspring in my body—but I fully expected to have a nanny to take care of them.

I knew the gate code, so I drove right up to the front door and waved at Rell, this big fine-ass dude who was basically their driver extraordinaire. I rang the doorbell and a few seconds later, was greeted by Renee, who looked gorgeous in a yellow sundress and bare feet. She smiled, pulled me into a hug, and said, "I literally can't believe this!" She gently pinched my arm. "Nicky, are you real?"

I rolled my eyes. "Would you stop and let me in so I can see my nephew?"

"I wanna feel bad about the fact that no one comes to see me anymore, but I can't blame y'all. Little Zo is like this miniature version of his daddy and I love it."

"That's because you're so crazy about his big-juicy-fine daddy."

"I sure am."

"Shit, I would be, too," I mumbled.

Renee shook her head as she led me into the living room where I almost gasped at the sight of my father holding Little Zo in his arms, cooing at him. What the hell?

I shot Renee a confused look. She just widened her eyes, and said, "Look who's here, Daddy."

My father looked up, and this bright smile spread across his face. "Hey, baby girl! You here to visit our prince, too?"

"Uh-um...yeah. Hey, Daddy."

At that moment, Lorenzo stepped into the room with a beer in each hand and grinned at me. "Hey, Nicky. Come to see Little Man?"

I nodded. "Yeah. Y'all already giving him beer?"

Lorenzo chuckled. "No, one's for me. The other's for his granddaddy."

"That's right," my father said in this goofy baby-talk voice. "I'm your granddaddy, your paw-paw!"

I watched in awe as he kissed the baby's forehead and then handed him to Renee. She kissed her husband and beckoned for me to follow her to the kitchen.

"Let me feed him and then he's all yours," she said, as we sat down at the table.

"Nay, what in all the fucks is going on? Who was that man in there spending time with family in broad open daylight? Holding Little Zo? And now he's in there drinking beer with Lorenzo, and—" A burst of laughter came from the living room. I frowned. "Laughing and talking to him like they're old college buddies? Girl, what the entire hell?"

Renee shrugged her shoulders. "I've been meaning to call you since you forgot my number, but anyway, Daddy's basically been coming over every day since I had the baby. He holds him, plays with him, and he and Big Zo have these long conversations. It's the weirdest thing ever. It's like he suddenly wants to be connected to family."

"Wow, did he have a near-death experience or something? I would think that'd be the only thing to make him suddenly become family-oriented."

Renee gave me this strange look, and I said, "What?"

"Nothing."

"Anyway, I caught that little remark about me forgetting your number. I've just been busy. I've—" The doorbell rang, and Lorenzo yelled he'd get it. "Wow, it's poppin' around here, huh?"

Renee nodded. "You can't imagine. Everybody wants to see this little boy." She kissed his forehead, and I smiled. She was so happy, and her happiness was way past due after spending years with an earthworm for a husband.

A few seconds later, Angie appeared in the kitchen doorway

looking cute in a white romper. I jumped up and hugged her, because I hadn't seen her in like forever.

"What's going on? Y'all thought y'all could sneak in a girls' night or I guess, day, without me?" she asked, as she pulled out of my hug and walked over to Renee. "Look at him! How can he just keep getting cuter and cuter?" she gushed.

"I know, right?" I agreed. "Shit, he makes my uterus ache, and y'all know that's a feat."

"It truly is," Renee said.

"Oh, I cannot wait to hold him! I've missed his little face!" Angie squealed.

"Nuh-uh, I call first. I came over here just for Little Zo," I protested.

Angie took a seat next to me and rolled her eyes. "Fine. So, how are things? He's what, two months old now? You and Zo getting adjusted?" she asked Renee.

Renee nodded. "Yeah, it was rough those first few nights after our mom and his mom moved out, but we've got a good routine going now, and Zo is so hands-on. He's so cute with the baby. He talks to him when he changes his diaper, tells him about the book he's writing. It's so funny."

"Wait, since he's two months now—" I lowered my voice. "—y'all done started back to screwing, haven't you?"

"Wow...that's what you got out of everything she just said?" Angie asked.

"No, I mean, that was my first thought when you said the grandmothers had moved out. So...have you?"

A little smile appeared on Renee's face as she began burping the baby. "Girl, he damn near attacked me before they could get out the door good."

I threw my head back. "Ahhh! I'm sitting here living vicariously through your ass right now. What I wouldn't give for some good sex!"

Angie and Renee both stared at me, then Angie finally said, "I know you're going to say I'm beating a dead horse, but um, you sure about this Travis thing?"

"Yeah, take it from me, marriage is hard even with good sex, bad sex will not make it any easier," Renee advised.

I sighed and shook my head. A little part of me wanted to tell them everything about me and Damon, the truth of our relationship, the way I craved him day and night, and the reasons there could never really be an us, but what me and Damon had was a secret that I'd held onto for so long, I honestly didn't know how to share it despite the fact that I wanted to, so I said, "There y'all go with that shit again. Look, me and Travis will be fine. I just gotta be patient with him. I was only tryna hear about some nasty sex in the meantime. Damn!"

As she handed me the baby, Renee said, "Oooh, and it was really nasty. It was the nastiest, filthiest, grimiest sex you can imagine." She grinned as she reclaimed her seat.

I kissed Little Zo's cheek, and sang, "Your mommy and daddy are freaks. Yes, they are. Yes, they arrrrrrrrre."

Angie chuckled. "Wow, y'all are really crazy up in here."

"You think this is crazy? You should've seen Daddy in there

---

playing with the baby," I stated.

Angie's eyes widened. "Girl, I saw Daddy in there guzzling beer and talking to Lorenzo. It's a three-ring circus up in this joint."

"It really is," Renee said. "So, how was LA, Ang?"

"It was great! Such a nice event! And you already know the women lost their minds over Ryan."

"Hell, I know they did. I don't know how your ass keeps from screaming every time he walks in the room," I said to Angie, but my eyes were glued to the chubby little boy in my arms. "Nay, he's everything. *Everything*," I added.

Renee beamed proudly. "I know. Isn't he?"

"Angie, when are you gonna have one?" I asked.

"Girl, please. Renee put the fear of God in me when she was having Little Zo. I'm too petrified to have a baby!" she answered.

"Hell, me too!" I said.

Renee rolled her eyes "I didn't cut up that bad."

"Sheeeiiiiiit!" Angie said.

Renee smirked and looked at me. "So, what you been up to, and did you take today off or something since you're here in the middle of the day?"

I took a deep breath and tore my eyes from my nephew, looking up at my sisters. "I quit my job. Travis finally gave me the go-ahead. Even added me to his credit cards."

"Wow," Renee said.

"And in return, you had to do what?" Angie asked.

I cleared my throat and shrugged a little, letting my eyes drift to the tabletop. "Set a date. September sixteenth."

Silence.

I looked from Renee, whose eyes were downcast, to Angie, who wore a frown as she stared at me. "Damn, can I get a 'congratulations' or something?"

"If this is truly what you want, congratulations, Nicky," Renee said.

"Yeah, what she said," Angie agreed.

I mustered up a smile. "So, you know you two have to be in the wedding."

"Yeah," Angie said. "Of course."

Renee nodded in accordance.

"Is Damon gonna be in the wedding?"

I sighed. "Really, Ang? You had to bring him up?"

"He's family! What's the problem?"

I bit my bottom lip and fought back tears. Shit, I was going to have to get ahold of myself. I'd gone like ten years without seeing Damon at one point. Why the hell was I so messed up about not seeing him now? It'd only been a couple of weeks.

I searched my brain for something bitchy to say, but all I could do was choke back tears, and mutter, "I should go." Then I handed Little Zo to Angie and left.

I went to a couple of stores, picked up some dinner for me and Travis, drove by Damon's apartment complex four times, and when I got home, found both Travis and Damon sitting on the sofa.

8

Nicole

I just stood there, my eyes glued to Damon, my heart racing. A
thousand thoughts flooded my mind at once, the chief one being that
I wanted to be in Damon's arms. I just wanted him to hold me,
needed him to hold me. And I wanted to cry. And after he held me
and I cried, I wanted to screw him until my coochie locked up. That
actually happened back in high school. We got carried away one
night when his mom had left town, leaving him alone in their house.
I'd snuck over there and we did it so many times, my coochie went
on strike and locked up on us. He couldn't even get a finger in there,
so we were forced to stop until the next morning.

Damon stared at me.

I stared at him.

Travis hopped up from the sofa, taking the bags from me and
kissing my cheek. "Hey, babe! Look who's having dinner with us."

"Hey, Nick," Damon said, with a smile on his face.

"Uh…hey, Damon." I turned and plastered on a smile for Travis.
"Hey, babe. What a surprise!"

He grinned. "Yeah, I ran into Damon at the gas station and invited
him over."

"Great! Let me go freshen up and set the table."

I damn near ran into the bedroom, shutting the door behind me. I slid to the floor, asking myself what the hell I was supposed to do. How in the complete fuck was I going to have dinner with Damon *and* Travis? It'd never been the three of us alone before.

A knock came at the door. I sprung to my feet and took my blouse off before easing the door open, peeking out at Travis. "Hey, can you give me a sec? I need to change. I went to see Little Zo and he peed on me," I lied.

His face scrunched up in displeasure. Travis hated bodily fluids, which was one of the reasons our sex was so lackluster. He wasn't fond of French-kissing. He also wouldn't go down on me, but honestly, that was a relief because he didn't like for me to go down on him, either. The one time I did, he wouldn't kiss me for a week afterwards. That was a relief, too. Plus, he never protested about having to wear condoms.

"Oh," he said, "okay."

"Yeah. Be out in a sec, sweetie."

"All right."

I pulled myself together, told myself I could do this. And hell, I was actually glad to see Damon, had missed him terribly. This was perfect. There was no way we could have sex under these circumstances, so the smile I wore when I finally emerged from the bedroom twenty minutes later was genuine.

I flounced into the living room in a flare dress with bell sleeves and a V-neck keyhole that fell an inch or so above my knees, and my bare feet. "Well, I'll go set the table and warm the food up."

"I'll help," Damon said cheerily, standing from the sofa and following me into the kitchen.

Travis trailed us and had opened his mouth to speak, but his phone rang. He murmured, "Dang, gotta take this," as he ducked back into the living room. From what I could hear of his end of the conversation, it was a work call and those tended to go on forever.

"What can I do to help?" Damon asked, as he rested a hand on my arm.

His touch made me melt and that pissed me off, so I snatched away from him and put the food in the microwave. "Go home."

He chuckled. "You're not glad to see me, Nick?"

I rolled my eyes as I opened the cabinet and grabbed three plates. Before I could move to get the silverware, Damon was behind me, pressing his erect penis against my butt. I froze. Just stood there before having the presence of mind to say, "Damon, don't—"

He wrapped his arms around me, leaning in to kiss my neck.

I closed my eyes, and said, "Dame…s-stop."

He reached around, slid his hand under my dress and up my thigh. "You really want me to?"

I didn't reply, just darted my eyes toward the doorway, tuned my ears into the conversation Travis was still loudly having in the living room, and gasped when I felt Damon's hand find its way into my panties. I moaned softly when his finger reintroduced itself to my clit. "Damon…he-he could come back in here any moment."

"Then you better hurry up and come, Nick," he breathed into my ear.

Helpless to stop him, I closed my eyes and ears. Shut my mind off from what was logical and let myself feel what I wanted and needed to feel. I leaned into Damon's body, spread my legs for him, and whimpered softly as he plunged two fingers inside of me. Faster and faster he fingered me, his hot breath on my ear, his tongue on my neck, his other hand in my panties torturing my clit. With both his hands fondling me like that, it felt like he was playing a lewd duet between my legs, and I loved every second of it. I inhaled deeply, trying to find my scent somewhere in the midst of the roast beef and garlic potatoes that were being heated up in the microwave. It was there, barely noticeable, but it was there. Then the aching pressure that was bubbling inside of me burst, and I bit my tongue to keep from screaming.

Seconds later, I was leaning over the counter catching my breath, Damon was at the sink washing his hands, and Travis was poking his head in the kitchen door, saying, "Babe, I have to run to the office. This case is falling apart. Not sure when I'll be back. Sorry about dinner, Damon. I was really looking forward to chatting with you."

"Man...me, too," Damon said, sounding disappointed as he dried his hands.

"Oh, babe...really?" I tried to sound absolutely crushed.

He stepped all the way into the kitchen and nodded. "Yeah. Be back as soon as I can. Man, dinner smells delicious. You guys enjoy."

Damon and I stood there and stared at each other as Travis moved around, grabbing what I was sure were his laptop and briefcase, and as soon as we heard the front door close, we were on each other like two feral animals, growling and clawing at each other. His mouth crashed into mine. My hand fumbled with the button on his jeans. Somehow, without ever disconnecting our mouths, his pants came off and so did my panties. Travis was probably still in the parking lot when Damon picked me up and glided inside of me. I closed my eyes, moaned, kissed him, tore at his shoulders, and tried not to cry. He felt…he felt like *home*.

He gripped my ass and clamped his mouth to my neck as he thrusted so deeply, I was sure I'd be sore later. I was also sure I'd have a hicky on my neck, but I didn't stop him, *couldn't* stop him.

"I love you, Nick," he murmured against my neck. "And I missed you."

That's when the tears came. I hugged him tightly and closed my eyes, letting them flow.

"You don't have to say it back, because I know how you feel. I know you love me, too. Maybe not as much as I love you, but you love me. You just wish you didn't."

I kept my mouth shut as he kept sliding in and out of the sticky wetness he'd caused only moments earlier.

"I'm sorry for ever hurting you. I'm sorry you think there can't be an us because of some stupid shit I did in high school. I wish I could take it back, baby, because I love you so much. I don't know how to love anyone else."

His voice was becoming more and more strained. I could tell he was about to hit his peak. So was I.

"I don't *wanna* love anyone else. You're the air I breathe."

"Damon…Damon…Damon…" I wailed, as I climaxed.

He held me to him so tightly, I was sure he'd break me, then he thrusted harder, deeper, until he was roaring in my ear, "Don't marry him, Nick!"

A minute later, we were still in the same position. He kissed me over and over again, almost as if it was a compulsion. Then, he finally set me on the floor on legs so weak, I had to hold onto him to keep from falling. As I bent over to grab my panties so I could put them on to catch the essence of him I knew would soon be leaking from me, he repeated, "Nick, don't marry him."

"I...I love him," I whispered, my eyes on everything but his face.

"Look at me and say that. Matter of fact, look at me and tell me you don't love me. Tell me it's him you want and not me."

I shook my head, my eyes on the microwave. "I can't."

He moved closer to me. "Then don't marry him. You want me to beg? Because I will. I'll get on my knees right here and beg if it means you'll leave and come with me."

"W-why'd you come here tonight?"

"Because he invited me, and I missed you. You've been avoiding me, remember?"

"This was so wrong. I've done a lot of shit, but I've never committed sexual acts with a man in another man's house with the homeowner in another room for part of it. Only you could make me do something like this. Only you..."

"Why do you think that is?"

"I-I don't know. Because you have the best stroke game in the world? Because your dick is ridiculously good? How am I supposed to answer that?"

"Truthfully."

I sighed and tugged at the edges of the sleeves on my dress.

"You want me to leave now that I got you off, because you're

feeling uncomfortable and guilty for fucking me in his kitchen—
Don't look at me like that; I know you, Nick—I'll leave if you tell
me the truth. That you love me."

I shook my head and dropped my eyes. "I can't. I won't. I don't
wanna feel what I feel for you, and I'm not going to say it."

He smiled as he pulled his jeans back on. "You just did, baby."

Ten minutes later, I was standing in the living room, staring at the
door Damon had just exited through, softly saying, "You were
wrong. You couldn't possibly love me more than I love you. I've
always loved you more. Always."

Several hours later, Travis had returned home and was in bed beside
me sleeping soundly. I, on the other hand, couldn't seem to find
sleep, so I lay there with the bright screen of my cell phone piercing
the darkness as I mindlessly perused my Instagram feed. I was
checking out Teyana Taylor's profile when a text came
through…from Damon.

*Up working and listening 2 Pandora Radio. Heard this song and
thought about u.*

There was a YouTube link at the end of the text.

I glanced at a still-sleeping Travis before turning over and digging
my earbuds out of my purse. Plugging them into my phone, I clicked
on the link. The song was *Blind Man* by Xavier Omär. I sank into the
bed, letting my head relax on the pillow as I closed my eyes and
listened to the song. When it ended, I instantly missed its beauty and

played it again. Before I knew it, I'd drifted off to sleep.

9

Damon

"Fake for Bae dot com? You say it's a store?" There was a dubious expression on Travis's face.

I nodded as I took a sip of water. "Yeah, we sell souvenirs from around the world."

Travis looked intrigued as he asked, "So why the name 'Fake for Bae?'"

"Oh, yeah. That." I chuckled, but before I could explain it to him, Nicky did.

"The whole purpose of the site is for guys or girls who've lied about where they've traveled to impress their mate to be able to buy authentic souvenirs as proof," she said, keeping her eyes off me. This little dinner at their place was a re-do of the one a week earlier, and she'd done everything in her power not to be left alone with me. If Travis got up to use the bathroom, I half-expected her to follow him in there and shake his dick for him. I was both frustrated and impressed. For all the shit I talked about her not being able to hold out, I was sitting there about to die from wanting to touch her.

"So, your business is built on deception?" Travis asked.

I shrugged. "You could say that. But it's lucrative. My best business so far, financially."

"Where do you get the souvenirs?"

"From tons of wholesalers around the world. Most of the stuff is cheap, too, so I make a good profit."

Travis nodded. "So you have the web comic, Fake for Bae, and what else was it?"

"I review video games and comics on my blog and a little YouTube channel. Not seeing much money from either yet, though."

Travis shook his head. "Three businesses. You must work all the time."

"Basically, I do."

"Wouldn't it be easier to just get a job?"

I reclined in my chair. "Did that. Eight years in the Navy. A couple teaching abroad. Now I wanna chase my dreams."

"Thanks for your service, Damon. But, it just seems crazy to me, putting in all that work with no real results."

"Well, Travis, that's what entrepreneurship is. We put in crazy hours, take lots of risks, so that years from now, we can live like no one else. I love what I do."

"Wow, I really believe you do."

"Travis is passionate about his work, too. Aren't you, sweetie?" Nicky asked, placing her hand on his arm.

I fixed my eyes on her, hoping she'd look up at me. But she didn't.

"I am, but I don't wanna talk about me tonight, babe. Hey, Damon, how'd you and Nicky meet?"

"She didn't already tell you?" I replied, my eyes on Nicky. Her eyes were on her empty plate. Nicky always had a crazy metabolism, could eat anything but never gained a pound.

"No…well, I guess it's never really come up. But I'm intrigued, never met a woman with a guy best friend before," Travis said.

I smiled, sensed her discomfort, and asked, "Nick, you wanna tell him?"

She glanced up at me. "No, go ahead."

I was surprised, because things between me and her had always been so private, but hell, she was engaged to this man. So I guess she was trying to be at least partially transparent with him. A part of me despised his ass for putting a ring on my girl's finger, even though I knew he had no idea how deep things ran with us.

"Well," I began, "we met at Jefferson Elementary when we were both in Mrs. Monroe's second grade class. I was this uber geek, a weird kid, really. Skinny, glasses, and short for my age at the time. No friends at all, because I was just awkward as hell. The second Tuesday of the school year, I wore a Dr. Spock t-shirt to school, and this pretty little girl—Nick—came up to me at recess and asked if I knew I was wearing a *Star Trek* t-shirt. She was so intense, I was kind of scared of her, but I said yeah, I knew. Then she smiled this big smile and we had this long, seven-year-old conversation about how the classic *Star Trek* was the best. She was so smart; I couldn't believe it. In the weeks that followed, we found out we had so much more in common. We both loved to read, read way above our grade levels, loved video games, and a bunch of other stuff. The only problem came when she wanted to talk fashion. I wasn't interested in that, but I knew I'd found a kindred spirit, even though I didn't know what that meant at the time. And she was so protective of me. If anyone ever came for me, Nicky would be in their faces in a second, ready to do battle. She was tiny like she is now and tough and mean as hell, be kicking ass while wearing these frilly dresses with ribbons in her hair. It was like I had my own little fashionable Dora Milaje guard."

"Dora who?" Travis asked.

"Dora Milaje," Nicky cut in. "They're Black Panther's royal guard, all women, bad-assery at its finest. Damon is a comic book fanatic. Black Panther is his favorite hero. He's probably watched that movie trailer a million times by now."

I grinned at her. "A million and a half."

She leaned forward with a big smile on her face. "You were hype as hell the first time you watched it, weren't you? You should've done a reaction video. I know you acted a fool when you saw it."

"Hell, yeah! I was so hype, I damn near threw my laptop at a wall!"

She turned to Travis, and quipped, "It's probably set as his home page on his computer. I bet when you click on the browser, that video pops on."

"You know me too well, Nicodemus."

"Stahhhhp! You know I hate when you call me that, with your whack, Marvel-loving ass."

"Aw, shit! You wanna go there? DC *sucks*! Your love of Wonder Woman can't save their sorry asses."

With raised eyebrows, she countered, "Wonder Woman could lasso the shit out of Black Panther, have him giving her directions to Wakanda."

"Sheeiiiiit! Wonder Woman can pull that sorry-ass lasso out

around Black Panther if she wants to. Be done messed around and got her ass tied up with that rope and fucked. Shit, that nigga is from Africa. He'll Bambaataa her ass!"

She laughed in that loud way she always did. I loved her goofy-ass laugh. "Dame! Why are you so damn silly?!"

I was grinning hard now. "Because bullshit makes me silly, and the mere thought that any DC character could step to a Marvel character and not get fucked all the way up is bullshit!"

"Batman will mess Black Panther's world completely up!"

I leaned forward with my mouth hung open. "You've got to be shitting me right now, Nick! Batman's rich ass ain't got nothing but a bunch of gadgets and cars and stuff. And he ain't even as rich as Black Panther! You need to put some respeck on T'Challa's name!"

We stared at each other for a second, and then we both fell out laughing.

Travis just sat there with this amused look on his face, then said, "Wow, you guys are hilarious."

"That's just me and Nick," I said. "Best friends for real. We can argue one second, laugh the next. Always been that way. All the way through school, from second to twelfth grade, we were like Siamese twins, always attached to each other. She's—" I almost said my other half, because that was what she was, but I could see the worry on her face, and as jacked up as this whole situation was, I shook what I was feeling off. "She's the best friend a guy could ask for."

He smiled as he reached for her hand and squeezed it.

"So how'd you two meet?" I asked.

"Babe, you wanna tell him?" he asked, then leaned in and kissed her cheek.

My eyes narrowed a little, and I had to fight not to reach across the table and slap his ass for putting his lips on my girl, but even thinking that was irrational and I knew it. I wished more than anything I could take back the past so I could be with Nicky.

She shook her head, gave him a fake smile, and said, "No, you tell him." Her eyes fluttered up to meet mine, an apology somewhere behind them. I tried to make my eyes tell her it was my fault. I'd asked the question and wanted the answer, no matter how much it would hurt to hear it.

Travis's eyes were still on her. "You sure?"

She nodded. "Yeah, you tell it better than I do. Go ahead."

"All right." He shifted his attention to me. "Romey U has this tradition where alumni speak at their annual high school senior days. I was tapped to speak at one and Nicky was my handler, so to speak. She was working in student recruitment at the university, and she got me to where I needed to be and everything. Damon, it was love at first sight for me. It-it was like I'd found my other half…"

I cringed, and as he went on and on about how gorgeous she looked that day and how hospitable she was to him and how he asked her out to dinner and how excited he was when she accepted, I smiled and nodded in all the right places, but all I could think was how I couldn't wait to get out of his beige-ass condo.

He finally took a breath, and I said, "That sounds real serendipitous and…stuff."

"It was!" He turned and kissed her on the lips. "I'm so lucky to have found her."

She smiled uncomfortably. "Me, too."

I managed something in between a grimace and a smile. "Congrats, guys. Can't wait to be in this wedding."

"Thanks. So, you thinking about settling down soon, Damon?" Travis asked.

I tilted my head to the side a little, glanced at Nicky, *my* girl, and said, "Travis, I would love to settle down with the woman I love, but I know if I looked her in the eye and told her how much I love her and miss her, fell down on my knees and begged her to forgive me for ever hurting her, promised to spend the rest of my life making it up to her and making love to her, told her how much I miss her smile, her goofy-ass laugh, the way she smells, the way she feels...she'd refuse me. I know she'd say no, so I can't settle down. I can't be with her, and to be honest, it kills me, because I don't want anyone else."

"Wow." Travis shook his head. "You really love this woman, huh?"

I glanced at Nicky again, saw the tears in her eyes. "I've loved her for so long, I don't know how to stop loving her."

"I hope you get her back." He leaned forward. "You're talking about the YouTuber, right? The one Nicky told me about?"

I smiled as I stood from the table. "Well, thanks for the great dinner that I know Nick didn't cook."

She blinked a couple of times and rolled her eyes. "Whatever, Damon."

Travis proffered me his hand. "Hey, glad you came over. We'll have to do this again soon."

"Definitely," I said, as I shook his hand.

A phone rang, and Travis groaned. "That's mine. Work, I'm sure." He kissed Nicky on the forehead. "Babe, you'll walk Damon to the door?"

She strained out a smile. "Sure, sweetie."

At the door, we stared at each other for a minute or two before I pulled her into a hug she didn't resist, kissed her ear, and whispered, "Goodnight, baby."

Then I left.

10

Nicole

The day of our meeting with the wedding planner, I stood in front of the mirror that hung on Travis's closet door and snapped a picture of myself wearing one of my favorite dresses, a skin-tight, champagne-colored mini t-strap one that was so short, it could almost be mistaken for a blouse. I paired it with nude stilettos and wore my bone-strait hair loose, letting it fall to my back. I'd developed a rather unhealthy Instagram addiction since I'd stopped working, so I uploaded the photo with the caption, "Wedding planning. #ootd #hiswcw #bridetobe," and shoved my phone in my purse.

I was heading out the bedroom when Travis walked through the door and stopped in his tracks. He stood there and stared so long, I laughed and twirled around. "You like?" I asked.

He nodded. "Yeah, but…My mom will be there."

I shrugged. "So will mine."

"Uh, yeah…what about that black dress I got you in New York?"

I knew what dress he was referring to, and I only got it because he kept saying how he loved it, but I knew I'd never wear it. It was definitely not my style. "What about it?" I asked.

"I think you'd look better in it."

"Well, *I* don't. And we don't have time for me to change. We need to be there in less than an hour."

"How long would it take for you to put it on?"

I blew out a frustrated breath. "What's wrong with what I have on, Travis? This is my style. I always wear something like this. You never had a problem with it before."

"I don't have a problem with it. I mean, you look great, Nicky. I just…you're going to be my wife soon. You gotta start dressing the part."

I frowned. "Dressing the part? What are you talking about? What does that even mean?"

He stepped closer to me and rested a hand on my arm. I almost snatched away from him, but stopped myself.

"Babe, I'm trying to build my career, planning to run for office in a couple of years. I need you to start dressing for that future." He leaned in and kissed my cheek. "Wear the black dress and some more…conservative shoes. Don't take too long."

I stood there for a minute or two, really, *really* wanting to curse his ass out. Instead, I snatched my dress over my head and stomped over to the closet. As I redressed, I vowed to myself that he was going to pay for asking me to dress like a damn Quaker.

*****

Claire Thorne was a tiny little swarthy-skinned woman who stood at about four-eleven and appeared to wear a size zero. She looked elegant in a flowy, Grecian-style dress that billowed to the floor, only allowing a peek at her sandaled feet and French-manicured toenails. She was an older woman. Judging by the heavy make-up caked on her face, I'd put her at sixty. Sitting in her swanky office with her Cat Woman eyeglasses balanced on the tip of her nose, her voice was light as she shared her vision for our wedding and its accompanying festivities. It all sounded wonderful, regal, and I should've been over the moon that I was getting a dream wedding, but I felt so uncomfortable in that dress Travis insisted I wear, and I didn't miss the look his mother gave my mother and father when they arrived. I had always known she didn't really like me, because my parents weren't educated or whatever like them. She never voiced her displeasure with my lineage outright, and when I asked Travis about it, he claimed she adored me and everything I stood for, but I caught the little snide remarks her black-version-of-a-Cruella-Deville-looking ass tossed out from time to time. Shit like, "A car salesman? Hmm, to think, the judge and I wasted all those years in school when all we needed to do was sell cars," or "Your mother is lovely, but I suppose a life of leisure will do that. I mean, who needs a career? Just because I've worked hard all my life doesn't mean everyone has to…"

I couldn't stand her ass, and she was going to keep disliking me, because my career-less ass was never working again. I had to get *something* out of this marriage.

I watched her smile at Claire as they discussed some reception venue, and then cut my eyes at my parents who sat there looking uncomfortable. My mother had been trying to get a word in for close to thirty minutes. These two hags were ignoring her, and that was pissing me off.

So, with Travis's clingy ass still sitting there gripping my hand, I leaned forward and cleared my throat. "I think my mother has something to say." I didn't smile or use the fake voice I reserved for the McClure clan. And they noticed.

"Oh, goodness! Did you say something, Mrs. Strickland?" Travis's mom asked.

My mother offered her a smile and nodded. My mom was so gorgeous, I honestly think Mrs. McClure was jealous of her, and she should've been. "Yes, you all were discussing wedding venues earlier?"

Claire bobbed her head a bit. "Yes, the Holy Trinity Chapel. A favorite amongst my clients."

Mama nodded. "I see, well, Nicole's sisters both married at True Vine Missionary Baptist, so it's sort of a tradition for our family now. I'm positive Nicky would want to wed there, too."

I smiled at her.

Mrs. McClure frowned. "True Vine? Never heard of it."

"It's actually located in Bullster, about fifteen minutes outside of Romey. It was my mother's church. It's small, but it makes for a gorgeous, intimate ceremony," Mama explained.

"Small? Intimate?" Mrs. McClure scoffed. "We are expecting well over three hundred guests from our side alone. How many people can this church accommodate?"

Mama shrugged. "Fifty? Sixty if they pull out extra chairs and set them next to the pews."

Mrs. McClure laughed lightly, cutting her eyes at Claire, who shook her head. "Oh, that won't do." Then she said with finality, "Holy Trinity, it is."

"Awesome!" Claire gushed.

"Uh—" I began, ready to totally break character and curse these geriatric hoes all the way out, but my daddy cut in.

"Wait a minute. How are you gonna make the final decision when I'm the one footing the bill?" He was holding Mama's hand, and that cinnamon skin he managed to pass on to me and Angie was so red, it was damn near glowing. Daddy might have messed over Mama over the years and been a less-than-stellar father, but at that moment, I could tell he wanted to pimp slap these two biddies.

"You're paying for it?" Claire asked, genuinely stunned.

"Hell, yes! It's my daughter's wedding. Why do you think I'm here? And another thing: this is her and Travis's wedding. The hell are we even here for? All that needs to happen is for them to make the decisions and hand me the bill."

Mrs. McClure gave Daddy a skeptical look. "You're going to cover everything?"

"Why? You think I can't? Because I guarantee you I can."

I was grinning from ear to ear.

Mrs. McClure looked flustered as she said, "No, I didn't—Travis, what do *you* want? Holy Trinity or this New Wine place?"

"True Vine," Mama corrected.

"Yeah, that," Travis's mom said, with a dismissive wave of her hand.

Oooooh, this bitch!

Travis looked from his mom to me with uncertainty in his eyes.

His ass was scared of her. "Uh, Nicky, what do you think?"

I *wasn't* scared of her, so I said, "True Vine."

Travis's shoulders slumped a bit. His mother's face soured. Claire dropped her eyes and shook her head yet again. Mama was smiling. And Daddy said, "That's what I thought."

Travis didn't have much to say on the way home, but I really didn't care. I knew there were certain rules when it came to being with him. Some I could deal with, like wearing this ugly-ass dress. But my mom being disrespected? That was the kind of shit I couldn't tolerate. My mom and Damon's mom always got along well. His mom was stiff as hell, but she was nice. I hadn't seen her in probably twelve years, and I really needed to drop in on her.

Why did my mind insist on comparing Travis to Damon? Now I was comparing their mothers? What the hell?

I sighed and had resumed perusing Instagram when a text message popped up.

From Damon.

I glanced at Travis and angled the phone where I hoped he couldn't see it. I also hoped it wasn't a dick pic, while at the same time wishing it was. I tapped on the message and smiled as I read it: *Hey. Miss u.*

I glanced at Travis again and replied: *So?*

Damon: *So I wanna see u.*

Me: *No.*

Damon: *U know u miss me 2. Tryna act all hard.*

I was grinning now.

Me: *Whatever.*

Damon: *Come over tomorrow while Jack McCoy is at work.*

I stifled a giggle.

Me: *Who?*

Damon: *Jack McCoy with his Law and Order ass. Come see me Nick.*

Me: (crying laughing emoji) *Ur so dumb.*

Damon: *U gonna come see me?*

Me: *Yeah.*

Him: (blowing kiss emoji)

Me: (rolling eyes emoji)

When I looked up, the car had stopped. We were in the parking lot of Travis's condo, and he was staring at me. "What are you smiling about?" I noted the seriousness on his face as he asked the question.

I shrugged. "Just a meme on Instagram."

He nodded slowly. "Nicky, do you understand your place in my life?"

I frowned, glanced down at the now darkened screen on my phone and back up at him. "Uh, I'm not sure what you mean."

"I mean, do you know who I am and what that makes you?"

My frown deepened. Why was his ass speaking in riddles? "You're Travis McClure, and I'm your fiancée? I mean, what are you talking about?"

"Right. I'm a *McClure*. There's a certain status that goes along with my name. Status, and a laundry list of expectations. Do you understand that?"

I sighed and rubbed my forehead. "Is there a point to this other than you stating the obvious?" Oooo, I wanted to curse him out! Travis had this stupid habit of trying to talk to me like I was a child, and I hated that shit.

"I just need you to be clear about things, Nicky."

I unfastened my seatbelt and turned my body to face him. "Travis, sweetie, I may not come from a lineage like yours, but I happen to be well-educated and very smart. I totally understand you're a McClure and I definitely know who I am. I've been acquainted with myself for more than thirty years now, but darling, whatever you're trying to say? You need to spit that shit out and stop beating around the bush." My voice was sugary sweet, but my eyes were narrowed.

"You know how I feel about foul language."

"Yes, but honey, you're trying my patience."

He blew out a breath. "Fine. I want my mother to handle all the wedding details hence forth."

Who the hell says hence forth? "Since my parents are paying for it, that would be a no."

"I don't want them to pay for it."

I stared at him.

"And I'm not getting married in that little church."

I scoffed. "Well, I am."

He shook his head. "See, this is why I asked if you understood who I am. Who my parents are—"

"Oh, I understand. And I don't appreciate how your mother ignored mine. That was disrespectful, Travis. My parents might not be judges and lawyers, but they're my parents, and I have a problem with the way your mother insists on looking down her nose at them.

You know what? Screw this! Let's just call the wedding off, and you go find you someone who likes being treated like a child." I snatched the car door open and stomped toward his condo.

Behind me, I could hear a door slam shut and then rapid footsteps approaching me. "Nicky!" he yelled.

I kept going, unlocked the door, and walked inside, slamming the front door to his place so hard the wall shook a little. Making my way to his bedroom, I headed straight to the closet and began snatching clothes off hangers. Maybe it was hearing from Damon, or maybe it was that I was tired of pretending to be sugary sweet. I don't know, but I was over Travis and the McClure family as a whole. Yeah, I wanted to be taken care of, but fuck this!

"Nicky?" he said softly, as he stood just inside the bedroom. "Are you leaving?"

I rolled my eyes. "No, I'm packing my shit for my health."

He flinched. He really hated the "s" word and the "f" word, as he termed them, so I added, "Yes, I'm *fucking* leaving, Travis."

"I'm-I'm sorry. Don't go."

I looked up at him. "Why the hell not? I mean, I'm obviously not good enough to be a McClure. So, to hell with it."

"I never said that."

"You didn't have to, and FYI, my daddy is richer than yours. So while you wanna look down on the Stricklands, just remember that shit, okay?"

I zipped up the duffle bag haphazardly stuffed with some of my clothes and hoisted it on my shoulder. "I'll come back for the rest of my stuff later."

I stepped to the doorway, but he blocked me. "Please…don't go."

I fixed my eyes on his chest. "Nah, I'm going. I'm over this, Travis."

He just stood there, so I raised my eyes to meet his, saw tears filling them, and softened a little. "Travis…"

"I'm sorry. It's just—my parents put all these expectations on me and I know my mom is mad about the church but I love you and I don't wanna lose you. I'm sorry. This is *our* wedding. We can do what you want."

I dropped my shoulders. I didn't necessarily love him, but I did care about him, and hell, I didn't want him to cry, so I said. "Okay."

"You'll stay?" he asked, sounding hopeful.

I nodded. "I'll stay, but you have to let me be me."

He rested his hands on my arms. "Okay."

"That means I dress the way I want."

He nodded hesitantly. "All right." Leaning in, he kissed me with more passion than he ever had before, and a few minutes later, I was on his bed, on my back…with his face between my legs.

11

Damon

I yawned as I flipped over on my back and opened my eyes. The phone rang in my ear for a third time before she finally answered.

"Hello?" Her voice was soft, timid, apprehensive. That wasn't my girl's voice on the other end of the line. Something was wrong.

"Nick?" I replied.

"Yeah…"

"Something wrong?"

"No…"

I sat up on the side of my bed, pulling the phone from my ear to check the time. 10:00 AM. "Were you still sleep?" I asked, but she didn't sound drowsy. She just sounded strange.

"No, I woke up early to have breakfast with Travis."

That shit hurt, but I recovered quickly. "Okay…is he there? Is that why you're sounding like this?"

"Like what?"

"Like…like something's wrong."

After a couple of seconds of silence, she said, "Things are better between me and Travis now, and I don't want to betray him anymore."

"Me calling you is betraying him?"

"What it could lead to is betraying him."

I held the phone for a minute as the realization hit me that she was serious. Something in her voice told me she was actually trying to make things work with him. I mean, yeah, they'd been engaged for a while and had set a wedding date, but I never really got the impression Nicky was serious about him…until right at this moment.

Finally, I said, "Nick, you don't wanna talk to me anymore? *Ever?*"

She didn't respond, and something inside of me shifted. For all the messing around and playing we did, I loved her. I truly did.

"Nick?"

"Damon, I…"

"We can't be friends anymore? Nothing?" My damn voice broke, and it felt like twelfth grade all over again, but that time, the pain I felt was my fault. Whose fault was it this time? Hers or mine?

"I don't wanna lose you, Damc, but I-we can't be around each other or talk without it leading to other things. Travis isn't perfect, but I do care about him and I know he loves me."

"I loved you first."

"I-I know, but—"

I sighed. "I know, Nick. I fucked up. But damn, I get nothing? Just fuck my feelings?"

"No! Look, I don't know what you want me to say."

"Say I can be in your life as your friend."

"I want that, Damon, but you know how we are together."

"Nick, if you don't wanna have sex anymore, then we won't. I'd rather give up sex than give up having you in my life. I missed you all those years we didn't keep in touch. You're a part of me."

After a minute or so of silence, she said, "Okay…but what do we do together then, because all we've done with each other since you've been back is…*that*."

She couldn't say the word. I didn't even want to think it.

"I have something in mind. I don't guess you're coming over today, so you wanna roll out with me tomorrow, or do you have plans?"

"No, tomorrow's good. And thanks for understanding, Damon."

"No problem, Nick. As long as you're happy, I'm happy."

Man, I really wished I meant that.

*****

Around five that evening, I was kind of just sitting in my living room, staring at my computer and trying not to think about Nicky. I should've been working, but I couldn't concentrate on anything. Listening to music usually helped me focus. But that didn't even work, so I just sat there.

A knock at my door damn near made me jump out of my skin, and although it jolted me, another set of knocks had to sound before I was able to truly realize what was going on, that someone was at my door.

I dragged a hand over my face before hopping up to check the peep hole. A smile stretched across my face when I opened the door and pulled Angie Boyé into a hug. "Hey!" I greeted her.

All the years Nicky had been my friend, Angie had become like a big sister to me, and in my current state of mind and heart, seeing her smiling face was like pain medication to me. "What are you doing here?" I asked, as I gestured toward my sofa, offering her a seat.

As I sat next to her, she lifted a plastic bag I hadn't noticed her holding. "Brought you some dinner. Nothing fancy. Ryan grilled some burgers, so I brought you a couple."

I took the sack from her and peeped inside to see two burgers wrapped in foil, along with small Ziploc baggies of tomatoes, onions, pickles, slices of cheese, and hamburger buns. "Man, thanks, Ang. I didn't know I was hungry until you got here. Crazy, right?"

She smiled. "It's a hazard of working from home. Crazy hours because it's so easy to lose track of time. You forget to eat, hold your pee, work so long that you find yourself falling asleep with your hand on the mouse pad of your laptop."

I looked around my place and back at her. "Damn, is there a camera hidden in here? Sis, you just narrated my life."

She chuckled. "No, I've just been living that life for a few years now. Well, at least until Ryan and I got married. He's spoiled, wanted to be sure he got his time with me, so he made us a schedule. We work fixed hours when we're not traveling and have official off days. It's been a good change."

I thought about that for a minute, then rubbed the back of my neck, and said, "I need to do the same thing. I'm wearing myself out."

"It can easily happen. Hey, how's it going, though? Is all your hard work paying off?"

I slumped back on my sofa. "Ang, I don't know. I mean, I'm making it, but I'm actually contemplating moving in with my mom to save some money, and you already know I'm not tryna do that. I'm thirty damn years old, almost thirty-one, plus I'm not tryna hear her mouth. She's never supported my wanting to be an entrepreneur, and it's not like we get along."

Angie was quiet with this introspective look on her face, then she finally said, "You know, the other side of my duplex is vacant, has been for a while now, since Ryan moved out. Ryan is against letting any men lease it, and I'm not trying to have no women up in there, but you're family, so I think he'd be okay with you living there."

"Uh, I'm sure I won't be able to afford the rent at your place, either."

"I wouldn't charge you any rent, Damon. I wanna help you."

"Angie, I can't—"

"You can and you will unless you wanna hurt my feelings."

I shook my head. "Angie…"

"Look, me and Ryan aren't hurting for money, believe me. We're good. The place is yours if you want it. You'll only have to cover utilities. Can you handle that?"

I closed my eyes and decided to take her offer for what it was, a gift. So I nodded and said, "Yeah. Thank you, Angie."

"It's no problem. Just don't tell Nicky I'm not charging you any rent. Her spoiled ass has been tryna move in there forever."

I chuckled. "I won't."

"Great! Let me call and make sure Ryan's okay with this, and if he's not, I'll just have to change his mind." She gave me a wink.

I smiled at her and shook my head again. At least I knew one Strickland sister still had love for me.

12

Nicole

There was this one time in tenth grade when Damon caught this virus. It'd been going around the school, and was so bad, it caused a lot of absences. This particular day, Damon missed school, a rarity for the braniac who absorbed information like a sponge. Damon and I both loved the learning aspect of school but struggled with the socialization arm of it outside of our friendship.

I made it to lunch before deciding to skip the rest of the day to see about him, knowing his mother had probably left him to fend for himself. Wanda Davis was a beautiful woman who married young and divorced young, and in between that, had Damon who eventually became a casualty as her need to be successful outweighed her need to nurture her only child. During the bulk of high school, while she climbed the corporate ladder, Damon was left all alone more often than not.

After I coasted into his driveway in the car that had been a sweet sixteen gift from my father and parked next to the hand-me-down Ford Bronco some uncle or cousin of Damon's had given him, I approached the front door, knocked, waited, then took the spare key out of the fake rock sitting in the flower bed next to the front door and let myself in. Damon was in bed, burning up with fever. Lips parched and delirious out of his mind. My heart squeezed in my chest at seeing him like that, at seeing *my* Damon like that. I'll never forget the look in his drowsy eyes when he saw me. I could tell he wasn't sure if I was really there, but still looked relieved at the mere possibility of my presence.

I jumped into action, recalling the things my mom would do when me or my sisters would get sick. I found some Tylenol in his mom's bathroom and coaxed him into taking it. Located some chicken noodle soup in the kitchen and damn near had to force feed it to him. Turned the ceiling fan on in his room, blasted the AC even though it was in the dead of winter, to try and cool his body down, and breathed a sigh of relief when his fever broke.

I stayed there with him, sitting on the side of his bed, until I was expected to be home, then snuck out the house after bedtime and went back to him. Gave him more Tylenol and soup and was happy to see he was much more coherent. When I sat on the side of his bed, watching him drift off to sleep again, his eyes popped open and he lifted his long arms, a smile on his face as he whispered, "Come here, Nick."

I moved closer, let him fold me in his arms as I lay next to him in the twin bed.

"Thank you for taking care of me," he said in a weak voice, as I closed my eyes and melded into his thin body.

"You're my guy, Dame. Gotta take care of you."

"You're my girl," he replied, his voice heavy with sleep.

When we were alone, we always referred to each other as "my guy" and "my girl." It was our thing.

I smiled and burrowed in to spend the night there with him. I'd already set his bedside alarm and brought some clothes with me. I'd leave his house and head straight to school if he was still improving. If not, I would stay right there with him. I already had my excuse ready for my mom. I'd just tell her I left for school extra early, before she got up, for a meeting or something.

As it turned out, I didn't need the alarm, because Damon woke me up with passionate kisses. We made love that morning. Not sex, but love. By then, we'd been together in that way countless times, but there was something deeper about this time. In his little bed, we shared something so intimate, so intensely emotional, it ached as much as it pleased us. There was a desperation intermingled with the carnality of our connection, and from that point on, sex with Damon was never merely sex again.

That morning was also the first time I realized just how much in love with him I was.

Those events played repeatedly in my brain as I waited outside of Travis's condo for Damon to pick me up and take me wherever he was taking me. I was outside, because I was nervous and anxious, and also because I knew myself well enough to know that being inside any dwelling with Damon was a bad idea.

When his Optima finally pulled up in front of me, he rolled the window down, stuck his head out of it, and with a grin on his face, said, "Damn, I missed you, too."

I rolled my eyes as I walked over to the passenger's side and climbed in, the familiar mixture of spearmint gum and Damon's cologne infiltrating my senses, causing my body to instantly react, as if my coochie had a mind of its own and thought, *oh, Damon's here so I better get wet.* Had he not already begun pulling off the lot, I might've snatched the door open and jumped out.

"Where are you taking me?"

He glanced over at me with that same goofy-ass grin on his handsome-ass face. "It's a surprise. A pleasant one."

I frowned as I fixed my eyes on him. "You better not be taking me somewhere to screw, Scotty."

"Aw, shit. You pulled out my middle name? Damn, I'm not gonna try anything, Nick. I respect your wishes. I just wanna spend some time with you. Okay? Relax."

I sighed. "I'll try."

I gazed out the window, willing myself not to look at Damon as he navigated the streets of our town, eventually hitting the highway. I wanted to ask him again where we were going, but instead, pulled my phone out and tapped on the Instagram icon. Ironically, the first photo in my feed was one of Damon, obviously taken that morning from the driver's seat of the car I was sitting in. He was smiling brightly and the caption read:

Getting ready to spend the day with my #dayone. Nothing makes me happier than being in her presence, if only for a second. #mygirlforever #truelove

My first thought was to panic and worry about whether Travis had seen or would see the post, but Travis despised social media and didn't partake in it at all. I glanced at Damon, my heart fluttering at the sentiment of his words, a storm brewing in my mind at the implication of the same words, and my body? It was frustratingly aroused.

My shoulders sagged. Honestly, I wanted this attempt at chastity between us to work. Damon meant the world to me. I loved him in many ways and didn't want to face a future without him in my life at least as a friend. But this wasn't going to work. He loved me, *really* loved me, and at that point, I realized it was wrong to expect him to remain in my life in any capacity—even if he wished to—while I built a life with another man. It wouldn't be right. I loved him too much to cause him that kind of pain.

I had opened my mouth to share these feelings with him when I looked up and noticed he was pulling to a stop in front of a building that seemed somewhat familiar to me. My eyes scanned the lot and then rolled over to Damon who was wearing another ginormous grin.

"Where are we?"

"The gym at the old high school in Crumpton."

I nodded. That's why it was familiar to me. Crumpton was a town that was located about ten miles down the highway, east of Romey, with about half its population. This high school located on the edge of town had been replaced with a newer one.

"Why are we here?"

He nodded toward the building. "You didn't read the sign?"

My eyes scanned the front of the building and zeroed in on a blue and white banner stretched over the aging metal double doors: *5th Annual Crumpton Comic-Con.*

My eyes widened as I turned to him and smiled. "A Comic-Con?"

He gave me this look that was familiar to me. It was one he'd given me many times but more so when we were much younger—a look of innocent adoration. It melted my heart and made me want to lick him from head to toe.

"Yeah, I know how much you enjoyed the one we went to back in high school, figured you haven't been to one in a while. Thought it'd be fun," he said.

I turned my head and stared at the banner, letting my mind drift back to the beginning of our senior year of high school when Damon surprised me by driving me to Nashville for their Comic-Con. It was so much fun, and I promised myself I'd wear a costume the next time I attended one. A Wonder Woman costume. On the way back to Romey, I buried my head in Damon's lap and thanked him for the surprise with my mouth, almost causing him to have a wreck. My eyes flickered and dropped to my lap at that memory.

I finally shut those thoughts out and glanced at him. "I haven't been to a Comic-Con since you took me."

He frowned slightly. "Really? Well, this is past due. Let's go."

He hopped out of the car and so did I, giving him a curious look as he walked to the trunk and lifted it. A second later, he tossed me a package. I looked at the photo of its contents affixed to the front and then at Damon. "You got me a Wonder Woman costume?"

He gave me a lopsided grin. "Yeah, that's what you said you'd wear if you dressed up for one of these, right?"

"You remembered…" I breathed.

"Of course I did. I remember everything about you, about us." He dropped his eyes a bit, reminding me of the shy, adolescent Damon and making butterflies flutter in my stomach.

I glanced back at the building. "Uh, how long is this…how long will we be here?"

"Don't worry. I'll get you back home before Detective Stabler starts worrying."

I rolled my eyes. "Stabler wasn't even a lawyer, Damon."

"I know."

I looked down at the package again and then let my eyes roam the rapidly-filling parking lot. Crumpton was a small town, but I knew people were willing to travel far and near to attend an event like this. This one appeared to be no exception. "Um, thank you for this, but I don't think I should wear it. It looks kind of revealing on the picture, and I don't want to do anything that might upset Travis." I hated to bring him up, but since he already had in a roundabout way…

Damon blew out a sigh as he shut his trunk. "He ain't here, Nick. Look, I just wanna have some fun…with you. Just for today, I don't wanna think about the fact that you're engaged to someone other than me. I don't wanna think about anything. I just wanna enjoy this day, and I wanna spend it with you." He reached for my hand. "Please?"

I took his hand and nodded. As we approached the building, I noticed the package in his hand, and asked, "What kind of costume do you have?"

"Come on, now. What kind of question is that, Nick?"

I grinned. "My bad."

*****

Once inside, we split up, each ducking into a restroom to change into our costumes.

I came out first, holding my neatly folded clothes against my chest as I stood outside the men's restroom waiting for Damon. When he finally emerged, I gasped. Damon looked…there are no words for how good he looked in that Black Panther costume that appeared to have been painted on him. Virile? Hot? Sexy as hell? None of that seemed adequate. And although a mask covered most of the top half of his face, I knew it was him because I could see his eyes and lips and I knew his body, had it embedded in my psyche, could identify it in a line-up, and at that moment, desired to climb his fine ass like a tree.

I swallowed, unfastened my eyes from him, and glanced down at my feet. "You didn't think to get me footwear, huh?"

His eyes followed mine to the Jessica Simpson strappy ballet flats covering my feet then slid up the red thigh-high stockings to the micro-mini dress—blue skirt with white stars and red bodice that made my cleavage pop, gold v-shaped belt and gold Double-W accenting my breasts—all the way to the gold headpiece.

I saw his Adam's apple bob up and down as his eyes finally met mine. "Um, it didn't come with the boots?"

"Obviously not." I looked down at my size-C boobs that appeared huge in the built-in push-up bra. "Where'd you get this from anyway? La Perla? This feels more like lingerie than a costume."

He shook his head. "You know I can't afford shit at La Perla. I ordered it off some website. Glad I did, too." He licked his lips and grinned. "Come on. Let's see what they got going on."

As I took his hand again, I asked, "We just gonna carry our clothes around?"

As it turned out, after Damon paid the ten-dollar fee for us to enter the actual event space, which was the gym floor, we were each given plastic bags with the Crumpton Comic-Con logo on them. We shoved our clothes in them and began checking the place out.

Seconds later, Damon was damn near tackled by some white chick in a Storm (from the X-men) costume who begged him to take a picture with her as we attempted to make our way down an aisle of vendors.

Shoving her phone at me, she shrieked, "I gotta get a pic with my soul mate!" using some black woman's voice and then wrapped her damn arm around Damon and leaned into him. And what did he do? Just stood his stupid ass up there with this goofy smile on his dumb face, wrapping his arm around this trick. I wanted to throw that phone at her nose and yank her off him, but instead, I snapped the damn picture and flung the phone back at her.

Thirsty bitch.

After she left, Damon took my hand, and asked, "You all right?"

I cut my eyes at him. "Why wouldn't I be?"

That shit happened at least a dozen more times—hoes in various costumes approaching us, wanting to take pictures with Damon. Brazen, desperate hoes. I mean, yes, he was fine, but damn! And the worst one was a chick dressed up as Daphne from *Scooby Doo*. That trick actually asked if he would kiss her. When I heard that shit, I walked off, went and grabbed a seat in a room that was set up to look like the bridge of the USS Enterprise from *Star Trek*. I took Dr. Spock's seat, of course, and sat there trying to calm myself, because all I could see was red. Yeah, I was engaged to Travis, but Damon was mine, fucking mine! Always had been, and…and, shit, I was pissed about those women ogling and groping him. Honestly, the only reason I didn't punch one of them is I didn't want to get arrested and tarnish Travis's reputation.

As I glanced down at my engagement ring, I sighed. What the hell was I doing? Travis could screw another woman in my face and I wouldn't blink an eye, but I was about to go all *Kill Bill* on someone over taking pictures with Damon. Why? Why did I have an insane urge to throat punch any and every woman who came near him?

Because you love him.

I sighed again, finding absolutely no peace in that truth.

I heard the door open behind me, but didn't turn around. I didn't have to, because his scent announced him, and my body reacted to the fact that we were in that room alone just as it always had. My pulse raced, my nipples hardened, and my core throbbed. I closed my eyes and tried to shake it off, wondering if he had to endure similar torture when in my presence.

"I figured you'd find your way in here when I saw it listed as one of the attractions. Dr. Spock, huh?"

Without turning to face him, I replied, "You know it."

"It's crazy out there, right?" he said, as he made his way to the wall plastered with a huge poster of darkness and stars, giving the illusion of us blasting through space. "I thought you'd be the one getting all the attention with the way that outfit looks on you, not me."

I shrugged. "Black Panther is popular right now with all the buzz from the upcoming movie, plus, you look…good in that costume.

Really, really good."

I watched a smile slowly spread across his face, revealing his beautifully aligned teeth, and I started having thoughts about the way he liked to suck on my top lip sometimes when we kissed. My stomach lurched, and I dropped my eyes.

He moved closer to me. "So, there's a panel discussing what could be coming in the next season of *The Walking Dead* starting in like a minute. I wanna check that out and then watch some of the amateur anime music videos playing in another room, then hit a few vendors, grab some comic books. You wanna come with me or do your own thing?"

I hopped up from my seat. "I'll come with you. Can we go by the little snack bar and grab something to eat? My treat."

"Yeah, yeah. Whatever you want, Nick. Whatever you want."

Damon

Nicky was jealous, a fact that was confusing, amusing, and arousing as hell. I could see it on her face and in the tenseness of her body every time some chick stepped to me. But as crazy as her ass was, she knew she had no right to flex with her current situation.

But she wanted to.

She most definitely wanted to.

As we left that *Star Trek* room, I grabbed her hand. A stupid-ass part of me wanted to reassure her that she was the only girl for me despite the fact that she had another man standing in my spot. I guess that's just how love works. My need to protect her heart was like a damn reflex even though she'd long abandoned her duty to protect mine.

We hadn't taken ten steps out of that room when a tiny woman dressed, or barely dressed, as Harley Quinn damn near bulldozed into me, screaming, "Black Panther!" Shit, she actually knocked the wind out of me for a second.

I steadied myself and chuckled lightly. "Uh, hi. Nice to see DC showing Marvel some love." I cut my eyes at Nicky, who wore a scowl as she stared at the woman. "Right, Nick?" I added.

Nicky tilted her head to the side and folded her arms over her chest with force, making her boobs jump a little, which made my dick jump a little.

"OMG, I need a pic with you! Selfie?" the woman gushed, then moved in close to me, wrapping an arm around my waist. After she snapped the picture, she looked up at me and smiled. Then she rubbed her hands over my chest, and said, "Mm, so this is what a vibranium suit feels like. Ooooooo!"

Nicky grabbed my hand and yanked me away from the woman. Shit, I didn't know her little ass had that much strength in her!

"Fuck this!" Nicky yelled. "We're leaving before I have to whoop a bitch's ass up in here! These thirsty tricks…I swear!"

Harley Quinn's eyes tripled in size. "Oh, are you two together? Odd pair. Black Panther and Wonder Woman…with ballerina shoes on? And where's your lasso?" She lifted her head, now wearing an amused smirk.

Nicky dropped my hand and rolled her head around to face Harley Quinn. "Yes, *bitch*, we're together. *Been* together. *Gon' be* together. So take your little pale, un-melanated, thirsty ass on! His needs are well taken care of. Believe me! And as far as my shoes? I will kick them off and beat your ass with the swiftness if you lay another damn finger on *my* man!" Nicky grabbed my hand again, started walking off, then stopped and turned back to Harley Quinn. "Oh! And you better be glad I don't have a got-damn lasso, *BITCH*, or else I'd strangle your shapeless ass with it!"

Nicky pulled me all the way out the door.

I hit the button on the fob to unlock the car doors and felt her drop my hand. She stalked to the passenger's door, snatching it open, and slid in the car, slamming the door behind her. I stood by the car for a second, trying to process what had happened, wondered if she'd said what she said just in the heat of the moment or if she'd meant it. Well, there was only one way to find out.

I pulled my mask off, and as I climbed behind the steering wheel, I glanced at her. She was still seething, and before I could speak a single syllable, she was on me, mouth and tongue invading mine. Her hands were everywhere, and shit, of course my body responded to the familiarity of it all, but my brain just wouldn't get on board. So, I broke away from her.

Panting, I shook my head. "Nick, wait!"

Her tongue snaked out of her mouth and swept across my lips. "Uh-uh," she murmured. She clawed at the collar of my costume until more of my skin was exposed, then clamped her mouth to the hollow of my neck, sucking so hard my dick threatened to bust through my costume.

I closed my eyes and sank back in my seat, my mouth hanging open as I suddenly felt my seat begin to recline and realized Nicky was letting it back. She climbed on top of me, straddling me, grinding against me and moaning loudly. I probably should've felt victimized, considering she was the one who'd sworn off sex between us, but instead, I felt perplexed as fuck.

"Take off this damn costume, baby. Hurry…" Nicky murmured into my neck. That's when my wits finally returned.

I shook my head. "Nick, hold on—"

"I can't hold on, Damon!" she whined. "Come on, baby. Take this off…"

Her lips covered mine, her tongue dipped inside my mouth, and it took all the strength I could summon to push against her chest and snatch my mouth from her. "Nicole!" I thundered. "Stop!"

She jumped and fixed her eyes on me, her mouth open.

"Shit! What are you doing?"

Cocking her head to the side, she gave me a smirk. "After all these years, you don't know?"

I sighed. "Nick, you said we couldn't do this anymore."

She shrugged. "I can't help it. You just look so damn sexy in this costume."

"What about that stuff you said in there…about us being together? You meant that?"

She nodded. "Yeah."

"You said we're gon' be together and that I was your man. You meant that, too?"

She nodded again.

"Nick, you're marrying Detective Tutuola, though."

She rolled her eyes. "I know."

"So I'm supposed to do what? Keep fucking you while you're married to him?"

"Didn't I already ask you that?"

"Yeah, and now *I'm* asking *you*. Is that what you expect me to do?"

"Yeah...I mean, if you want to."

"Wow," I scoffed.

"What?" she said innocently. "It could work."

I turned and looked out the window, slowly shaking my head. "Get off me."

I didn't look at her, but could hear the confusion in her voice as she asked, "W-what?"

I faced her, looked her dead in the eye. "Get. Off. Me."

She stared at me for a moment. "Are you mad?"

I chuckled wryly. "Why would I be mad, Nick?"

"Y-you seem mad..."

"Would you be mad if I asked you to do some shit like that? To be my official and permanent side chick? Huh?"

She slid from my lap to the passenger's seat, and as I inclined my seat, I said, "Yeah, that's what I thought. Let me get you home to Adam Schiff's ass where you belong, because you damn sure don't belong in this car tryna fuck me...not anymore." I was angrier at myself than her, because *I* was the reason she expected me to go along with some moronic shit like that. After all, I'd been screwing her behind her fiancé's back for months, because historically, I was mindless when it came to Nicky. But that shit was canceled. Over.

From the corner of my eye, I could see the tears rolling down her face. Maybe I'd hurt her feelings or humiliated her, or maybe she was upset about me rejecting her sexually for the first time...ever. I had no idea, and I also didn't give a damn. I was done playing Nicky Strickland's games, because my ass always ended up on the losing end. Always. If she wanted to marry that lame-ass lawyer, she could marry him, but I was done being her *relief.*

As I pulled up in front of her fiancé's condo, I turned and looked at her. Her tears had stopped, but her eyes were slightly swollen and my anger had subsided a little. "How you gonna explain the outfit to him?" I asked.

She sighed heavily. "His car's not on the lot. He's not here. Still at work. I have time to change."

I nodded. "Well, at least you don't have to buy a wedding dress now."

Nicky frowned deeply. "Huh?"

"You said you were gonna dress as Wonder Woman when you got married. Remember?"

She shook her head and dropped her eyes to the floorboard. "That was years ago, elementary school. How can you remember that?"

I shrugged. "How can I not?"

A loaded silence fell over us, something that was a rare occurrence for me and Nicky. After a couple of minutes, she broke it with, "Damon, thank you for today, but I think it's best we just stop all contact. It's too hard..."

"Yeah…I agree," I said, with a slow nod.

Her eyes shot over to me. I had a feeling she was hoping I'd put up a fight, but I was past that with her. Her eyes left mine as she reached for the door handle.

"Nick, before you go, can I ask you something?"

She dropped her hand and turned to look at me, apprehension in her eyes. Slowly, she nodded.

"Why is it that you can't forgive me enough to be with me, but you can forgive me enough to screw me? And don't say sex isn't emotional for us, because it is, has been for a long time."

Her forehead creased as she turned toward the windshield. A minute or two later, she softly said, "I do forgive you, Damon. I just…I can't forget. The pain won't go away. The only time I don't think about what happened or feel the pain from it is when we're together *like that*. Everything bad goes away when we're intimate. All I feel is good. Most days, it's the only time I do feel any good in my life." Her eyes found mine again.

My heart stammered in my chest. "If I could go back in time and change things, fix things, I would, Nick. I swear to God I would."

She dropped her head. "I know you would. But…you can't. You can't." And with that, she opened the door and headed toward the condo, leaving me feeling like I did twelve years ago when my decisions wrecked us beyond repair.

13

Nicole

I sighed my relief audibly when the perky waitress reappeared, quickly lifting my empty champagne flute, alerting her of my need for another mimosa. Out of the corner of my eye, I saw Mrs. McClure's disapproving glare, but I gave exactly zero shits about it. If I was going to make it through this brunch meeting, I was going to have to be damn near drunk. The same applied to marrying her son.

What the hell am I doing?

I was so miserable, I couldn't think straight. It'd been two weeks since Damon took me to the Comic-Con, which was also the last day I saw or heard from him, period. He hadn't called or texted, respecting my wishes, and I couldn't find the courage to make contact with him. So, there I sat as my mother, Travis's mother, and Claire were hashing out last minute wedding details since the big day was rapidly approaching. Oh, and Travis's younger sister, Piper, was there, too, offering her input for some unknown reason. I had pretty much checked out of the meeting, not really caring about the decisions that were being made anymore.

Because, shit…I was really marrying Travis McClure.

My stomach swirled at the thought of it all. How did I get here? What was I doing? Why the hell didn't I stop this train wreck?

I didn't have the answers to any of that. All I knew was the man I loved, the only man I'd ever loved, was also the only man who'd broken my heart, and he'd done such an efficient job of it that I couldn't see through the fog of pain enough to stop what was an inevitable disaster. I wasn't fooling myself. I knew this wouldn't work with Travis. But I had to try. I had to at least attempt to move on, to be normal for once. I mean, I'd tried promiscuity, alcohol, a school addiction, and flat-out denial. None of that had erased the pain or my love for Damon. Maybe going full steam ahead with this sham of a marriage would.

It had to.

I really was unhappy, but at least I looked good in my black romper that was dotted with pink flowers and boasted long flouncy split sleeves. It was short and flirty and paired with matching pink leather ankle strap Kenneth Cole sandals, made my legs look kilometers long.

Damon would love me in this. Shit, he'd rip this sumbitch off me and screw me until I started singing the Negro National Anthem, have my ass singing soprano, alto, AND tenor.

I threw back my fresh mimosa and snickered at that thought.

My mom looked up at me and offered me a warm smile, reaching over to squeeze my hand. "Glad to see you so giddy about your wedding, sweetie."

My eyes widened, and when I realized all eyes were on me, I nodded enthusiastically. "I am! Can't wait to become Nicole Strickland-McClure!" I gushed that falsehood so convincingly, I almost believed it myself.

"You're gonna make a beautiful bride, Nicky. My brother is truly a lucky man to have found you," Piper said, with a huge smile on her face. I didn't know her well, had only been around her a few times like when Travis and I went to family dinners, but of the McClures, she seemed the most genuine.

So I returned her smile. "Thanks, Piper."

"Yes, well, I'm just glad this is almost over. It's been most stressful for me, especially since we could only invite a few people to the actual nuptials due to the size of the church," Travis's mom huffed and shook her head.

If this bitch ain't a broken record.

"Oh well," I muttered.

Mrs. McClure's mouth flew open, but before she could offer a rebuttal, Claire started talking about the rehearsal dinner. Mrs. McClure took to that segue, which was a good look for her, because I had just enough alcohol in me to curse her out properly.

When brunch was over, I was too tipsy to drive, so I had my mom drop me off at Travis's, where I finished off a half-empty bottle of wine and slept the day and my misery away.

14

Damon

She played me again.

There I sat my ass at the table across from her…and *him*, feeling infuriated and uncomfortable as hell at the same time. And betrayed, extremely betrayed. She invited me to have dinner with *her*, damn near begged me to come. She never mentioned *him*, but there he was.

Shit. I knew better than to come here.

I blew out a breath, puffing my cheeks as I pushed the food around on my plate. Shrimp scampi with pasta was one of my favorites, but my damn appetite was nowhere to be found.

"You like it?" she asked. "I called and got the recipe from Lisa Strickland. I know you always loved her cooking."

I was actually partial to Angie Strickland's version of the dish, but gave my mom a nod, and said, "Yeah, it's fine," deadpan and without looking up at her.

Then this nigga decided to pipe up. "Then why aren't you eating, son?"

Son? Did this motherfucker really just call me son? Was he serious?

I dropped my fork and squared my shoulders as my eyes met his. With raised eyebrows, I asked, "You really wanna know?"

"Uh-um, Lisa told me Nicky's getting married?" Mama chimed in, trying to avoid the inevitable. I hated Kyle Davis's deadbeat ass with a passion. Why she kept trying to put us in the same room was beyond me. Well, that wasn't true. I knew for a fact these little family reunions always coincided with them fucking. They'd been divorced since I was a kid, but had this on-again, off-again sexual relationship that had been going on for years. And when it was on-again, the phone calls from my mom would start. I don't know why I kept falling for this shit. I guess I wanted to believe she wanted to spend time with me for once and not just to reassemble this jacked-up family of ours.

"Yeah," I finally answered her, my eyes still on my sorry-ass father.

"She said you're in the wedding? Why haven't you mentioned it to me?" my mom asked.

I shifted my eyes to her and shrugged. "When would I have told you? We don't talk all that often."

Her eyes scanned the room nervously. "You could call more. I-I wish you would."

"Yeah, well, I don't know your schedule and I know you stay busy with work. So I just don't bother."

"Damon, you're my son, my only child. I would love to hear from you more, no matter my schedule. I can stop whatever I'm doing to talk to you."

See, that was the thing. Back in the day, some years after my dad left, my mom became this fembot. She was all about work and nothing else, eventually left me to fend for myself for weeks at a time during a phase in my life—my high school years—when I really needed a mom. Hell, if it wasn't for Nicky and her mom, I would've starved most days. Back then, when I would call my mom, she'd have her secretary take a message but would never call me back. After a while, I stopped calling her altogether. Barely contacted her when I was in the Navy, and it took her pleading with me for me to finally come home for a visit when I was living in South Korea. When I did come home, she was on this same family reunion bullshit. When I needed her, she was unavailable and I suppose I got used to that, so used to it that I was rarely in contact with her even now that I was back in town. Old habits die hard and hurt feelings linger. I suppose that was what Nicky was feeling.

Nicky.

For years, Nicky was my insulation from my parents' indifference toward me. Now there was no more Nicky, nothing to keep me sane.

Shit.

"Yeah, I'd like to hear from you more often, too."

I smiled and shook my head at those words coming from my sperm donor's mouth.

"Something amusing you?" he asked. "I'm serious, son."

"Son? Right. What's amusing is you sitting your ass over there pretending you give half a shit about me, knowing the second you two stop fucking, you're gonna go right back to doing what you do best, ignoring my ass."

"Damon!" my mother shrieked. "What has happened to you? You used to be so mild-mannered and respectful."

I angled my head to face her. "What? You don't like my

language, my attitude? Well, I guess you shouldn't have let me raise myself if you want my respect. Since neither of you could be bothered with me during my formative years, this is what the fuck you get."

Her mouth dropped open. My father's eyes were still on me, but he didn't speak.

"And since when did you start welcoming phone calls from me, Wanda? Didn't it used to irritate the shit outta you when I was a kid and I called you for things like…dinner?"

There were tears in her eyes as she said, "How many times can I apologize for the past, Damon?"

"Until it stops hurting!" I yelled, startling myself.

"Hey! You watch your tone with your mother!" my father bellowed.

I stared at him for a second, then started laughing. I mean, I doubled over and had tears in my eyes, laughing for a good two or three minutes. Finally, I sputtered, "Okay, right. Now you care about her being disrespected? After you cheated on her, left, and never paid a dime of child support? After years of y'all's booty calls y'all thought I didn't know about? After you haven't attempted to be in my life on a real level in years, I'm supposed to be intimidated by you raising your voice?" I chuckled and sighed, then yelled, "WELL, I'M A MAN NOW, KYLE, AND I CAN SHOUT, TOO!"

"We're getting remarried. That's why I called you here," my mom advised in a hurried voice.

Well, that shut my ass up. I stared at her, then him, for probably ten minutes, trying to process what she'd said, but it was like some part of my brain stopped functioning, and when it resumed operations, it started firing off all these crazy thoughts like, how did he deserve all these chances with my mom when he'd never done right by her? Why did she keep letting him back in? Why did she love him and not love me?

Why couldn't I be with Nicky?

Why couldn't she give me another chance? All I needed was one. *Just one.*

The last three thoughts made me bolt from my seat and just stand there for a moment. I might've been messed up in the head, but I knew I was a better man than Kyle Davis. So why the hell couldn't I get a happily ever after?

I scanned the dining room again, let my eyes rove over my parents a final time, and turned to leave without saying another word. My mom called after me, but I heard Kyle wisely tell her to give me some time.

Once in my car, I released a breath and rested my head on the steering wheel. Times like these, seeing Nicky would help me. Not just for sex, but for her ear. She knew how messed up my family was, and talking to her would help calm me. It always had, but that was out of the question, so I did the next best thing. I drove to Aunt Monda's house to get high.

15

Nicole

As I strutted into Club Indigo in a skin-tight pair of black leather leggings, a loose-fitting white racerback tank top, and a pair of black and white polka-dot platform pumps with my relaxed hair hanging free, you couldn't tell me shit.

In lieu of a bachelorette party, my sisters opted to treat me to a night out on the town, starting with a late dinner at my favorite Indian restaurant and ending here, where I pumped my fist to the sampled beat of *Wild Thoughts* as we made it to a table near the center of the club. It was a Wednesday night, just three days before my wedding, and after the stiff bridal shower I had endured earlier that day—hosted by Travis's mother—this was just what I needed. To let loose, get lit, and erase my mind of anything but feeling good, even if for just a couple of hours.

"Woo! I'm about to get turnt in this bitch tonight!" I announced once all three of us were seated. "I'm gonna head to the bar. Y'all want anything?" I asked.

"Water for me. I don't feel like pumping and dumping breast milk tonight," Renee shouted over the music.

"A Long Island Iced Tea for me," Angie yelled.

I raised my eyebrows. "You ain't playing, huh?"

She grinned. "Nope. Ryan's ass ain't gon' know what hit him

when I get home. And here." She reached into her purse and pulled out a couple hundred-dollar bills, handing them to me. "Drinks on me tonight."

I snatched the notes from her hand, twirled them in the air, and bounced to the bar. The crowd was sparse since it was the middle of the week, making it easy to carry our drinks back to the table. Once in my seat, I gulped down a generous amount of my Appletini, and said, "First, thank you two for this. Second, I can't believe Zo and Ryan let y'all come to a club. I'm surprised Zo's possessive ass isn't here with you, Nay."

She rolled her eyes. "Girl, you can't imagine the work I had to put in to get here tonight. I'm sixty-seven percent sure he put another baby in me this afternoon."

I giggled as Angie said, "Ryan, too! We literally spent the whole day screwing! Hell, I couldn't cheat on him if I wanted to. Not that I want to, and I'm *still* gon' molest his ass when I get home."

I drained my drink as I sniggered at both of them.

"What about Travis? He okay with you being out clubbing tonight?" Angie asked.

I gave her a smirk. "Girl, please. I didn't tell his I'm-a-McClure-and-I-have-a-reputation-to-uphold ass I was going to a club. He thinks we're having a girls' night at the Higgs estate, like a slumber party."

"You lied to him?" Renee asked, eyes wide.

"Uh, yeah! Look, I have a lifetime of stiff parties, *Matlock* marathons, and bad sex ahead of me. I can admit that, have even accepted it, but tonight? I'm gon' kick it Nicky Strickland style!

I'ma get drunk as fuck and might even get laid if I find a willing partner."

"I'm okay with the getting drunk part, will even fund it, but you ain't leaving with no dude," Angie said.

I sighed audibly, and although I was actually looking forward to a pre-nuptial one-night-stand more than anything, I said, "Fine."

As we sat, I was content to drink and chair dance until the DJ went retro on us and pulled out one of my favorite anthems. When I heard Juvenile declare that Cash Money records was taking over, I hopped up, screamed "Oh, hellllll yeah!" and jigged all the way to the dancefloor. I threw my ass in a circle, raised my arms, and rolled my hips as I rapped along to *Back that Azz Up* and didn't flinch when some random dude materialized behind me and grabbed my hips, dancing on my butt. I was too buzzed from the two drinks I'd consumed at that point to care about some strange man's proximity to me or my ass. Besides, he served a purpose, the same purpose the liquor had served, which was incidentally the same purpose any man whose name was not Damon Scott Davis served—a pain reliever. But those were always inadequate forms of treatment, because while Damon was the source of my pain, he was also the only effective remedy.

The thought of him made me squeeze my eyes shut and twerk my ass on dude so hard, I eventually felt his erection against my butt, and boy was it impressive! So I decided to glance over my shoulder to get a look at his face—not half bad-looking, but there was no way I stood a chance at getting that tonight. I could feel Angie's evil eyes on me. Nevertheless, I shouted, "I'm Nicky!" over my shoulder as he thrusted against my booty to the rhythm of the song.

"Dontae!" he yelled back.

Shit, if the DJ played *Bodak Yellow* or *Bad and Boujee*, Dontae's ass might've gotten a taste of some Nicky right then and there on that dancefloor.

I smiled and nodded, and once the song was over, I patted Dontae on the shoulder and returned to the table, fell into my chair, and tried to catch my breath, not realizing he had followed me.

He smiled. "Uh, can I get you another drink?"

Before I could accept, Angie's cockblocking ass said, "No, she's covered and getting married in a few days. Move on."

Dontae said, "Damn…a'ight," and skulked away.

"Wow, thanks, Angie," I said.

"You're very welcome, baby sis."

"He actually seemed nice."

Her eyes widened. "Yeah, I could tell from the way he was sexually assaulting your ass, *your literal ass*, on the floor out there."

"OMG, you're screwing with my buzz. I'ma go get another drink."

I had barely made it back to the table, sat down, and taken a sip of my margarita when Renee asked, "Is that Damon over there?"

Damon?! Huh? What? Where?!!!

My pulse accelerated. My mouth went dry. My core throbbed. My head popped up, and I followed Renee's line of sight to him—tall and fine in distressed jeans, a plain red tee, and red Chucks.

Got-dayum! Damon was sexy as hell!!

I crossed my legs. "Yep. That's him."

"Damon!" Angie attempted to shout over the music. With any luck, he wouldn't hear her.

He did.

Shit.

His head snapped in the direction of our table, and a gorgeous smile spread across his face. I squeezed my thighs together.

God, I loved that man.

I really, *really* loved that man.

Probably more than I loved myself.

As he was making his way to our table, I noticed his cousin, Theo, behind him.

While Damon greeted and hugged my sisters, I hugged Theo, who smelled like he had just bathed in marijuana smoke. A second later, Damon was pulling me into a tight hug that I melted into and whispering, "Hey, Nick," in my ear, before quickly pulling away from me. Damn, that stung, but I guess it was my fault.

He turned to Angie, and said, "What y'all Strickland sisters up to tonight?"

Theo cleared his throat.

"Aw, shit. My bad. Ladies, except Nick, 'cause she already knows him, this is my cousin, Theo Winters. Theo, you know Nick, and these are her sisters, Renee and Angie. Angie's my new landlord."

I looked up from the floor, which I had been studying to keep from ogling Damon, and basically shrieked, "What?!" My eyes shot to Angie.

She shrugged. "He moved in last week. I figured you knew since you two are so close."

I glanced at Damon who was staring at me, then my eyes found the floor again.

"Uh, okaaaay…Well, we're here to celebrate Nicky's impending nuptials," Angie said. "What are you two up to?"

"That's what's up," Damon said. "Theo just became a father. His little girl is a couple of weeks old. I brought him here to celebrate."

"Congrats," we all said. Well, I more or less mumbled it. Not that I wasn't happy for Theo, I was just *unhappy* for myself.

"Well, let me buy this dude a drink. Enjoy your night, ladies," Damon said.

"Thanks! You, too," Angie and Renee sang.

As he walked away, I guzzled the rest of my drink and looked up to find both my sisters staring at me.

"Not tonight, y'all. Do not go there tonight," I hissed.

Angie raised her hands. "I wasn't going anywhere."

Renee just zipped her fingers across her closed mouth.

When Childish Gambino's *Redbone* came on, I hopped up and quickly hit the dancefloor again. Dontae must have had me on his radar, because he was on me in seconds flat, rubbing and grinding, and I just giggled and teased him with my moves. I danced with him through two more songs and was going to head back to the table until I heard Xavier Omär's *Blind Man* and was instantly inundated with images of Damon—his smile, his laugh, his body. Felt his touch, even smelled him and instinctively glanced around the dancefloor for him but didn't see him. And then, I just stood there, so confused and overwhelmed that I didn't resist when Dontae pulled me to him and started moving seductively in time with the music. Instead, I wrapped my arms around him, closed my eyes, and swayed to the song, ignoring his grip on my ass. When he tried to nuzzle my neck, I spun around so that my back was against him, and he held me around my waist so that I could once again feel his erection on my butt. I closed my eyes again as we moved to the music, let myself get lost in it and my thoughts of Damon until I felt him stop, release me, then back away. Before I could turn to see what was going on, another pair of arms encircled my waist. Familiar arms.

Damon's arms.

My body reacted in its usual way in his presence, ready to receive what he had to give me and eagerly reciprocate. His tall body melded into mine as he held me tightly, grinding to the music, moving in time with my rolling hips as I looked up to see Dontae leaving the dancefloor. I wondered what Damon had said to him, so I asked.

"I told him you were my girl and that this was our song and to get gone," he said matter-of-factly right into my ear, as he tightened his arms around me. I closed my eyes again, relaxing against his hard body, satisfied with his answer.

Damon had always been a good dancer, a *great* dancer, but in the past, lacked the confidence to dance in public. But there on that dancefloor, he fully proved his confidence issues were a thing of the past as he moved seductively in perfect rhythm with the song.

When he leaned in and nuzzled my neck, I sighed. When he began to suckle on it, I reached up, rested my hand on the back of his head, and rolled my hips harder. When he spun me around and pulled me to him, I rested my head on his chest and looped my arms around him. And when he stopped and seized my mouth with his, I melted right there on that dancefloor.

I turned my back to him again, my heart thumping in my chest. We were in public for all to see. I was engaged to another man who had a reputation to protect, I'd just kissed a man I'd sworn I had no feelings for in my sisters' presence, and I…didn't care. At all. I was lost in the moment, warmed by his body pressing against the back of mine. I fit perfectly against him. *We* were perfect, made for each other. If I'd never known that before, I was sure of it at that moment.

I loved Damon Davis from the depths of my soul. I truly did.

Our dance became more than a dance. There, fully clothed under the pulsing purple lights on the dancefloor in Club Indigo, Damon and I made love to that song. What we shared that night rivaled all the other intimate moments we'd shared over the years.

The song ended, and so did whatever trance I'd slipped into. We stood there and stared at each other as another song began to play. In his eyes, I saw love and longing, regret and desire…not to mention lust, a whole lot of lust. So much lust, I had to fight not to drop to my knees before him and unbuckle his pants and suck him into amnesia without regard for us being in a public place. When he opened his mouth, I panicked, afraid to hear what he had to say or what I'd do in response to it, so I turned and damn near ran to my table on unsteady legs to find that both Zo and Ryan had joined us. But I couldn't address that, all I could do was blink back tears, grab my clutch from the table, and say, "I'm ready to go."

16

Damon

The church was nice—small, old, but well-kept. Low key, just like I remembered it. The first time I stepped foot in that church was years ago, high school, when I sat right by Nicky's side at her grandmother, Ms. Hannah's, funeral. Today was my second visit to True Vine.

I sighed as I tore my eyes away from the altar where the preacher was softly talking to Nicky and Travis. The entire wedding party had run through the ceremony twice, the rehearsal was drawing to a close, and several people had already left. *Most* people had left, but I couldn't leave because I was finally hit with the realization that Nicky was actually going through with this shit. The love of my life was marrying another man. How the fuck did things go this far? How the fuck did I let them get this far?

I was paralyzed with a feeling I couldn't describe. As bad as I wanted to leave, burning rubber and screeching tires, I couldn't move. I just couldn't move.

I felt so damn helpless in that moment. As long as we were having sex, I felt I had a little control over the situation, but now? I felt powerless.

Shit. Maybe I shouldn't have cut things off with her. That thought was followed by a whole textbook full of stupid, panicked notions. I needed to unglue my ass from that pew and jet.

"Hey." A soft voice startled me and I shifted my eyes from Nicky, who I didn't even realize I was staring at again, to see Angie dropping onto the pew beside me.

I swallowed, offered the woman who'd always been as much my sister as she was Nicky's a smile, and said, "Hey. Still here?"

She nodded. "Yeah. Nay had to get back home to feed Little Zo, so I'm hanging around to take Nicky home. She and Nay came here together since Nicky is staying at her and Zo's place until the wedding."

I nodded, involuntarily turned to look at Nicky again, and said, "Oh."

We were quiet for a minute or so until Angie said, "Well, I'm headed out. Just wanted to make sure I spoke to you before I left."

As she stood, I managed to get to my feet. "I'll walk you out," I offered. "I need to get home, too."

Once we were at Angie's car, my eyes found their way to the front of the church where Nicky and Travis now stood engaged in a private conversation.

"You really love her, don't you?" Angie asked softly, snatching my attention back to her.

I frowned slightly and opened my mouth to do what I always did when someone insinuated Nicky was more than a friend—lie—but Angie cut me off.

"Nuh-uh, don't bother giving me that 'we're just friends' crap Nicky always gives me. Please don't insult my intelligence like that. I know better, Damon. I can see it all over you *and* her. Well, I've always seen it in you, just wasn't sure about her. You two love each other. And if I wasn't sure before, that dance you two shared at Club Indigo? Whew! That definitely told me the truth. Wasn't nothing 'friendly' about that dance or that kiss."

I sighed as I rubbed the back of my head. I don't know what it was, whether it was the fact that I was tired, stressed the hell out about this wedding, or if I just needed to say it out loud to someone other than myself and Nicky, but after a beat of silence, I looked Angie in the eye, and said, "Yeah, I do. I love her as much more than just a friend."

I don't know what I expected her to do, but I definitely wasn't expecting her to stand there and stare at me or to open her car door and tell me to climb in, but I did as she said. Once I was inside her car, she climbed in beside me and punched me in the arm—hard.

"Ow! Damn! What was that for?!"

"For you standing by and letting my little sister destroy her life. How can you let her do this?!" she hissed through clenched teeth.

With wide eyes, I said, "Uh...I was under the impression you were already acquainted with Nicole Strickland. But you can't be, because if you were, you'd know I ain't *letting* her do shit. Nicky does what she wants when she wants. She's never been the type to ask for permission, and you know that."

"So...what? You're not even going to *try* to stop her?"

"You think I haven't? You think I want the love of my damn life to marry another man?"

Angie's expression softened. "Love of your life? Does she know that's how you feel? Maybe if you told her—"

I shook my head and dragged my hand over my face. "She knows, Angie. I've told her multiple times. If she doesn't know anything else, she knows I love her and want to be with her."

Her eyes diverted from me to the windshield. "And she loves you, right?"

I nodded. "Yeah. We've been in love since...since high school. Or at least that's when I knew she loved me. I've loved her much longer, since we were kids."

Angie returned her gaze to me. "Then why is she doing this? Money?"

"I think that's part of it, but...look, Ang, there's history between me and Nick that—shit. I fucked up back in the day and she can't or won't get over it. She won't let it go, so we can't be together. It's not something I want to discuss, but it...it was bad. When I say I fucked up, I mean I *really* fucked up."

"When? You've been gone for years. You just got back."

"High school. Senior year."

Her neck reclined. "Nicky's holding something against you that happened in high school?"

"Yeah."

Angie shook her head. "Damon, I knew my sister was touched, but that's just insane."

"Not really. I see why she feels the way she does. If it was the other way around, I'd probably still be messed up about it, too." *I am still messed up about it...*

"But you wouldn't hold on to it like she's doing. That's not in your nature. You'd forgive her and move on." She sighed. "I wish there was something I could do to stop her silly ass. She's about to make the biggest mistake of her life."

I didn't respond. Didn't know how to. So I just stared out the window for a second and then opened the passenger's door. "Thanks for this, Ang. It helped to tell someone what I'm feeling. Things with me and Nick have always been so secretive, you know?"

Her forehead creased. "Yeah, but why?"

I closed the door and faced Angie. "If I share this with you, you gotta keep it to yourself. You can't tell Nicky I said any of this."

She nodded.

"Me and Nick...we really did start off as best friends. We completed and complemented each other in a lot of ways. Then, when we were in junior high, we started having sex." I paused for a second, seriously feeling like I was betraying Nicky's trust. "Um...and we kept that a secret, because as friends, we had unlimited access to each other. We were sure our parents—that was back when my mom still gave half a shit about me—would shut that down if they knew our relationship had...evolved. So we kept playing the best friend role and having sex."

"Wait, but you had girlfriends and she had boyfriends."

"I know. Nicky thought we needed to experience having boyfriends and girlfriends. Shit, she always came up with these crazy ideas and I was so gone over her, I just went along with them. But anyway, the thing between us was weird and didn't make a lot of sense, but it was *our* thing. It worked for us. And besides, neither of us were ever serious about anyone else. They were just decoys, really."

She shook her head.

"We even agreed to only have sex with each other."

"Wow."

"I know, sounds stupid as hell to me, too, now. But back then, it seemed all right. Anyway, the whole secret thing just stuck. Old habits, you know?"

"Yeah. But there's one thing I really don't understand."

With a lifted brow, I said, "What?"

"How could you agree to be in her wedding?"

I rubbed my eyes with the thumb and index finger of my right hand. "Hell, I didn't think she'd go through with it. Plus, Nick has a hard time, uh…controlling herself around me, and I like getting in her space, messing with her. Being in the wedding and a part of the rehearsals and stuff gave me a prime opportunity to do that. And I figured I'd just go along with it when Travis invited me to be in the wedding, until she came to her senses, and now? I think I just need to be there to see if she'll actually do it."

"I really hope she doesn't. I hope she wakes the hell up and realizes she needs to be with you and not Travis."

"Me too, Angie. You have no idea how badly I want that."

Nicole

I wasn't surprised to see Damon sitting in Angie's car, because I'd been watching him the whole night, hoping no one, especially

Travis, noticed. It wasn't that I wanted my attention to be on him, but shit, I loved the man and was deeply attracted and connected to him. As badly as I wished none of that was true, it was, and it was hard to ignore him.

When I made it to my sister's car, I leaned in the driver's side window, my eyes instantly finding their way to Damon. "Hey, Damon," I said softly.

With his eyes on the windshield, he said, "'Sup, Nicky."

I blinked hard, unsure which hurt more, that he wouldn't look at me or that he called me Nicky instead of Nick. Before I could decide, he opened the door and hopped out, informing Angie that he was heading home. Then he left without even tossing another word at me.

Well, that *really* nipped at me, and I kind of just stood there staring after him until Angie tapped my arm, and asked, "Hey, you ready to head out?"

I shook my head. "Uh…I actually came to let you know I'm leaving with Travis. His mom planned a last-minute dinner thing she wants me to come to. He'll drop me off at Renee's." My voice was laced with more displeasure than I intended to convey.

"Oh, okay…"

I sighed. "What?"

With raised eyebrows and faux innocence, she said, "Huh?"

"Why are you looking at me like that and sounding like that?"

"How am I looking and sounding, Nicky?"

"Like you got some shit to say that's gon' piss me off."

"Well…"

I straightened and clasped my hands to my hips. "Just say it. Travis is waiting for me."

"Okay. What the hell are you doing, Nicky? Are you seriously going through with this? You're going to marry a man you don't give even a modicum of a damn about when me and you both know you love someone else?"

I tilted my head to the side. "Here we go with that shit again. And who is the someone else? Damon?" Then a thought hit me. "What were you two talking about in here anyway?"

She just looked at me.

"Shit, he told you about us, didn't he? What'd he say?"

"Enough for me to know you're breaking his heart by doing this. His and yours."

I backed away a bit, shaking my head. "You don't get it. You don't understand."

"What don't I understand, Nicky? He told me he hurt you—"

"What?!" I yelped. From the corner of my eye, I could see Travis making his way to me, but I couldn't think about that. Had Damon told her—

She waved her hands in front of her face. "He didn't—*wouldn't*— offer any details, but he did say he hurt you and you're holding it against him. He even understands why, but Nicky, you're wrong, and I'm sure you know you're wrong. You love him. It's all over you, baby sis. You gotta let the past go and do what's best for your heart."

I pushed my lips into a pout and glanced at Travis as he approached me. Lowering my head, I whispered, "I don't love

Travis, so there's no way he can break my heart like Damon did. I *am* doing what's best for my heart."

As I straightened, Travis reached for my hand and kissed my cheek. "You ready?"

I gave him a smile. "Yeah, babe."

Travis looked at Angie. "Hey, Angela. I'll be sure to get her to Renee's."

Angie nodded. "Okay, great," she said unenthusiastically.

I shot her a look as I let Travis lead me to his car.

*****

Dinner was held at the McClures's stately suburban Romey home, the one with the living room wall full of certificates, diplomas, and college graduation portraits. The one with the oil painting of Travis's parents hanging over the fireplace. It was an intimidating home with a frigid environment. My parents might not have had the best marriage, but home always felt like home for the most part. My sisters and I could laugh and talk there and depend on our mother to make us feel welcome. Hell, even Daddy was sure to give us a hug and a smile and a "baby girl." But this…this museum Travis's family called a home, was far from a real home.

Judge McClure—as everyone, including his wife, addressed him—sat at the head of the table, face stern yet rather blank throughout the meal. Mrs. McClure sat to his right, with Piper sitting to her right. On the other side of Piper sat her boyfriend, a young law student named Dennett. To the judge's left sat his only son, Travis, with me right beside him. The formal dining room was noiseless with the exception of the sound of expensive silverware scraping against fine China or ice settling in our glasses of sweet tea. Sitting there in all that sterility made me miss my overtly dysfunctional family.

I sighed lightly as I cut into an asparagus spear. If the food had been even remotely satisfying, this meal wouldn't have been so unbearable. It was prepared by their live-in maid, Wilma, who apparently couldn't cook worth shit.

"So…Saturday's the big day. You ready, Trav?" Judge McClure's voice boomed against the walls, making me almost miss my mouth with the asparagus.

Travis smiled and grabbed my free hand under the table. "More than ready. I can't wait for Nick to become my wife."

Wait. What did he call me?

Judge McClure snorted. "How about you, Nicole?" He didn't bother looking up at me. He never really made eye contact with me the few times I was in his presence, even when addressing me. It was odd, but I didn't care.

I squeezed Travis's hand and smiled at him. "I-I can't wait to be Mrs. Travis McClure." Hell, I almost convinced myself again. Maybe this could work out. Maybe I could grow to really love Travis. I mean…maybe.

"Well, I for one am so excited about this wedding! Nicole, you are going to look so beautiful in your dress!" Piper gushed.

"Thanks, Piper. I really love it," I replied.

"Hmm, well…I believe everything will be lovely. We might be

able to pull this off despite the size of the church," Mrs. McClure said, as she took a sip of the saccharine-sweet tea.

Here she goes with that bullshit again. Bitch.

"Mm, yes. That was a concern of mine, too. Grace, did you tell the Stricklands we were willing to pay for a larger venue? I mean, if their budget was an issue…" Judge McClure rumbled, addressing his wife.

Got-damn, I'm right here and I can hear your ass. I twisted my hand free of Travis's and cleared my throat. "Uh…"

"Let it go, Judge. It's settled. That's where Nicky and Travis chose to exchange their vows. I shouldn't have brought it up," Mrs. McClure muttered.

Not to be outdone, I added, "And it had nothing to do with a budget. My father would've paid for me to get married at Madison Square Garden if that was what I wanted." And it was the truth. My father was nothing if not generous. He was a terrible father, but one who spoiled me all the days of my life. Paid for me to pursue and earn four advanced degrees. He wasn't shit, but I'd be damned if the McClures were going to belittle him. They could suck my ass if that's what they thought.

Judge McClure eyed me for a moment—surprisingly—then nodded. "I'm aware of your father's wealth, Nicole."

"Then why did you insinuate otherwise?" I asked.

Travis, his mom, and his sister all gasped simultaneously.

"Did I?" the judge asked.

I hadn't spent much time around the judge, as he always seemed occupied or out of pocket, which meant he didn't know me, but he was about to learn. I might have faked my way into this engagement pretending to be some Pollyanna, but that shit was over. It wasn't like Travis would back out because I got an attitude with his father. Backing out now would be embarrassing and fuel too many rumors. I might not have loved the man, but I knew him. Travis was too concerned with his image to let some closed-door confrontation cause him that level of discomfort. So I had no reservations about putting the elder Mr. McClure in his place. "You mentioned a budget, right? There was no budget. The only stipulation my father made was for me and Travis to make the major decisions concerning our wedding."

He stared at me for a moment and then gave me a smirk. "I see. Well, I apologize if I offended you in any way. That was not my intention, Nicole." He turned to Travis. "Son, if you're done with your meal, I'd like to speak to you for a moment."

Travis nodded, gave me a nervous look, and left the table with his father.

I continued fighting through my bland dinner, enveloped in my thoughts, thoughts of Damon Davis and his big, long—

"Nicole, a word of advice?"

I looked up to see Grace McClure's gaze affixed to me and her daughter's eyes downcast. Dennett's face was in his plate.

"Excuse me?" I said, as I reclined in my chair, deciding to give up on the charade of enjoying the food.

"I'd like to give you a word of advice," she repeated.

Did I ask this hag for some advice? "Okay…"

"You don't want to get on the judge's bad side."

And why are you calling your husband, a man I presume you used to screw at some point in time, "the judge"?

"What exactly does that mean?" I asked, with a lifted brow.

"It means that as the patriarch of the family, he wields a great amount of influence, especially over Travis. If you upset the judge, you upset Travis, and I'm sure you don't want strife in your marriage at the onset. Do you?"

I scoffed. "Right. Thanks." Standing from my seat, I added, "Tell Travis I'll be waiting outside for him. I need some air."

After fifteen minutes of waiting, I was contemplating calling Renee and seeing if maybe their driver could come pick me up when a soft voice broke into my thoughts.

"Hey, I'm sorry about my folks. They're...they suck."

I turned to face Piper. She was a couple of years younger than Travis at twenty-nine, tall, and painfully thin. I was small, but still had curves. Piper was virtually a stick, but she was sweet and genuine, and of all the McClures, I hated being around her the least.

How are you going to survive being a part of this family, a family that doesn't even like you?

I shook those thoughts off and gave her a smile. "It's okay. I can handle them."

Her eyes widened. "Oh, no doubt! You handled them both back there. Travis is probably being reprimanded, though. You weren't at all what our parents were expecting him to bring home." She ended that statement with a little giggle.

"Really? What were they expecting?"

"They see Travis as the next Barack Obama, so of course they expected him to come home with a Michelle, some Ivy League superwoman lawyer."

"Hmm, is that what they expect you to be? Is Dennett your Caucasian Barack?" I asked.

"Their expectations of me are very low. I don't have Travis's brains, so they just hope I can manage to marry well." She shrugged. "Dennett's the heir to his family's very successful business, and he'll be a lawyer, so he definitely fits their bill."

"But not yours?"

She glanced back at the house before shaking her head. "Nope," she said, lowering her voice. "I like guys like your friend, the one who's going to be in the wedding. Damon, I think is his name. The tall one with the tattoos? Now, *he* is gorgeous!"

My eyes danced all over the place as I tried not to look like I wanted to curse her out. "Uh, yeah…Damon's always been handsome."

"Not just handsome. *Fine!* And he's your best friend? There's no way I could've kept a man who looks like that in the friend zone!"

I frowned and swallowed hard. "Uh…well, we've known each other since we were little. He didn't exactly look like that back then."

"Okay, but damn! Look at him now!" She moved closer to me. "Hey, you think you could hook me up with him?"

"Huh—what? W-what about Dennett?"

She rolled her eyes. "He's so bad in bed, it's not even funny. But that Damon? He looks like he can screw like a champ!"

My mouth just kept opening and closing like it was on a hinge.

What the hell could I say? "Okay" was not an option. Yeah, I was marrying her brother, but Damon's dick was not up for grabs on my watch. Piper's little fake innocent closet ho' ass was going to have to look further.

"Oooh!" she practically shouted. "He's gay!"

"Hell, no!" I said, before I could stop myself. "Uh, no. He's definitely not gay."

"Well, what's the problem?"

"Problem? Uh…um…oh! He's-he's in a relationship, a long-term, committed relationship."

Her shoulders sagged, and the look of wonderment fled from her eyes. Good. Her ass needed to look elsewhere, because that dick was mine, damn-it! Mine!

How's it yours when you're marrying another man in less than forty-eight hours, Nicky?

Shut the hell up!

I was arguing with myself in my head. I was losing my damn mind.

"Hey, sorry it took so long. The judge wanted to pick my brain about a case he's presiding over," Travis said, appearing out of nowhere and wrapping an arm around me. "Let me get you to your sister's so you can get your beauty rest." He pressed a gentle kiss to my temple.

I was so relieved to see him. Piper was on the edge of receiving an irrational ass whooping from me.

Once we were in his car, I settled in the seat and peered over at him, noticing the look of introspection on his face. "Was your father picking your brain about a case...or me?"

He chuckled. "Well, he did mention you. Said something about you being a tiger and a more than suitable mate for me."

My eyes widened. "Really?"

He nodded. "Yeah. A life in politics is hard, babe. Your fire will be an asset to me, to our marriage."

My eyes shifted from Travis to the darkened scenery outside the car. "Wow."

He chuckled again. "Yeah, you really impressed him, Nick."

I cringed. "You know...that's the second time you've called me that."

"Called you what?"

"Nick."

"Oh...so?"

"So, could you not call me that?"

"Why? Damon calls you that. I figured it was another nickname for you, like Nicky."

I bit my bottom lip. "It's not."

"It's not another nickname?" He sounded so perplexed.

"It is, but not like Nicky. Everyone calls me Nicky. Only Dam— just don't call me that."

Merciful silence filled the car, and I hoped Travis would just do as I asked and let it drop. Then he said, "Is something going on between you and Damon?"

The tasteless food I'd ingested at the McClures's began to curdle in my belly, and my mouth suddenly became devoid of moisture. "Huh? W-what? Why do you say that? What do you mean? What could be going on between us?" all came out in a rush. Hell, I may as well have just told him we'd been fucking. I mean, I might as well have given him full disclosure complete with a chart outlining when, where, and our most frequently used position.

"Did you two have an argument?"

Yeah, because I asked him to be my side dude after I marry you because I love him and his penis. "An argument?"

"Yeah, you two didn't say two words to each other at rehearsal, and when I spoke to him, he was real short with me."

"Oh…"

"What's going on?"

"Uh, I think he's having…relationship problems. I know how he is with stuff like that, so I just keep my distance."

"Oh. Missy Mae?"

"I think so."

He did drop it this time, thankfully. I'd told so many lies on Damon in less than an hour, I was actually beginning to grow a conscience.

Once inside Renee's and Zo's castle (I'm not even exaggerating with the label "castle"), I lay in the huge bed in one of their guest bedrooms, unable to sleep. I wondered if I shouldn't have opted to stay at my mom's, then reminded myself that her and Daddy were probably screwing all over the place at that very moment. Nah, I was good at Renee's and was glad Travis and I decided to live apart and abstain from sex during the week or so leading up to the wedding. I truly needed the break.

After tossing and turning for more than an hour, I buried my head in my pillow and groaned. Then I flipped over and stared at the ceiling. Without even thinking about it, I reached for my phone in the bed beside me and tapped on the Instagram icon. I checked my profile, smiled when I saw that my followers had grown to a little over six thousand, and then went to the feed and scrolled through the posts, stopping when I got to a pic of Damon, *fine-ass* Damon, at the gym—shirtless. The caption read: *Late night gym session. Trying to clear my mind.*

I stared at the picture until my eyes grew heavy and I was finally able to fall asleep.

17

Nicole

I looked good—no, I looked smoking hot in a white bodycon mini
with a plunging V neckline covered in white lace. Was it appropriate
wedding rehearsal dinner wear? Probably not, but I didn't care. It
was *my* dinner, the night before *my* wedding. My last night as a free
woman, a Strickland, so I was going to wear what I wanted to wear,
sit in that private room in the Tranquil Valley Country Club, drink as
much wine as I could stomach, and try my best to enjoy myself.

At least my sisters and their husbands were there, and my mom
and dad, so I wouldn't be relegated to pretending to engage with the
McClures and Travis's two frat brothers, who were serving as
groomsmen along with Damon. Damon, who was either late or not
coming at all. Since we weren't talking to each other, I had no idea,
but I knew I missed him.

Terribly.

Just seeing him would've shifted my mood, but there was nothing
I could do to make that happen.

As I sat next to Travis, who was in deep conversation with Ryan,
I had to ask myself for the millionth time why I couldn't truly
forgive Damon and just…be with him. It was what I wanted. It was
probably even what I needed. But I couldn't. I couldn't let it go, and
I had sense enough to know it was to my detriment. I knew I'd never

be happy with Travis.

I fixed my eyes on my plate, took another sip of wine, and had totally zoned out for a good ten minutes when I heard Angie say, "Hey, Damon!"

My heart thudded in my chest and my head snapped up. He looked…gorgeous in his usual casual attire—t-shirt (this one was vintage *Rugrats*), jeans, and Chucks—the sexiest and most underdressed person in attendance. He smiled as he greeted Angie and everyone else at the table, gave me a little nod, and then I saw *her*.

What. The. Entire. Fuck?

Okay, so he brought a date. That was bad enough, but this bitch? Really?

As he pulled her chair out for her, I could feel my face heating up and my hands began to shake. I could not BELIEVE this shit! I sat there and scowled at him. I mean, if looks could kill, Damon's ass would've been wearing a toe tag.

"Congratulations, Nicole!" this bitch chirped.

I gave her a smirk. "Ivy," I said, "I didn't realize you still lived in Romey."

"Yeah!" she gushed, with this big-ass grin on her red-ass face. I didn't have anything against light-skinned people. Hell, Ryan was damn near white and he was in the top three on my list of the finest men in the world. But I could not stand this beige ho'!

She continued with, "Well, I was in LA for a few years—that's where my little girl was born—but I moved back here like five, six years ago? Had the good fortune of running into Dame recently and now I'm getting to see you, too!"

Dame? Really, bitch?

"You have a daughter?" I asked, my eyes darting to Damon, whose eyes were glued to Ivy.

Asshole.

"Yes!" Her ass was just too happy for my taste. She pulled out her cell and thrusted it at me. "Kimora. She's eight. Me and her dad didn't work out, but I'm blessed to have my baby girl."

I stared down at the phone until Travis nudged me.

My eyes widened as I handed the phone back to her. "Oh! Travis, you know Damon, and his date here is uh, Ivy…Smith?"

"Oh!" She giggled. "It's Ivy Amato now."

I nodded. "Ivy, this is Travis McClure, my fiancé."

As Travis and Ivy exchanged greetings, I grabbed my cell from the table and fired a text to Damon: *Really? U brought her? HER? Seriously. Like for real?*

I glanced up to see him checking his phone. A second later, he sent: *What?*

Me: *U know the fuck what!!!!*

Damon: *What's the problem, Nicole?*

Me: *The problem is that basic ass giggly bitch sitting next to u!*

Damon: *What are u talking about?*

Me: *I'm talking about u disrespecting me by bringing somebody u fucked to my party!*

Damon: *Disrespecting u? Ok.*

Me: *Fuck u!*

Damon: *Nope. I'll pass. That's what u got Captain Cragen's ass for. He can keep unfucking u since u like it so much ur marrying him.*

My eyes shot up to him and narrowed at the smirk he wore as he stared at me. I guess I must have glared at him too long, because I felt Angie, who sat beside me, kick me under the table. My reaction was to shoot to my feet.

"Nicky?" Travis asked, sounding confused.

"I need to go to the restroom. Be right back, Travvie."

"I'll go with her," Angie said.

"Me, too," Renee stated.

Inside the ladies' room, Angie asked, "What is going on with you and Damon, and why is it going on at your rehearsal dinner?"

"You look cute," I said, noticing her pant suit for the first time. I turned to Renee. "And you, too, Nay!"

"Nicky! The hell is wrong with you?!" Angie shrieked.

Renee stepped closer to me. "Yeah, the whole table was staring at you and Damon. What's going on?"

I frowned. "They were?!"

Before either of my sisters could breathe another word, the restroom door burst open and Damon charged in, making Renee jump and yelp. He breezed past us, slamming stall doors open, I presume checking to see if anyone else was in there with us. Then he was in front of me, so close I could almost taste him. I closed my eyes and inhaled.

"The fuck is wrong with you?!" he shouted. "You upset about me bringing Ivy to this bullshit-ass dinner while you sit there next to Olivia Benson wearing his ring?! What kind of twisted shit is this?!"

My eyes popped open and found Angie. "Can y'all, I mean, can we—"

She grabbed Renee. "We'll be outside guarding the door or something." She knew Damon, and as upset as he was, she knew he wouldn't hurt me.

Once we were alone, I said, "Damon—"

"You can't be serious right now, Nicky! I've sat my stupid ass up here and watched another man kiss you, listened to you talk about how he can't fuck, which means you've been giving it up to him regularly, and you wanna trip about me bringing a date?!" His nostrils were flaring. I don't think I'd ever seen him so angry, but I didn't care.

"It's not about you bringing a date, it's about you bringing *her* and you know it!"

He laughed, or chuckled. This negro *chuckled!*

"The hell are you laughing at?! You cheated on me with that bitch!"

He moved even closer to me, getting in my face and making me want to stick my tongue down his throat despite my anger. "She was my girlfriend! And you had a boyfriend at the time! You and I weren't a real couple, Nicky, because that's the way *you* wanted it! How the hell did I cheat on you?!"

"We had an agreement! You screwed her, Damon! You weren't supposed to screw anyone but me!"

"I was a kid! Damn, Nick! This is insane! I was seventeen, eighteen years old and I didn't look like this and she was throwing pussy at me! Of course I screwed her! But that was twelve fucking years ago!"

"You hurt me!"

He opened his mouth and then closed it, stared at me for a moment, and finally said, "You're doing this, marrying him, to hurt me. That's it, isn't it?"

"W-what?"

"You don't want him. I doubt if you even like him. You want me, but you're trying to punish me, right?"

"No. I accepted Travis's proposal before you moved back."

"And you made sure to call and tell me about it."

My mouth fell open. "Be-because you're my friend! You think I'm doing this just to spite you?"

He nodded. "Yeah, I do. You wanna hurt me, but what you don't realize is I've been hurting this whole damn time, baby." He cupped my face in his hands. "I have loved you since I was seven years old, Nick. You have my heart. You've *always* had my heart, my mind and body, too. I spent all these years wanting you, missing you, thinking about how different things would've been had I reacted another way, but I was a kid, *a kid!* And I was scared shitless. You can't keep holding some shit I did all those years ago against me. It's not fair!"

I shook my head as my eyes filled with tears.

"I'm a man now. I'm not the same person I was in high school and neither are you, baby. I need for you to let this shit go and leave here with me. I need you to be with me, to choose me right here and right now." He leaned in until his lips hovered over mine. "I need you to call this wedding off, baby. I love you, Nick. You could search the whole world and you'll never find a man who'll love you more. There's no way you could." Then he kissed me and my eyes fluttered closed.

"D-Damon—"

"I'm not afraid to beg and plead, because I need you, Nick. Look, I have been patient, I've put my pride aside. Shit, I gave up my dignity and became your side dude, a walking dick to you, because for a while there, I honestly thought I deserved to be treated that way, and I just knew you'd stop this shit. Do you have any idea what it did to me knowing that non-fucking motherfucker was touching you, that you were giving yourself to him? That shit kills me, Nick! And I can't take it anymore. You gotta call it off, baby. Forgive me and call it off. Be mine, Nick. Be with me…"

I stared at him and shook my head. "I-I can't."

He sighed and dropped his hands from my face. "Okay…okay. Then it's over. I'm done asking—*begging* you to forgive me. No more friendship. No nothing. I'm done. I won't ask again, and I won't watch you do this shit. I'm not coming to the wedding."

"But-but you're *in* the wedding."

As he started for the door, he said, "Not anymore. Have a nice life, Nick, because I'm damn sure moving on with mine."

*****

I was hysterical after Damon left the restroom, seemingly

unending tears soaking the lace covering my bosom. When I finally stopped crying, Renee had to go announce to everyone that I wasn't feeling well, because there was no way I could show my face. Plus, I was so upset about what Damon had said, I was in no condition to play the happy bride anyway. Renee was sure to let them know it was nothing serious and that I would be at the wedding with bells on. I think she told them I was fatigued from all the pre-wedding activities. That was true, but I was also…heartbroken.

Irrevocably so.

I wanted to call the wedding off and go to Damon. I wanted that so badly, I found myself sitting on the side of my bed in Renee's house staring at my car keys on the dresser. To stop myself, I did what I always did when I threatened to break weak. I remembered why I couldn't forgive him. And after I played those memories in my brain several times, I grabbed my phone and called an old analgesic of mine—Maurice.

Damon

"I'm pregnant."

Her voice was barely above a whisper. We sat in her car after school that day after she'd caught up with me as I was climbing into my truck, about to leave.

I sat there, my heart hammering in my chest, my stomach bubbling, my head spinning. Pregnant? I turned to face her, saw the tears in her eyes, and closed mine. "How?" I asked. It was a stupid question, but one with layers.

She looked up at me. "My birth control failed, I guess."

"Failed? You guess? How, Nick?"

She shrugged as her tongue darted out to wet her lips. "I don't know for sure. I read somewhere that antibiotics can cancel out the pill. Remember when you got strep back in February?"

I nodded. I was always catching whatever bug was being passed around at school, and Nicky always took care of me when I did. She always took care of me, *period*.

"Well, you gave it to me, remember? And I had to take antibiotics and we were…having a lot of sex like we always do, Dame. So I guess that's how it happened."

I nodded again and fixed my eyes on our fellow classmates as they laughed and talked on their way to their cars. Carefree, that's what they were, probably thinking about stuff like ordering graduation invitations and going to prom, oblivious to what was unfolding inside Nicky's car.

"You sure it's mine?" I asked.

Her eyes narrowed as she inspected me. "What?!"

I flinched a little at the volume of her voice. "Is it-is it mine? I mean, there's no way it could be anyone else's?"

"Who the fuck else's would it be, Damon?!" she shrieked. "Of all the stuff I thought you'd say, I never thought it would be something this stupid! I've never been with anyone but you! Ever!"

I held up my hands. "Okay, okay! I'm sorry, but I had to ask. I mean, you have a boyfriend, Greg, and—"

"I'm not having sex with Greg-fucking-Porter, Damon, and you know that! Just like you're not having sex with Ivy Smith!"

I looked away from her.

"Are you?" Her voice was lower now, almost timid.

I didn't answer.

"Are you, Damon?"

I looked at her and closed my eyes.

"You're fucking Ivy?! But we agreed!"

I sighed and brought my hand to my face, gnawing on my thumbnail, a nervous habit of mine. One of many I had as a kid.

"Damon!"

"I'm sorry! I thought you were doing it with Greg!"

"Why would you think that?"

I shrugged. "I don't know…"

She leaned against the back of her seat and closed her eyes, letting her tears escape. "I don't believe this. I do not believe this."

I reached for her, pulling her to me, relieved when she didn't resist. "I'm sorry, Nick. It didn't mean anything. I'll break up with her if you want. I don't even really like her. I just…are you sure you're pregnant?"

She nodded against my chest. "I haven't had a period since February. It's May. And I took a test this morning."

I blew out a breath. "Okay. What do we do? I mean, what do you want to do?"

"I don't know," she wailed. "I made an appointment at the free clinic. I guess we can figure it out after that." She looked up at me. "It's next week. Will you come with me?"

"Of course I will. And I'll break up with Ivy. Whatever you

want."

"You don't have to do that, at least not until we figure out what we're gonna do."

"Okay."

I didn't talk to Nicky again after that day. I avoided her, made sure I didn't bump into her in the halls of our school. We didn't have any classes together, so it was easy to duck her. I ignored her phone calls. Locked the deadbolt so she couldn't let herself into my house with the spare key.

And I missed the appointment at the free clinic.

On purpose.

I abandoned her, completely turned my back on the woman carrying my child, the one person who had always been there for me without fail. I let her down, because...I panicked. I didn't know what to do or how to handle something like this. I knew she was telling the truth and that the baby was mine. I felt that in my heart, and I wanted to be there for her, but I was scared, *petrified*. What was I going to do? How would I be able to take care of Nicky and the baby? Sure, I had plans to go into the military when I graduated, but how would I support them emotionally with my fucked-up upbringing? I didn't know how to be a father, because I didn't have even a halfway decent example. I didn't want to screw my kid up like my parents did me. And what if she decided not to keep it? I didn't think I could live with that either.

I didn't know what to do! So I hid from it, all of it, and a week after her appointment when the house phone rang—I didn't have a cell back then, but Nicky did—I had the bad luck of my mother being home. I had been able to avoid her phone calls up until then, but my mom answered and brought the phone to me, informing me it was Nicky.

"Hello?" I damn near whispered.

"What happened to you last week? You missed my appointment."

I held the phone.

"I lost the baby."

My mouth dropped open, but nothing came out.

"Damon, did you hear me?"

I swallowed the lump in my throat, and said, "Yeah, I heard you. W-what-what happened?"

"I don't know. I started bleeding this morning, skipped school and went back to the clinic instead. Found out I lost the baby."

"Oh…"

"I'm sure you're happy now," she said, sounding hurt and angry. Very, very angry.

"No…Nick, I'm sorry."

"For what? Deserting me? Avoiding me? Ignoring me? Treating me like I did it by myself? Not even having the decency to show up at the appointment? I made them wait, because I thought no matter how you'd been acting, you wouldn't let me down like that. But you did, after everything we've been through together. You are my best friend, my *only* friend, and you didn't show up when I needed you to." Now she was crying into the phone.

"Nick, please don't cry. I'm so sorry. I just…I'm sorry." I couldn't tell her I was scared, *terrified*. I was lame enough as it was to everyone else. Nicky was the only person that treated me like a human besides Ivy. I couldn't show anymore weakness around her than I already had over the years.

"Where were you during my appointment, Damon?"

"With Ivy," fell out of my mouth before I could stop it, and it was a lie. I'd already broken up with her.

She gasped into the phone. "She's more important to you than our child?!"

"No! I just. Nick—"

"I hate you! I never want to see your face or hear your voice again! Do you hear me?! I. HATE. YOU!"

And then she hung up, and that was the last time I spoke to Nicky until my visit to Romey three years ago. I wrote her letters apologizing the summer after we graduated. Tons of them, begging for her forgiveness over and over again. Some she kept, but the last few she returned unopened, and she never wrote back. Eventually, I gave up, went on with my life, but a piece of my heart was always with her, would always be with her. But as I sat on my sofa in the early morning hours of her wedding day, I knew it was time to move on again. It was time to let her go.

For good.

*****

"You sure you wanna do this?" I asked, trying to hide my nervousness.

Nicky nodded, bit her bottom lip, and glanced at my bedroom door for the hundredth time. "You sure your mom won't come in here?"

"She's not here. I told you that. She's at my dad's, I think."

Her eyes raced around the room. "Oh, yeah…"

I smiled. "You're nervous."

Her eyes widened, and then she gave me a smirk. "No, I'm not."

I was down to nothing but my boxers. Nicky had on panties and a t-shirt that matched. I guess she noticed me staring at her underwear, so she quickly stood and stripped, then laid back on my bed. "See," she said, in an unsteady voice. "I'm not scared. Your turn." Her eyes fell below my waist.

I glanced down at my boxers, where she could easily see the effect her nakedness had on me. I bit my thumbnail for a second, took a deep breath, and dropped my underwear.

Nicky's eyes stretched wide and her mouth dropped open. "Is it—should it be that big?"

I glanced down at myself and shrugged. "I guess. I mean, yeah? I mean, it's the only one I got so…yeah."

She blinked a couple of times and closed her mouth. "Okay, come on."

I crawled into bed, kissed her, and with a mixture of terror and excitement filling me, gave my virginity to Nicky and took hers from her. Later that night, while she was fast asleep, I told her I loved her for the first time, although I'd felt that way about her for years…

I jumped up from the couch at the sound of someone banging on my door. I had fallen asleep with images of that first time with Nicky playing in my mind the entire time, and since this was the first time I'd been able to sleep in days and had been rewarded with such a sweet dream, I was pissed at whoever was trying to break the damn door down at that time of morning, whatever time that was. I checked my phone on the way to the door—6:00 A.M. Checked the peephole and just stood there for a second, rubbed my eyes, and looked again. Then I shook my head and opened the door.

"I'm not fucking you on your wedding day, Nicole."

She frowned, twisted her lips, and said, "I'm not here for that." She was dressed in all white—pants and a blouse—for her wedding day, I guess. She looked…beautiful.

I leaned against the doorjamb. "Why are you here, then?"

"I want—I *need* to talk to you."

"I'm not coming to the wedding. I'm not watching you marry that dude."

"I understand that. I should've never gone along with that in the beginning. If the tables were turned…Can I come in?"

"Shouldn't you be on your way to the church. Don't you get married in a few hours?"

"Damon, please, I just need to talk to you. Won't take long, I promise."

I hesitated and then let her in, standing in front of her with my arms folded at my chest. "What's up?"

"I-I wanna apologize to you."

"Trying to clear your conscience before you marry Lennie Briscoe's ass?"

"Damon, *please*. This is hard enough for me. Can you just let me do this?"

I sighed and fell onto the couch, motioned to the loveseat. She sat on it and stared at the floor for a minute or so before raising her eyes to meet mine.

"I'm sorry, Damon, for…everything. But mostly for not forgiving you. I know I said I had, but that's not really true. What you said last night hit me and it hit me *hard*. All this time, I've only thought about what *I* went through. I was scared…and alone without you at a time when I needed you the most. And you were always there for me. We were always there for each other, so the last thing I expected was for you to turn your back on me, and it really hurt, because you were all I had. I mean, it wasn't like I was gonna tell my mom or my sisters about the baby until I had to."

"Nick, I'm sorry. I really am," I said, as I watched her eyes pool with tears.

"I know you are. I know, and I realize now that you were just as scared and confused as I was."

I didn't respond, but was relieved she understood what I was feeling back then.

"I would've had the baby. Had I not lost it, I was gonna have it, because I loved you so much." She wiped a tear. "I wish I'd told you, made you understand how I felt about you. I was just young and stupid and wrapped up in the fun of our secret, of being someone else's girlfriend but your lover. I don't know. I guess it made me feel edgy." She blew out a breath and smiled faintly. "But I loved you. I did. So much, and I think that's why it hurt to know you'd been with Ivy, because at the time, I never even considered giving myself to anyone but you."

"It was only once, and it was nothing like being with you.

Nothing has ever compared to that," I said softly. "Nothing ever will."

She nodded. "I know the feeling." She was quiet for a moment, and I knew her well enough to know she was deliberating over something, making an internal decision in my presence. Finally, she said, "I don't know if you've heard about my reputation, but I've been really, really...promiscuous over the years. My mind went in a tailspin after I lost our baby. I went from trying to deal with the possibility of having a baby at eighteen, to finding out the baby was dead with no idea how to cope with any of it, and then there was you, me pushing you away and us being apart for the first time in forever, and I was just...lost. You were a part of me, a *real* part of me for so long that I didn't know how to properly function without you. I slept with so many men. *So many...*" She shook her head. "I can't tell you how many men I was with over the years. I didn't slow down until Travis, and even then, I couldn't be with just him, as you know."

I nodded, my eyes glued to her.

"I eventually convinced myself I was looking for a husband, trying to screw my way to the altar." She laughed lightly. "Now I fully realize I was trying to purge you from my system, to replace you and make the pain of being without you go away, but I couldn't. And then you moved back, and things were like they were before sexually. It was only a part of you, but it was enough to keep me going, to make me feel better, to take some of the sadness away."

I could feel tears filling *my* eyes now, but I fought them back like a soldier.

"I love you, Damon. I love you from the depths of my soul. I have always loved you, and I will always love you. I'm sorry I mistreated you, asked you to accept me being with Travis while I slept with you, because you deserve more than that. You deserve all of me, or maybe something better than me, because I'm all kinds of fucked up."

"Nick—"

"You definitely deserve something, *someone* better than me, but you have the misfortune of being in love with me. And you were right, I *have* been trying to punish you, to hurt you. It was wrong, and it stops now. I love you too much to keep hurting you. But more than anything, I'm afraid of you, Damon."

"Afraid of me?" I asked, my brow creased.

She nodded. "I'm afraid of being hurt again, by you. You see, you're the only man who can hurt me, because you're the only man I have ever loved. You're the only man I *will* ever love. You own my heart, all my love, and with that kind of possession comes a lot of power. You can easily break me. You've done it before, and I don't ever, *ever* want to feel that pain again. I'm terrified of your power and your hold on my heart."

"Nick, baby—"

She shook her head and stood from the loveseat, wrapping her arms around herself. "Nevertheless, I'm helpless to the fact that I love you, and I'm tired of running from it. I-I'm supposed to get married today, but what I really want, what I *need,* is to be with you, if you'll let me…if you still want me."

I stared at her, trying to get a handle on what she was saying.

"You wanna be with me just for today? You rescheduled your wedding or something? I told you, I'm not—"

"I canceled the wedding."

I stood and rubbed the back of my head with my hand. "You did what?"

"I canceled the wedding. I'm not marrying Travis, even if you decide you don't want me anymore. But I hope and pray you do, because I'm tired of not being with you. I love you."

I stared at her for probably five whole minutes, my heart racing in my chest.

"Damon?" she said, uncertainty in her voice. "Are you going to say something?"

"I...I don't know what to say."

She moved closer to me and rested her hand on my chest. "Say you want to be with me. Please say you want to be with me."

I gazed down at her, inhaled her scent, and closed my eyes. "I do, I just..."

"What is it?"

"I never thought this would happen. I wanted it to, but I just...Is this real? I mean, is this a dream or something? Am I gonna wake up to find out you're married and my brain played a trick on me?"

She reached up and brushed my lips with hers. "Does this feel real?"

18

Nicole

He was standing there staring at me again, and my mind raced, trying to find something to say or do to convince him that this was real, that I wanted to be with him. But, after all the years that had passed and all the games I'd played with his heart, I couldn't blame him for his apprehension. So I decided to stand there and give him the time he needed to let it sink in.

He closed his eyes and covered them with a hand he eventually dragged down his face. Then he pinned his eyes to my face, slowly taking it in, bringing his hand to my cheek to touch me. His eyes roamed my face for the better part of six or seven minutes, examining each inch, seemingly each skin cell. And then he smiled his beautiful smile, and quietly uttered, "This isn't a dream. It's real."

I blinked back tears as I nodded. "It is, and I love you, and I'm yours if you'll still have me. All yours. Forever."

He rested his forehead against mine and chuckled softly. "You have no idea how long I've wanted to hear you say that, how many nights I prayed for it. And now…I don't know what to do. I don't know what to say."

"Say you'll have me," I whispered. "Say you love me."

He squatted a little until his face was even with mine. "I do love you, Nicole Strickland. I love you so much." He kissed me gently and backed away a bit. "Everything that happened, me turning my back on you when you needed me? I'ma spend the rest of my life making that up to you." He slapped a hand to his chest. "I'm a man now, and I know how to treat a woman, *my* woman. I know how to love you now, and I will never hurt you like that again. I promise."

"I know you won't. I know you won't…and I won't hurt you, either, ever again."

He captured my mouth again as his hands gripped my hips, slid to my back, down to my ass, up to the sides of my face, returned to my back, and back to my face as if he wasn't sure where to touch me. Then he backed me onto the love seat, straddling me while cradling my face in his hands, devouring my mouth so aggressively it felt like his tongue was at war with mine. He kissed me so fiercely and for so long, I found myself struggling to breathe, but I didn't care. Feeling the passion emanating from him, from *my* Damon, felt so good, if I died from suffocation, I'd die a happy woman.

When his mouth finally left mine, it traveled to my neck where he planted soft kisses and murmured, "I'ma make you so fucking happy, Nick. I swear I am."

"You already do, Dame. I love you so much."

He lifted his face, allowing me to see the tears spilling from his eyes. "I love you, too, baby. Forever."

I reached up and wiped his face. "Damon…"

His mouth covered mine, devouring me again, his hands feverishly rubbing my breasts through my blouse, the weight of his big body hovering over mine on the small loveseat. I closed my eyes and moaned, my body vibrating from sensations only derived from being in close proximity to Damon Davis. I was wet and aching for him, ready for whatever he wanted to do with and to me.

He reached down and rubbed my yoni through my pants, eliciting a low groan from me as I thrusted toward his hand.

"You're so damn hot! I can feel it through your clothes," he murmured against my mouth.

"See what you do to me?" I whined. "Only you."

That's when he lost it, started yanking on the button closure to my pants. "Take this shit off," he growled.

My hands scrambled to my pants, unbuttoning them. Damon stood from the loveseat and helped me to my feet so that I could kick out of my pants, then he snatched my blouse open and yanked it off me. He reached around me and unhooked my bra, tugging it down my arms. I went to pull the matching panties off, but he swatted my hand away, reached down, and ripped the flimsy material apart at the waist band before cupping my treasure in his big hand and sliding a finger over my clit. I flinched and moaned in response. Reaching for him, I tried to get ahold of his t-shirt to pull it off him, but he backed me onto the loveseat at the same time, giving me no other option but to sit back down.

He fell to his knees, opened my legs, and before I could take my next breath, he was pulling me to the edge of the loveseat and his mouth was on me, tongue lapping every inch of my yoni from labia to labia, sending electric jolts and warmth throughout my body. "Oooooooh, shit, baby!" I whimpered.

He reached up and grabbed my left nipple while slipping a finger into my wetness, adding a second finger almost instantly, working me over as his tongue moved in a circular motion, devouring my essence. With every scrape of it against my sensitive bud, I jerked and moaned.

"Damon," I whispered. "Damon…"

He licked, making slurping sounds, then pulled my clit into his mouth and sucked loudly, his fingers still playing a tune in my flooded core, his other hand pulling and tugging on my nipple. I felt a quickening build inside of me, making my thoughts foggy and erratic and my heart gallop in my chest. "Ooooooooh!" I yelled, as my legs began to quiver and my core pulsated around Damon's fingers. "Shiiiiiiiit!" I screamed, as he implacably licked me, making the waves of the orgasm stretch on and on and on.

When he finally lifted his head, he smiled at me, then reached up and pulled my head to his to kiss me, smearing my mouth with my own juices in the process, giving me a taste of myself. I whimpered against his mouth. He stood, threw his clothes off and then reached for my hand, pulling me to him and wrapping my legs around his waist. Standing was his favorite position since returning to Romey. I think he liked having me in that helpless position, knowing I had to depend on him to keep me from falling, knowing this position required me to trust him completely.

He entered me as he consumed my mouth. No hesitation, no preparation, no prologue or foreword. Just all of him inside of me in one swift stroke, causing me to scream into his mouth. The fullness of him felt like Heaven, and as he gripped my ass and pummeled me over and over again, punishing my yoni, I took the pain and relished in the pleasure that shadowed it. Damon moaned into my mouth, then found my neck and began sucking on it—hard. That hurt, too, but Damon knew I loved the sensual pain he inflicted.

"I love you so much, Nick. I love you so…damn…much!" he grunted, with each thrust.

He was hitting my spot, repeatedly, but it was no accident. Damon knew me, knew my body like no one else, knew where my spot was and just how to hit it.

"Shit!" I screamed, as another orgasm swelled in my core. "Baby!"

"Yeeeeah, Nick…give me another one, baby," he urged, giving me the full measure of him with each roll of his hips. Shit, he didn't have to convince me. My body had a mind of its own and was seconds from blowing.

"Ahhhhhhhhh! Kocham Cię tak bardzo!" I screamed, so deep in ecstasy, I swear I was losing my mind. I dug my nails into his shoulders and shuddered violently before burying my face in his neck.

"Oooooh, shit!" he groaned. And with that, he delivered a couple more thrusts and emptied inside of me with a roar.

19

Nicole

Two hours earlier…

"Damn, I missed you. You disappeared on me." Maurice's mouth was on my ear, his hand up my shirt.

Sitting on the side of his bed, I leaned back on my hands as he damn near climbed on top of me. His eagerness told me he wasn't lying about missing me.

"Uh…yeah. I know," I replied.

He moved his mouth to my neck. "I tried to call…"

I grabbed the back of his head and tried to relax. I was so uptight, you'd think I'd never been with him before.

As he trailed kisses from my neck to my mouth, he said, "I been feenin' for your little ass."

I rolled my eyes. "Like you been sitting your ass up in here doing without."

He raised his head, forehead creased as he licked his lips. Maurice was handsome—dark-skinned with piercing hooded eyes and an athletic build. He was a personal trainer and on my sex scale from zero to Damon, he was pretty close to the top, but he was known for being a player, worse than me. And he was a proven pathological liar. No way could I take his ass seriously as far as a relationship went.

"Naw, I ain't been doing without, but ain't none of them you. Ain't none of them got what you got. Shit, I told you I'd leave all of them alone for you."

Yeah, right. "Mm-hmm."

He pushed me onto my back and hovered over me. I still had on my clothes. He wore only his boxer briefs and his signature cologne—Paco Rabanne's *1 Million*. I was hours from marrying Travis, but I needed this. I knew just one good orgasm would calm my nerves and ease the ache crowding my heart. Maurice was no Damon, but he could get the job done in a pinch. So there I was, chasing my pain relief yet again.

I lay there as Maurice untied the string at the waist of my pajama bottoms, then I lifted my butt so that he could pull them down my legs. He kissed my stomach as he eased his hand inside my panties, and I shut my eyes, still trying to relax. Then an image appeared behind my closed lids, causing me to gasp.

"Yeah, baby. You like that?" Maurice asked, I suppose believing I was reacting to his hand in my panties doing what it was doing. But that wasn't the case. My mind was playing scenes of Damon with women, various women, first Ivy then others—faceless women. Reel after reel flashed in my mind of him laughing, smiling, holding their hands, making love to them…telling them he loved them. And then…and then I saw him in a white tuxedo, standing at an altar waiting for a woman who was not me.

The scene disappeared, and his words echoed in my mind:

"...*Then it's over. I'm done asking—begging you to forgive me. No more friendship. No nothing. I'm done. I won't ask again...*"

"...*Have a nice life, Nick, because I'm damn sure moving on with mine.*"

That's when I realized what the hell I was doing and just how stupid and useless it was. At that moment, all my transgressions were crystal clear. I bolted upright, making Maurice, who at some point in time had dropped his underwear, stumble. His dark eyes were full of confusion as I scooted to the foot of the bed and snatched my pants up from the floor.

"Look, Marcus, I'm sorry. I can't do this," I basically mumbled.

"Maurice!" he shouted.

I squeezed my eyes shut. "Shit, my bad. I can't do this, Maurice."

"Are you fucking serious, Nicky?!"

As I hopped into my pants, I said, "I know. I know this is completely messed up. I wouldn't blame you if you ignored my calls from now till the end of time. As a matter of fact, you should probably hate me for this. But I can't do it. Not anymore."

He grasped the back of his head, his eyes bugged. "*You* called *me*! You called me after you told me you couldn't see me anymore. And you got the nerve to call me some other nigga's name? I can't believe your ass!"

I grabbed my keys from his dresser and shook my head, muttered, "Neither can I," and headed for the door.

"This is some foul shit, Nicky!" he called after me.

"I'm sorry!" I shouted, as I slipped out of his apartment.

In my car, my hands trembled as I started the engine and pulled off the lot. I glanced at my phone, which I'd left sitting in the passenger's seat, and sighed, feeling nervous about what I was about to do, what I *needed* to do. Shit, it was something I *had* to do.

I made it to one of my daddy's car lots and pulled over, unsure of why I thought this would be a safe place to stop. Hell, was there a safe place for a woman to sit in her car alone at four o'clock in the morning? Maybe it was just the familiarity that made me feel secure, the name *Strickland Motors* painted in bold red script on the side of the building that consisted of nothing but windows.

I put the car in park and stared out the window at nothing really, trying to get my bearings and gather the nerve to dial the number. I almost changed my mind, but as soon as my hand touched my keys, I was reminded of the visions—Damon with someone else, spending the rest of his life with someone else, *my* Damon loving someone other than me, and I snatched my phone up and dialed the number.

"H-hello? Nicky?" His voice was laden with sleep, and I felt bad for doing this over the phone, but it had to be done and I couldn't deal with the dramatics of doing it in person.

"Hey, Travis? I'm sorry to be calling so late…or early, but there's something I need to say to you and it can't wait."

Silence, and for a second, I thought he'd fallen back to sleep.

Finally, he said, "Yeah? What is it?" The dread in his voice was palpable. I really felt like shit for doing this to him. His family may not have been the nicest to me, with the exception of Piper, they might have seen me as beneath him, and perhaps I was in many ways, but Travis had been kind to me. He might not have made my heart race, but he was a good person and would make a good husband to someone, just not me. His best would never be good enough for me, because I wasn't available. Hadn't been for years. I belonged to Damon Davis—all of me.

"I can't marry you," I finally said in a voice so soft, I wasn't sure he heard me.

"Babe, it's just pre-wedding jitters. Everyone gets them. You'll be—"

"No-no, that's not it." I was shaking my head so hard, I feared I'd get dizzy. "This is something I should've done a while ago. I-it was wrong to accept your proposal knowing I shouldn't have. I-I can't marry you and I'm sorry it took me so long to tell you."

"Nicky, don't do this. I know it's scary. I'm afraid, too. I—"

"Travis, I *cannot* marry you. *Ever.* I just…can't, and I'm sorry. I'm so, so sorry, from the bottom of my heart."

I ended the call and left for Renee's house where I showered, dressed, and sat on the side of her guest bed for a few minutes, taking the time to text my mother about my canceled wedding— knowing she'd share the information with the rest of my family— before heading to Damon's, full of trepidation and anxiety, hoping it wasn't too late, hoping against hope that he still wanted me.

20

Damon

Now…

We made love two more times before we both passed out on the loveseat, me with my body sprawled across it, feet on the floor, Nicky curled up on top of me. I woke up first and could tell from the way the sun streamed through the blinds on the huge living room window that it was early afternoon. I smiled down at Nicky as I rubbed my hand over her bare shoulder. She was still here. It wasn't a dream, and my damn heart felt like it was about to burst. I had wished for this, wanted it for so long, it became like that dream people have for their lives that they know is nowhere within their reach. The ultimate fantasy, the if-the-planets-align-perfectly-and-a-miracle-happens fantasy. The improbable fantasy. Nicky was that for me.

And now she was here…with *me*.

She was mine.

Finally, mine.

She stirred, stretched on my body, then lifted her head and smiled at me. Looked into my eyes, and said, "Forever."

I returned her smile. "And ever."

When we used to say that to each other as kids, we were

referencing our friendship. Now those words solidified our love.

"I love you," I said, as I kissed her forehead.

She gave me another smile. "I love you, too." Resting her head on my chest again, she sighed. "I could lay here with you like this until the end of time."

"Hmm, me too. But your stomach keeps growling, so I think I should get up and feed you."

"My stomach is not—" She was interrupted by a rumble so loud, she started giggling. "Shit, I guess I *am* hungry."

I laughed. "I really put it on you, didn't I? Got you all hungry and shit." Before I could finish that statement, *my* stomach growled.

Nicky burst out laughing. "Who put what on whom, huh?"

Still grinning like a fool, I said, "I'm just hungry from all the energy I used dicking you down."

"Whatever! You act like I didn't do any work."

"Oh, you put in some work. You gon' put in some more, too, because—"

Boom! Boom! Boom!

We both jumped. Nicky actually jumped off of me and stood naked in the middle of my living room.

"Damon? You in there?!" It was Angie. For a second, I thought Travis had seen Nicky's car in the driveway and was coming to start some shit about the canceled wedding. My ass was going to gladly finish it.

Nicky's eyes searched the floor, and then she grabbed my t-shirt and pulled it over her head. As I pulled on my sweats, I said, "Really?"

She shrugged before reaching up and kissing my cheek.

I shook my head as I walked over to the door and cracked it open. "Hey, Ang. 'Sup?"

She tried to glance behind me. "Uh, I see Nicky's car out here. Is she okay?"

"Yeah, sorry about the noise...uh, my bad. She's good, though."

She cocked her head to the side and rolled her eyes. "Fool, I'm not talking about you two in here screwing like a couple of wild hyenas, although that's...disturbing. I'm talking about her state of mind after calling her wedding off on the day of? My mom called and told me about it."

"Oh." I glanced behind me at Nicky sitting on the loveseat in my shirt. Then I lowered my voice. "Uh, Ang, I think the fact that we've been in here screwing like a couple of wild hyenas is a dead giveaway that she's in a good state of mind."

She nodded slowly. "Right...well, if you two decide to take a break, Ryan's about to fire up the grill since we don't have a wedding to go to. Renee and Zo are coming over. Y'all are welcome."

"All right, cool."

I closed the door and rushed to Nicky, grabbing her face and kissing her. "Hey, what was that you said in Russian when we were doing it this morning?"

She chuckled. "It was Polish."

Nicky could be so crazy sometimes, it was easy to forget her extreme intelligence. She had a degree in Slavic languages and could speak several of them fluently. My ass lived in South Korea for two years and could only speak enough of the language to minimally survive. "Oh, my bad. What did you say in Polish?" I asked, with a grin.

She dropped her smile and looked into my eyes. "I said, 'I love you so much.'"

I stared at her for a moment, my damn chest feeling like it was about to explode or collapse or something. Then I picked her up and tossed her over my shoulder as I made my way to the bathroom.

She yelped, and said, "What are you doing?"

"I'm about to fuck the shit out of you in this shower before we get ready to head over to your sister's to eat."

Nicole

Sitting on the back deck of my sister's side of the duplex wearing one of Damon's t-shirts and a pair of jeans I'd left at his place months earlier, I giggled from my seat on his lap as he nipped my neck with his teeth, and then looked up to see four pairs of amused eyes staring at us.

"I hope y'all's asses are enjoying the show," I said, with a smirk.

Zo and Ryan quickly looked away, as did Renee, but Angie gave me a mirroring smirk.

"What, Angie?" I sighed.

"Nothing," she sang. "You two are just the cutest, sweetest, craziest, most dysfunctional sight I've ever seen. You really are some twisted besties."

I pursed my lips and stuck my tongue out at her. "I'm happy for the first time in ever, so I'm not even gonna pull a comeback from my bitch repertoire for you. I'ma let you slide today, big sis."

"You know what, I'm happy for you two. Both of you. I'm not even gonna trip on the fact that you were engaged to another man less than twenty-four hours ago. Shit, I'm ecstatic you dodged that bullet, just wish you'd done it before today," Angie responded.

"Yeah, I know. I wish I could've come to myself earlier, too," I said.

Damon squeezed me to him and kissed my arm. "I'm just glad you did at all. Glad you're mine now, baby."

I turned and fixed my eyes on his mouth, "Me, too," I said, before kissing him, a peck that soon morphed into nothing short of public foreplay as he gripped a handful of my ass and moaned into my mouth.

Angie cleared her throat. "Okay, okay, we're gonna have to set some ground rules here. I'm all for y'all being together, always have been, and I know you two are adults, but shit, I still see Damon as my little brother. Y'all are gonna have to bring it down to a good PG around me until I can get adjusted to this new dynamic between you."

"Aw, baby, leave them alone. They gotta get used to being a couple," Ryan cooed, as he pulled her from her lawn chair into his lap. "You know how it is when you're in love and can't keep your hands off each other." He looked into her eyes before sliding his hand up her thigh. "Right?"

Renee yelped, and I could see Zo had gotten all in her personal space.

"Y'all some nasty-ass married people," I murmured.

Damon laughed as he kissed my neck. "Must run in the family."

"You have no idea," Angie said.

"Ugh," Renee groaned, as she clutched her stomach. "I can't even look at feathers anymore."

"Or chaps or lassos, huh?" I goaded, snickering at the men's confused expressions.

Angie hopped out of Ryan's lap. "Enough of that. Baby, crank the music up and I'ma go grab the cards and dominoes. We 'bout to kick it for real!"

Thirty minutes later, I was licking barbecue sauce from my fingers while I watched Ryan decimate Zo and Damon in a game of dominoes. Ryan was talking so much shit in that drawl of his, even his opponents were cracking up.

As he slammed a domino onto the patio table, scoring another ten points, he shouted, "Tennessee Toddy, all ass and no body! I don't know why y'all agreed to play bones with me. You know what they call me back home in Louisiana? *Boyé the Muthafuckin' Domino Dominator!* I almost feel sorry about the ass-kicking I'm putting on y'all. I mean, damn, are y'all even trying?"

Zo and Damon both shook their heads, and I fought not to laugh out loud. Ryan was truly a fool.

Renee was on the phone with Zo's mom checking on Little Zo while Angie was draped over Ryan's back with a big grin on her face. After Renee's call ended, she came and sat by me, asked, "So what's the plan now, Nicky? Are you moving back home? Staying with Damon?"

My eyes shot to Damon. We hadn't discussed that. Well, we hadn't really discussed anything. We'd spent most of our first day as a couple together screwing like rabbits. "Uh…" I began.

"She's staying with me. I've waited too long for this to play around with it. I want her with me, if that's okay with her." Damon's eyes found mine.

I smiled so brightly, my cheeks hurt as I nodded at him. "I want that, too, but I gotta get my stuff from Travis's place. I called the wedding off over the phone."

"I'll take you. Tomorrow," Damon asserted.

"No, Dame. I can't do that to him. He's actually a good guy, a *harmless* good guy, and I feel bad enough for jilting him almost at the altar. I can't show up at his place with the reason I left him by my side."

"He knows I'm the reason?"

I shook my head, no.

"Well, you're not going alone."

I had always had the stronger personality of the two of us, and in the past, I'd basically called the shots. He was showing me he was in control now. A man. And it turned me the hell on, but still…

"Damon—"

Ryan cut me off with, "I'll take you. When we wanna do this?

Tomorrow? I got you sis-in-law. Damon is right; you don't need to go alone. You don't know what state of mind dude is in right now. Harmless or not, no sense in taking a chance like that."

"I'll go, too. And we can take Rell," Zo offered.

"Hey, good looking out, y'all," Damon said.

"It's all good," Zo replied.

I sighed. "Okay, all I need is a job now so I can pull my weight, so I guess that's what I'll be doing in the immediate future. Job hunting."

Damon shook his head. "Nah, I know you're not about that job life. I got you. Things have been evening out since I moved next door. You don't have to get a job, Nick."

I reached over and rubbed his arm. "But I wanna work and help you. I'd work ten jobs for you, Dame."

"Awww," Renee sang, as she clutched her chest.

Damon smiled as he leaned in close, pecked me on the lips, and mouthed, "Love you."

I mouthed back, "Love you, too."

"Hell, as much as you stay on social media, I need to hire you to post on my accounts. With the way me and Ryan travel now, I don't have the time," Angie whined.

"I keep up with my accounts, though. You could do it," Ryan said.

"You keep up with your accounts, because your spoiled ass likes the attention."

"So?"

Angie rolled her eyes. "Anyway, I'd pay you top dollar to post like once or twice a day on Instagram alone. I'll send you pics or whatever, and you can come up with captions and hashtags, because you're good at that."

I tried to push back the excitement that bubbled inside of me. I *was* good at social media, especially Instagram. "Are you serious, Ang? I'd love that!"

"Dead serious. Could you post on Facebook and Twitter for me, too?" she asked.

I nodded. "I can just link them up with Instagram so one post goes across all three platforms."

Angie threw her hand up. "Shit, whatever. Do you. It's a deal!"

"Thanks, Ang!"

"Hey, could you do that for my Author Street and Zo Publications accounts? I'll pay, too. My ass hates anything with the word social attached to it. I haven't posted on either in months," Zo said.

"Yes. Please help him," Renee cosigned.

"Yeah, sure!" I gushed.

"Oh, and I'll get with Cass about you taking over Genesis's accounts, too. Cass has been handling them, but with her having to get the new midwife acclimated to things, she just doesn't have the time anymore. And there's no telling when I'll go back to work to help," Renee stated.

"That'd be great, Nay! Thanks, everyone! I'm so excited about this!"

Everyone smiled and assured me it was no problem. Then Angie said, "Nay, I thought you were going back to work in a couple of weeks. Can't stand to leave little man yet, huh?"

Renee shrugged. "That and the fact that I'm actually pregnant again. Just found out this morning."

"What?!" Angie and I shrieked in unison.

"Damn, Zo! You the man!" Ryan shouted, as he jumped up from his seat and gave Zo dap. "I ain't even had a chance to put one in Angie yet and you on number two? Shit!"

"Congrats, you two!" Damon said, with a big grin on his face.

"Dang, Baby Zo is what? Four months old? Wow!" Angie said.

"Dayum!" was my contribution. "Your fertility issues are over!"

"I know, I know. But this is the last one. I'm getting too old for this. One of us is getting snipped after this one," Renee declared.

"Shiiiiiiit, not me!" Zo said.

At that, all of us fell out laughing. Well, everyone except for Renee, who just shook her head.

21

Nicole

Awkward.

Being in Travis's place again so soon after canceling our wedding was extremely awkward, especially with Ryan waiting in the living room with Travis, and Zo basically following me around the place as I gathered my things. I had to beg Zo to leave Rell's big intimidating-looking ass in the car, not wanting to scare Travis all the way to death.

No matter how many times I tried to convince my brothers-in-law and my man that Travis was harmless, they refused to let me come alone, and I honestly felt bad showing up with bodyguards. I might've only had a heart for Damon and my family, but I lived with and halfway maintained a relationship with Travis for more than a year. I cared about him and really hated that I hurt him. He looked so sad when he opened the door for me.

I sighed as I zipped up my suitcase and scanned the bedroom one last time.

"Ready?" Zo asked, as he took the suitcase from me.

I nodded.

As we both headed to the bedroom door, Travis stepped into the room with Ryan on his tail. "Nicky, can I speak with you for a moment?"

Ryan's and Zo's eyes were on me as I said, "Travis, there's really nothing for us to talk about." I needed to get the hell up out of there. The guilt was eating my ass up.

He clutched his forehead, a stress-related habit of his, and then dropped his hand to his side. "Nicky, you called our wedding off the morning of, *over the phone*. The least you could do is give me five minutes of your time. Give me something more than 'I just can't marry you.'"

My shoulders fell, and I looked from Ryan to Zo. "Can you give us a few minutes."

Neither of them moved.

My eyes bounced between my brothers-in-law again. "Five minutes. Please?"

"We'll be right outside the door," Zo said to me, then turned to Travis and added, "*Right outside the door.*"

They left, pulling the door almost closed behind them, and Travis and I just stood there in silence, eyes locked.

Finally, I said, "I'm so sorry, Travis, but I…it would've never worked."

"I knew you didn't love me."

I was unsure of how to respond to that. So I didn't.

"And I knew we weren't compatible, polar opposites, really. I knew you weren't being faithful, saw the passion marks on your neck and your thighs. But I overlooked all of that, because I really thought we had something special. A-a partnership."

"Um, we did. But things changed. *I* changed. Believe me, it was for the best that I ended things. You'll find someone better. Your

Michelle Obama. I'm not what you need."

"Who is he?"

I shook my head. "I'm not going there. It doesn't matter. All that matters—"

"Damon?"

My mouth flew open.

He scoffed. "Wow. You know, my mother told me there was more to you two, that it didn't make sense for two people who look like you and him to just be friends unless one of you was gay. She was right."

"Uh, Travis. I need to go."

"All that stuff he said about the woman he loved, that was about you, wasn't it?"

"Travis—"

"He can't take care of you. He doesn't have the means. He's broke."

I sighed. "Travis, I'm not discus—"

"You humiliated me. You know that? I invited him into my home. Made him a part of our wedding, and all the time, you were…doing whatever you were doing with him. I look and feel like a fool now."

"I-I really am sorry," I uttered softly. "I'm not a good person and I know it. I'm sorry. That's all I can give you, my heartfelt apology."

As I eased past him, he said, "Karma's a bitch, Nicky. Be careful."

I flinched at hearing him use that kind of language, hesitated, closed my eyes for a moment, then left.

*****

"Hey, sweetie. I was trying to give you a little time, but me and your dad are worried about you. How are you holding up?"

I sat up in the bed, resting my back against the headboard and pulling the sheet over my naked body. Damon was in the shower and instead of joining him, which would undoubtedly lead to sex regardless of the fact that we'd just done it, I decided to return my mother's phone call from earlier that day.

"I'm fine. I'm just sorry Daddy spent all that money for nothing."

"Oh, honey, he's not worried about that. Are you, Angelo? She's worried about the money you spent on the wedding."

Daddy was there? My sisters and I still had no idea what our parents were doing other than being nasty freaks. Where was their marriage going?

A second later, my father's voice filled my ear. "Baby girl, don't you worry about the money. I'm just glad you changed your mind and didn't marry into that sadity-ass family. Here's your mother back."

"Sweetie, are you sure you're okay?" Mama's worried voice returned.

"Yeah, I'm actually...great. It was the right decision. Definitely the right decision."

"Good. I can't say my heart was broken over the turn of events, just wanted to make sure yours wasn't either."

I scoffed. "It's not. My heart is perfect right now," I said, as a

naked Damon sauntered back into the bedroom. I licked my lips as
my eyes followed him.

"That's wonderful! Well, I know Damon is taking good care of
you. Angie told me you've been staying with him. It's really a
blessing he moved back. He's always been such a good friend to
you."

As he pulled his underwear on, I said, "Um, Damon and I are
more than friends. Uh…he's why I called the wedding off, Mama."

"Oh? Oh! Ooooooooh!" Mama went through several rounds of
revelation, all revealed in the changing inflection of her voice. Then
she said, "Awwww, sweetie. Finally!"

Damon sat on the side of the bed, his eyes on me.

"Finally?" I responded. "Y-you knew?"

"I knew that how you two felt about each other went far beyond
the scope of a simple friendship. I also had my suspicions that was
why you were so wild. Or at least I believed that was one of the
reasons, besides genetics—you loved him and he wasn't here."

"Wow," I said, as Damon lifted from the bed and left the room.

"Well, you *really* just put my mind at ease." I could hear the smile
in my mother's voice.

I eyed the doorway and lowered my voice. "You don't think
there's anything wrong with moving on so fast. I've…never been in
a real relationship before, not one like this. I…I love Damon, Mama.
Like really love him. I don't wanna mess this up." I had tears in my
eyes. *When did I get so emotional? Damn!*

"You two have known each other forever. This is no ordinary
relationship. It's one with history, one you've been building since

grade school. Just…don't stop loving him and always respect him. You won't mess it up."

"I do respect him and I *can't* stop loving him. I know, because I tried."

She chuckled. "I truly know what you mean. Well, I'll let you go. Tell Damon I said hi. You two will have to come over for dinner soon. Actually, I need to plan something for the entire family."

"That'd be great, Mama."

Before I could end the call good, Damon was back. He handed me a cup of my favorite orange tea and climbed in bed beside me. "That was your mom?" he asked.

"And my dad."

"Talking about the wedding?"

"Yeah. They're cool with it, and us."

He smiled. "Good. How'd it go with Anita Van Buren today?"

I shook my head. "Could you at least stop calling him female *Law and Order* character names?"

"Fine. How'd it go with Munch?"

I giggled lightly. "You're so damn silly. How many episodes of those shows have you watched?"

"Every episode from every iteration. What y'all talk about?"

"Not much since I went there with bodyguards, which was totally unnecessary."

"I'm not tryna hear that, Nick. Dude is weird. And I'm like, eighty percent sure he's gay or something. I mean, what straight nigga don't like eating pussy and getting head? That shit is abnormal."

I sighed, but he was making a crudely valid point. "He figured out about us, told me to beware of karma."

He stared at me. "You worried about that?"

I shrugged. "It *was* foul how we got together. Me hurting Travis, you hurting Missy…"

Damon scooted over until his body was touching mine and placed his hand on my cheek. "How we got together was in Mrs. Monroe's second grade classroom. We are soul mates, two halves of a whole. This?" He swept his index finger from my chest to his a couple of times. "This is fate, an inevitability, a blessed union, and a motherfucking long time coming. We were meant to be. What we did was put them out of their misery. We freed them from what could only be loveless relationships, because neither of us had a heart to share with them. My heart has always been yours and yours, mine. Look, baby, we've already had our pain. So fuck him and his idea of karma. We got what we deserve—each other."

Then he kissed me, and his shower was soon rendered useless as his sweat dripped onto my body…again.

22

Nicole

We adjusted quickly to being a couple rather than two people creeping behind someone's back. Us being together felt…natural, and I discovered a lot about Damon now that I wasn't screwing him on the run. Like, he played music most nights while we slept. He'd turn the bookshelf stereo in his room on to soft music just before we turned in. Mostly old-school R&B, as well as Alternative R&B and Neo Soul. He also like sleeping naked, spooned behind me…or inside of me.

He would go out and buy us breakfast every morning after he hit the gym. He loved the sandwiches I made us for lunch. We'd collaborate on dinner. He liked for me to walk around half naked but preferred full nudity. We had a lot of sex, to the point I was afraid we'd go overboard and it would become mundane to him, but it was always so hot, I quickly pushed that thought to the back of my mind. Damon worked almost incessantly, but promised he was trying to cut back and create a better balance for his life. I didn't really mind, because managing Angie's, Zo's, and Genesis's social media accounts in addition to Damon's—which I managed pro bono, of course—was time-consuming work that I loved. I also loved the way we could both work for hours, right there in that duplex, side-by-side.

Us being together? Nothing was better than that, period.

Damon

"Hey, Aunt Monda," I said, as she pulled me into a hug. I wrapped one arm around her while still clutching Nicky's hand.

"Hey, baby! Always good to see you!" She glanced behind me. "And there's my girl!"

Nicky smiled as my mother's sister rounded me and yanked her into a hug. Through a giggle, she said, "Hey, Aunt Monda."

My aunt released her and beamed. "Girl, I haven't seen you since you two were teenagers, skipping school over here, getting high off my weed and screwing in Theo's room thinking I didn't know it."

Nicky's mouth fell open. I just laughed. She and my aunt were a lot alike with their slick mouths. Plus, I wasn't shocked. She'd told me back then that we weren't fooling her with our "friendship."

"Oh, girl. Shut your mouth. I'm just glad y'all ain't fronting no more. Theo told me y'all are together now," Aunt Monda said, giving Nicky a smirk.

"Uh…" Nicky looked up at me and grinned. "Yeah, we are."

"Mm-hmm. Well, I know you here for Theo. He in the back with Onika and the baby."

"All right, Auntie," I said, as I squeezed Nicky's hand and led her down the dark hallway.

Theo was back in his work room at his computer with his baby girl, Tia, asleep in his arms while Onika sat in a corner on the floor, face buried in her cell phone. She was a big girl, light-skinned and tall with a pink bonnet on her head, wearing a t-shirt and a pair of baggy gray sweat pants.

"Whaddup, fool!" I greeted my cousin.

Theo jumped a little, causing the tiny baby to stir. "Shit, Dame! I forgot you was coming. Nigga, you scared me!"

I offered him a lopsided grin. "Didn't I just text you like five minutes ago? Man, you too young to be this forgetful."

"Maaaaan, ain't getting no sleep. Lil' Mama a night owl," he said.

"Hey, Damon!" Onika yelled. "Tell your cousin it's normal for babies to be awake at night so he can stop talking shit about my baby."

Before I could agree with her, Theo snatched around in the chair and glared at her. "It's my baby, too. And I love to sleep. She look like you; she could at least inherit my sleeping habits."

These two fools...

"Can I hold her?" Nicky's voice was so soft coming from behind me, I barely recognized it.

"Nicky? Nicky Strickland?" Theo said, as if one, he'd just noticed her, and two, I didn't inform him she'd be with me in my text.

She smiled as she eased by my body into the room and gave Theo a half hug. He handed her the baby, and said, "'Nika, this Damon's girl. The one I told you about."

She looked up from her phone again, and her eyes lit up with recognition. "Oh, yeah. Hey. You cute. Little. No kids?"

Nicky gave Onika a tight smile and shook her head. She glanced at me before sitting in the folding chair I usually occupied when I talked business with my cousin. I felt a little tear in my heart, because I knew she was thinking about our baby. I wished things had turned out differently. That was a burden I almost wished I could carry alone but knew it would be too much for me.

Nicky and Onika fell into an easy conversation as Theo showed me the finished artwork for the next month's chapter of *Foreign Son*. My lazy-ass slacker cousin's talent always amazed me, and I was thankful he was able to meet the deadline I'd set for us despite his daddy duties.

"Wow!" Nicky said, now standing behind where I was bent over the computer. "Theo, I'd forgotten how talented an artist you are. This looks so good!"

Glancing back to see that Onika now had the sleeping baby, I stood upright, moving back a little to give Nicky a better view of the computer screen.

As I wrapped an arm around her little waist, she said, "You do all of this digitally?"

Theo nodded, pointing to the Wacom tablet that was attached to his computer and its accompanying pen. "I use this and Manga Studio software. Both are pretty cheap, but they get the job done."

"Man, this is terrific! And you do the story, baby?" Her eyes were on me now, filled with wonder.

I grinned. "Yeah. You act like I never showed you our site before."

She shook her head. "You did months ago, when I was…I wasn't in the right head space back then to fully appreciate it. But now? I'm so proud of you two!"

I wrapped my arm around her shoulder and kissed her temple. "Thanks, Nick."

"You're welcome," she said, as she reached up and kissed my lips. "Hey, is your site mobile friendly?"

"Yeah," Theo answered before I could.

"Good! I'ma take some screenshots of the current chapter and tag everyone from Stan Lee to Oprah on Instagram, Twitter, and Facebook. You say *Fake for Bae* is your top-earning business, but this is your meal ticket. *This* is incredible, and I'm about to make sure everyone knows about it."

I couldn't do anything but smile. It felt good to know my girl had my back. So good, that once I got her back home, I ate her like I was a death row inmate and she was my last meal.

*****

"You gonna get that?" Nicky asked, glancing up from her computer where she was scheduling posts for her clients, including me, with Hootsuite.

"Nope. It's just my mom. Not in the mood today."

She was quiet for a moment, then my mom called again, the third time in less than an hour. "She's marathon calling you. Could be an emergency."

"I'll call her back later."

"Why not now?"

I finally looked up from my computer to see her eyes on me. "Because I know she's on some bullshit, probably tryna plan another fake-ass family dinner, and I'm not in the mood."

"But how do you know that for sure?"

"Because I know my mother, Nick. When she's on that shit, she always calls back to back like it's urgent, but it never is."

"But it could be this time."

I refocused on my computer screen and blew out a breath. "It's not."

"But you don't know that."

"Nick, I'm done discussing this. I'll call her back later."

I thought she'd left it alone, but after a stretch of silence, she said, "You got some chick programmed as 'Mama' in your phone?"

My head snapped up. "What?"

She closed her laptop and squared her shoulders. "I said…is some *bitch* calling you and you got her name in your phone listed as 'Mama'?"

I closed my own damn computer. "And why in THE FUCK would I do that?"

"To throw me off that ho's scent."

"Are you serious, Nick?"

"Do I look serious?!"

"Let me get this straight. You think I'm cheating on you with a motherfucker I got programmed into my phone as 'Mama'?"

"Yes!"

"Nick, have you lost your damn mind? Then what do I have my mom in here as?" I asked, holding up my phone.

She shrugged. "Wanda? Mrs. Davis? I don't know!"

"You think I'm cheating on you?"

"Is it Ivy?"

My eyes damn near popped out of my head as I stood from the sofa. "Ivy? I'm not messing with Ivy!"

Nicky hopped up from her seat beside me, raising her voice. Only inches separated us. "But you *are* messing with someone else, huh? What's her name, Damon?!"

"Her name is Nicole Lisette Strickland! Shit! Crazy ass woman!"

"Did you screw Ivy before we got together?"

"Huh? Nick! No!" I could see tears filling her eyes, and it felt like the room was spinning. What the hell was going on? "Nicole, I have not touched any woman but you since I've been back in Romey, and that ain't some chick calling me. It's my mom." I tried to go for the calm approach, because her ass was bugging completely the hell out.

"Prove it," she challenged, her eyes narrowed at me.

"Prove—you don't believe me? You know me better than this, Nick! Come on!"

"If that's your mother, I don't see why you can't just call her back and show me it's her." Her ass was pouting now.

"Because I don't like my mother, and you of all people know that! Damn!"

She just stood there and looked at me.

I scoffed and shook my head as I held the phone up to her face, dialed my mom's number, and put it on speakerphone, mumbling, "You are crazy as hell," under my breath.

After my mother answered, I said, "Hey, Ma, I just wanted you to know I got your calls. I'll call you back later. Can't talk now."

"Oh, okay?" my mother's confused voice said.

I ended the call and stared at Nicky's insane ass with raised eyebrows. "Nick, I have waited my whole damn life to be able to call you mine. Do you actually think I'd do anything to mess this up?"

She dropped her eyes. "No. I...I'm sorry."

I held the phone out to her. "Here, call all the damn numbers in there and see if I'm using your sister, Angie's, name as code for some chick. And your mom's name. And Aunt Monda. And the chick that works at Kroger's that sells the bootleg DVDs on the side. I got her number from Zo. She's in here as Ally, but I don't even know if that's her real name. She's old and she's black. I've never heard of an old black chick named—"

She heaved a sigh and with slumped shoulders said, "Okay, okay! I said I'm sorry! I believe you! I-I overreacted, overreached, acted a fool for nothing. But I can't help it! I've never been in a relationship with someone I love before. I mean, I love you so much it's driving me crazy."

"You think? Look, I feel the same way about you, but damn! Can you at least *try* to trust me? We in here screwing twenty-five hours a day and you think I got time to cheat on you?"

"No...I'm sorry, Dame," she whined.

I shook my head and moved to leave the room, but stopped when I heard her say, "I'll do anything to make it up to you." She stepped closer to me and dropped to her knees, grabbing the waistband of my jeans.

I dragged my bottom lip between my teeth and smiled down at her as she unbuttoned and unzipped my pants. Just that quick, I forgot about being mad at her.

23

Nicole

I was sitting in my parents' formal living room with my eyes across the space focused on the three men huddled near the piano no one in the Strickland family knew how to play. Well actually, my eyes were fixed on Damon as he stood there in black jeans, a plain white tee—instead if his usual vintage comic book or cartoon t-shirt—a black sport coat and black and white Chucks, holding a lowball glass of brandy, because apparently, grown-up Damon liked brandy. He looked gorgeous, and as Angie filled me and Renee in on her and Ryan's most recent trip to a beauty convention in New York City, I tried to calculate when during the course of the evening Damon and I could sneak into a bathroom for a quickie. I was on fire for him.

"Nicky? Did you hear me?" Angie's voice sounded so far off…

I jerked my head around to give her my attention. "Huh?"

Angie grinned. "Girl, I thought I had it bad! You can't keep your eyes off of Damon. How did I miss this before? All this time I thought he had a crush on you, but your ass been in love, too, huh?"

I shrugged. "Whatever."

"Right. *Whatever*. Nicky, I can't believe you kept this from us all these years!" Renee said.

"How you know it's been years—oh, yeah…I forgot Damon spilled the beans to Angie's loose-lipped ass."

"Yep," Angie confirmed.

I rolled my eyes. "Yeah, I'm crazy about him, always have been." My eyes made their way back over to him in time to catch him smiling at me. "I just had to get out of my own way long enough to accept it."

"I think it's beautiful, two people who've known each other since they were kids together and in love. I mean, you two are at a huge advantage. You already know everything there is to know about each other," Renee said.

"Yeah, it was definitely easy to slide into a relationship with Damon, but there're still things we have to learn about each other. We were apart for years, nearly our entire adulthoods. We've changed a lot, but the basics, the core of who we are as people, are the same. I know him at the deepest level, but I'm enjoying the way he's matured. The things that are different about him now—his confidence, the way he curses like a champ, his body, his openness about his feelings—all of that just makes me love him more." I was so deep in thought, more or less speaking out loud to myself than to them, that it took me a second to notice the shocked expressions they wore. Feeling self-conscious, I said, "What?"

"Nicky, that was the most beautiful, heartfelt, mature—"

"And normal," Renee said, interrupting Angie.

Angie nodded. "Yeah! And *normal* thing you have ever said. *Ever.*"

I smiled. "You didn't let me finish." I glanced around the room and lowered my voice. "And his dick? Sheeeeiiiiiiiiit! His skills are on POINT! He was good before. But now? I'm a straight-up fiend for him! The other night, he had me reciting the Pledge of Allegiance *and* the damn preamble to the constitution. I was 'We the People' like a motherfucker! My man can batter the chicken and fry the shit out of it! In a skillet, *not* a deep fryer!"

"There she is," Angie said, turning to Renee. "Our sister is back."

Renee shook her head. "Yep, that's her."

I planted a smirk on my face and was about to double down on my debaucherous speech when a booming voice snatched our attention.

"Sorry for the delay, everyone! Me and Lisa must've uh…lost track of time," Daddy announced, giving Mama, who clung to his side, a wink. Renee groaned softly. I giggled.

"Glad you all let yourselves in! Well, my baby did the honors of preparing us a delicious meal tonight, so let's eat!"

A few minutes later, we were all seated at the dining room table enjoying my mom's specialty, the only thing she made better than Angie did—lasagna.

"I can't believe you didn't bring my little buddy," Daddy said, his eyes on Renee and Zo, who were sitting across the table from me and Damon. I had been disappointed about Little Zo's absence, too, but had kept it to myself. I loved his little chunky butt.

"My mom wanted to keep him, and besides, me and Renee needed a real break, a night out, Pops," Zo said, and I wondered when he started calling Daddy *Pops*. Here lately, Daddy and Zo were damn near inseparable. I threw a look at Renee. She gave me a little shrug in return.

"Hmm, I guess I'll let y'all pass today, but I'll be by tomorrow so me and the little guy can spend some quality time together."

This time, Angie, who was sitting to my right, nudged me and muttered, "What the hell?"

I mumbled, "Girl…"

Then the table was filled with small talk about Angie's and Ryan's most recent trip, the book Zo was working on, my blossoming social media management business that I'd monikered *NLS*, and even Damon's websites. It was a nice, normal dinner, and it felt like Mama and Daddy never separated, almost like Daddy was never an absent father or an unfaithful husband. They both seemed…happy, content, much like the rest of us sitting around the table. There was a peace in that room that I'd never felt in that house in my entire life. It wasn't that my childhood was filled with strife; it was just always cloudy with a distinct sadness that hovered over the place because of my father's actions. But on this particular evening, for the first time in years, I couldn't feel that sadness.

As I lifted a forkful of key lime pie to my mouth, my father stood and cleared his throat. I set my fork down, and along with everyone else at the table, focused on Daddy.

"I first want to say how happy I am to be able to have this time with my family tonight. I love you, all of you. *Of course*, I love my baby girls, and I'm just—" He paused as his voice quivered a bit. "I'm glad to see they've chosen good men. Especially you, Nicole. I could've thrown a party when you canceled that wedding. I thought I was gonna have to put my foot in somebody's a—"

"Angelo!" Mama scolded.

"Sorry, baby. Uh, Damon, I never knew you that well, because

I…wasn't around much, but my Lisa loves you, and that's all I need to know. I'm glad Nicole has you," Daddy said.

"Thank you, sir. I'm truly the lucky one. Nicky is the answer to my dreams."

With my mouth gaped open and my eyes wet with tears, I fell into Damon and hugged him tightly.

"Well," my father continued, "Lisa and I thought this would be a good time to tell you all that after more than three years of separation and a lot of begging and pleading on my part, she has agreed to give me another chance."

Gasps and a chorus of "whats" rang throughout the room. I don't think any of us were exactly shocked about this development. If my sisters were anything like me, they were just surprised at Daddy's demeanor, the calm in his voice, and the way he kept shooting adoring glances at Mama. Daddy was just…different.

"Now, I know what you're thinking, but I promise you this: I'm not the same man I was before me and your mother separated. I've learned a lot about myself, your mother, and even you girls since Lisa kicked me out. And these two new sons of mine?" He shook his head. "Seeing the way Ryan loves and respects Angie and the way Lorenzo loves and respects Renee? Well, you two young men showed my old ass how it's supposed to be done, how to do it right." He turned and faced Mama. "Lisa, baby, you are my everything. You stood by me when I was nothing, didn't have nothing, and even after that when all I gave you was a comfortable, lonely life. You gave me three beautiful daughters and raised them into wonderful women. You are too good for me, but I'm blessed to have your love and your heart. I promise to take better care of it this time. I love you. Thank you for taking me back."

Mama leaped from her seat into Daddy's arms, and my heart swelled for them, for all of us.

24

Nicole

I fought to regulate my breathing as I blinked back tears. Sitting in the passenger's seat of Damon's car, the loudest thought in my cluttered mind was: *I knew this wouldn't last.*

It couldn't. Things had been too good for too long. Two months had passed since we'd officially been together. Two months of peace, spent soaking in each other's love. I'd been happy, *too* happy. And then…this.

But I wasn't surprised, knew it was merely a matter of time before my past crept into my present, especially since that particular part of my past wasn't so far in the distance.

I chanced a glance at Damon, at the man who made me swoon like a character in a romance novel. The man who made my heart race and my coochie liquify. I could see the tenseness in his jaw, and my eyes didn't miss the way his big hand kept gripping and releasing the steering wheel. He was pissed and rightfully so. Hell, I'd be pissed if I was him. If the tables were turned, I'm not sure things would've turned out so well. Sure, he was probably going to get back to the duplex and throw me and all my shit out of his place, and I couldn't even get mad about it, but if I had been him and not one, not two, but four different dudes, all my former fuck buddies, had come up to our table while we were out to dinner, my ass would've gone ballistic, but not Damon. He sat there and watched as I explained to West, Quincy, LeVontae, and another guy whose name eluded me that yes, my number had changed—a precaution I took shortly after moving in with Damon, because who had time to block that many niggas—and no, I wasn't going to give them the new one, because I was in a relationship with the man sitting across the table from me. Three of them took that information, apologized to Damon, and left. But West, who was a dude I screwed for the novelty of the fact that he had a gold grill and no job, just stood there, glanced at Damon, and said, "The fuck he got to do with us? I'm tryna kick it wit' you, not marry you. Shit."

Damon frowned and quickly stood from his seat, fists clenched at his sides, ready to do battle. And while West was a fool and a certified thug, Damon was bigger, taller, and had anger issues due to his parents' neglect and indifference. Plus, he loved me and was possessive of me before I was even really his, had marked me long ago. So I knew West was about to get his ass whooped. However, instinct told me to sit *my* ass down. I wasn't about to jump up and get between them and give Damon the impression I was defending West. *Screw that.* West was just going to have to take that ass-whooping, and I'd have to figure out which of my abused credit cards to use to bail my man out. And then, once I got him home, I was going to have to do all kinds of freaky shit to make it up to him. I mean, regular head wasn't going to cut it, despite the fact that I had the ability to make him speak in tongues.

But West wasn't as dumb as I thought he was. Damon could look very meek and unassuming at times, much like teenage Damon, something that actually turned me on, and I think that's what West saw in him when he decided to flex. But when Damon hopped up, and said, "I ain't got *shit* to do with you, but I got *everything* to do with her, and if you don't take your ass on somewhere, I'ma fuck you up right where you stand, yank that grill out your mouth and shove it down your damn throat," then lowered his voice and added, "Try me. *Please* try me," West didn't say another word. Just turned and left with a scowl on his face. We finished dinner in silence. Utter silence. Uncomfortable silence, during which my eyes and throat burned from fighting back stinging tears. My ho' days had caught up with me. I was about to lose the only man I'd ever loved, and it was all my fault.

It was one thing for me to tell him I'd been loose. It was another for him to see the evidence.

My heart rate doubled when Damon pulled into his driveway behind my car and shut off the engine. He sat there for a moment and stared out the windshield. My mind screamed at me to say something, but all I could come up with was, "I'm-I'm sorry."

His eyes swung over to me and rolled over my face for a second before he opened his door and climbed out, slamming it behind him. I reluctantly opened my door and followed him, waiting at the bottom of the front steps while he unlocked the door. Angie and Ryan were out of town, so at least they wouldn't witness my walk of shame as I moved out of another man's house in less than three months' time.

He went inside, leaving the door open…for me? Or maybe so he could throw my shit outside. I wasn't sure what to do, so I just stood there staring at the open door.

I could argue that my sister owns the place and refuse to go...

A minute or so later, Damon appeared in the doorway. I waited for a suitcase to land at my feet, but instead, he said, "You coming in?" with raised eyebrows and an unreadable expression on his face.

I gulped and nodded, ascending the steps and moving inside the dimly-lit apartment, shutting the door. Still facing the door and feeling his presence behind me, I softly said, "I'll understand if you want me to go. I'll get my stuff and—"

Damon's body collided with mine, pinning me to the door, his body weight knocking the air from my lungs and clipping my words. I turned my head, and released a breath, my heart slamming into my ribcage in response to the unexpected contact.

I could feel his breath on my neck, hear his harsh breathing, feel his hands on my arms. Then I felt his tongue on the back of my neck, and I closed my eyes. A low moan flew from my mouth on a ragged breath. His hands slid down my arms to my hips, then he reached around and unfastened my jeans, sliding his big hand inside my underwear to grasp my yoni. "This is what they want," he murmured. "But they can't have it. Can they?"

I shook my head as his hand gripped me tightly down there. "No," I whimpered. "That's what I told them, baby. Y-you heard me."

He tightened his grip on my treasure. "Mm-hmm. Why can't they have it, Nick?"

"B-because it's yours."

"Always been mine?"

I nodded as he pressed his erection against my butt while still gripping me.

He flicked his tongue against my earlobe. "I can't hear you, baby."

"Y-yes."

"Always gon' be mine?"

"Ahhhhh, shit! Yes!" I whined, as he loosened his grip and used a finger to stroke my clit.

He pulled his hand out of my jeans and pushed them and my panties down my legs, squatting behind me and kissing both of my butt cheeks in the process. Then he smacked my ass and spun me around to watch him undress while I pulled my blouse over my head, revealing the nakedness underneath as I'd opted not to wear a bra. He moved closer to me, knocking me back against the door as his mouth met mine in a tongue-lashing kiss. His body pressed against mine again as he palmed my breast, squeezing it as his other hand cupped my yoni tightly again, maybe even tighter than before. Possessively, as if there was any question in my mind who it belonged to. It'd belonged to him since the damn eighth grade.

And he knew that.

All I could do was moan into his mouth, because the passion he was emitting was overwhelming, *stifling*. Here I was, thinking I was a second from being single again, and according to this current assault, Damon was turned on by the evening's events.

As he reached around and gripped my ass with both hands, mouth still devouring mine, my legs instinctually wrapped around his as I scaled him and began grinding against him. He ended the kiss and stared at me as I gripped his shoulders, my breathing lurid.

"Nick, I don't give a damn how many men you fucked before you were officially mine. A hundred, a thousand, I don't care. I wasn't sitting around counting sheep and shit all those years myself. I did me. You did you, but this thing we got now? That's all that matters. I love you. Some thirsty niggas won't change that as long as their asses stay in the past. Okay? Shit, I don't want somebody no one else wants. And the fact that they've had it and can't get it anymore? That's just icing on the cake. I'm not letting you go, Nick. I'm *never* letting you go. No matter what."

I didn't bother trying to stop my tears. I just nodded, said, "I love you, Damon. Only you," and closed my eyes, yelping when he lifted my body, sitting my legs on his shoulders, my cookie directly in his face. I grabbed his head to steady myself as he buried his face between my legs. My head fell back as I let go of his head and braced myself against the wall. I was thankful for the duplex's high ceilings since I was perched on shoulders that rose over six feet from the floor. Damon devoured me, his stiff tongue attacking my bud relentlessly. I screamed like a mad woman as he licked me to the edge and shuddered as an intense orgasm rolled over me. He continued licking me as I whimpered, and when the thrumming in my core finally ceased, he lowered me to his waist, wrapping my legs around him and eliciting a gasp from me when he entered me with a groan of pleasure. His palm hit the door behind me as he thrusted deep inside me while burying his face in my neck. I held him tightly as my back slid up and down the door. "Damon!" I shouted, as he glided in and out of my wetness. He felt so good, different from any other man who'd ever touched me, and only two minutes, maybe three, after entering me, he incited another internal tornado that was quickly swirling out of control, causing me to hold my breath while my mouth hung wide open. My hearing ceased as my body rocked, and when it returned, I could hear Damon yelling, "Damn, Nick! Shit!"

My pulsing vagina was pulling on him, making him release earlier than he'd intended. But shit, that was his fault.

After a few more thrusts, he grunted, screamed my name with a tortured look on his face, and then his forehead collapsed against mine as we both tried to catch our breath.

"Nick, I told you, you gotta stop milking me and shit like that," he mumbled. "I can usually fight through it, but when it's that intense, I can't hold out."

"How can I stop it?" I asked. "You're the one making me come."

"Damn, I guess you're right. My bad."

I laughed. "Are you apologizing for giving me an orgasm?"

He gave me a lopsided grin. "I don't even know what I'm saying right now. I'm in a pussy fog."

"A what?!" I threw my head back and cackled loudly.

"You laughing, but that's why those dudes won't leave you alone. Too bad it's mine now and their asses can't have it."

I looked him in the eye and smiled. "That's right. It's yours forever."

"And ever, baby."

25

Damon

"Nick, come on. You see I'm tryna play this game." I leaned my head to the right, trying to see the TV screen.

She kissed my neck, her hands on my chest as she slowly rocked in my lap. We weren't naked, but she was definitely trying to get there. "I'm not stopping you from playing it," she murmured.

"But you're keeping me from concentrating, baby. There used to be a time when you'd be playing this game with me instead of distracting me."

"I'm out of practice, and you know I hate losing." Her lips met mine, totally grabbing what concentration I had managed to hold on to, and as I closed my eyes to return her kiss, I could hear the wails of my avatar as he was being overtaken by a pack of zombies.

"Dame, man! Are you even trying?" Theo's voice poured through the headset covering my ears.

Our kiss ended, and I switched the mic on my headset back on to respond to my cousin. "Nicky's over here messing with me. Let me hit you back, man."

"A'ight. Tell her I said wassup."

"I will." I pulled the headset off, tossed it on the couch beside us, and grabbed Nicky's hips. Looking into her eyes, I said, "Theo said hi."

She rocked in my lap again. "Mm-hmm."

"You made me lose."

With a lifted brow, she said, "So you'd rather play with Theo than play with me? Your best friend?"

I shook my head. "No, but I need to do a review of this game. Now it's gonna take me longer. This is work, not play."

She kissed me again. "This is work, too."

I grinned. "Nah, this is most definitely play. Work has never felt this good. But it'll have to wait till later."

She gave me a dubious look. "You don't wanna wait till later, and you know it. I can *feel* that you don't." She shot me a sly grin as she reached down between us.

I sighed. "Nick, come on, baby. Let me do this and then we can do *that*." I nodded toward my crotch.

Her spoiled ass rolled her eyes and slid from my lap to the couch. "Fine. I got work to do anyway. You just better hope I'm still in the mood later on."

I chuckled. "Baby, you're *always* in the mood."

"Whatever," she muttered, as she hopped up from the couch and headed toward the bedroom.

Thirty minutes later, Nicky rushed back into the living room as I was on my computer trying to write up my review of the game, and shrieked, "It worked!"

I looked up at her and stared for a second. "Why are you wet and naked?"

"I was in the tub and I decided to check your social media accounts, see if I needed to reply to anything, and I saw this on

Instagram." She held her phone up to my face, but shit, I couldn't take my eyes off her.

"What?" I asked, as I licked my lips.

"Look at the phone, Dame!"

"Damn, okay. You ain't gotta yell." I took the phone from her and read the DM. Then I frowned, looked up at her, at the wide-eyed, excited expression she wore, and back at the phone again. The message was from Karyn McNooner, a native Chicagoan and creator of the ground-breaking and controversial *Backwoods* comic strip. The same strip that became a popular animated series and movie, with wildly successful merchandising. The Karyn McNooner who'd won an Emmy for her writing contribution to an episode of *The Backwoods*. The same Karyn McNooner who, because of her success, was one of the most influential voices in modern African American culture. *This* Karyn McNooner wanted to set up a meeting to discuss the future of *Foreign Son*.

MY *Foreign Son*.

Mother. Fucker!

I looked up at Nicky with the biggest grin on my face, and said, "Damn…Your crazy ass tagging all those celebrities in those *Foreign Son* posts all over social media paid off!"

She nodded and giggled as I jumped up from the couch, grabbed her wet body, and kissed her all over her face. "Thank you, baby! Thank you!" I shouted.

She kissed me back three or four times. "Hey, I was just doing my job. You gonna call Theo?"

As I buried my face in her neck, I said, "Yeah, right after I handle some business with you."

She purred as I wrapped her legs around my waist and walked us to the bedroom.

*****

It was quiet, peaceful as we lay there in my bed, and I was…content. No, I was happy as hell. It's funny how things happen sometimes, how stuff falls into place when you least expect it. I spent a lot of years trying to figure myself out, trying to understand my place in the world. I never really had any guidance, no one to point me in the right direction, the path set out just for me, because my parents never gave a damn, or when they did offer some guidance, it was the college-then-job thing that never really fit me. No one ever truly cared about my wellbeing, my state of mind, or my future…but Nicky.

Nicky.

I squeezed her closer to me and kissed her forehead, peered down at her to see that even though it was past midnight, she was still awake.

"What're you doing up?" I asked.

She lifted her head and smiled. "What are *you* doing up? Too excited to sleep?"

"Yeah…excited, anxious, scared as shit. Can't wait to hear back from McNooner. See exactly what she's talking about."

"Me either. Baby, I'm so happy for you and for Theo, too. You guys deserve this chance. This is gonna be huge, Dame. I can just feel it. I know y'all are about to blow up!"

"Hmm, thanks to you."

"No, thanks to the talent you two have. All I did was stalk McNooner into noticing it."

I chuckled. "Well, I appreciate the hell out of your stalking skills."

She laughed. "You're welcome. So tell me, baby, how does it feel to know your dream is about to come true?"

I looked down at her with her eyes wide, her smooth skin free of make-up, her hair covered with a silk scarf, her mouth spread in a beautiful smile, and at that moment, I saw the old Nicky, the little girl who kicked ass on the regular for me. And teenage Nicky, the Nicky who believed in me before I knew how to, who took care of me when my parents wouldn't, and who took my heart and loved me like no one else ever has.

In fact, she *was* my heart. All that I was and wanted to be was because of crazy-ass Nicky Strickland.

I searched her eyes for a second and then I reached for her, pulling her up so that her face was even with mine. "Nick...baby, don't you know that all my dreams came true the day you became mine, *really* mine? This stuff with the comic or anything else that follows? Shit, none of that even matters other than it being a means for me to take care of you. If McNooner cut me a check for a million dollars right now and I didn't have you, it wouldn't mean shit. You are everything to me. You're my happiness, Nick."

I could see the tears in her eyes as her brow furrowed. "Damon, you make me feel like I'm a prize or something, and I love you for it." She rubbed her finger across the scar on my forehead, knowing how it turned me on when she did that.

"You *are* a prize, baby. My treasure. My future. My forever."

She kissed me while climbing on top of me until her naked body straddled mine.

I shook my head as I ended our kiss, flipped her onto her back, and slid down her body.

"What are you doing?" she asked.

I spread her legs and buried my face between them. "Thanking you again."

26

✦

Damon

"Congrats, man! Renee told me about you hearing from Karyn McNooner. That's big stuff!" Zo nudged me so hard, I bumped into Nicky, damn near knocking her out of her chair. I knew he meant no harm, but dude was humongous and obviously didn't know his own strength.

"Thanks, man," I said, rubbing my arm. "But we've still gotta meet with her and see what's up. I feel good about it, though."

I felt Nicky wrap her hands around my other arm as she leaned forward to look at Zo. "Damon's about to be a star. I just know it!"

I chuckled. "Comic book creators don't usually become stars, baby. As a rule, we're faceless geeks."

"Look at McNooner and Stan Lee. No one thinks they're faceless geeks. Stan Lee has mad swag for an old white man!"

I nodded. "True, but I'll just take financial stability, and if I get it, I'ma spoil your ass even more than you already are."

Nicky, who looked fucking mouthwatering in a tight, short, white dress, causing me to look even more out of place in my usual formal attire of black jeans, black tee, black blazer, and black chucks—not that I gave a damn about being out of place—pouted, making me want to kiss her, so I did. "I'm not spoiled," she said.

I leaned in close to her ear. "You're spoiled on this D, and you know it."

"Yep, and I want it right now."

I was smiling too hard. "Shit, come on then. We can leave right now. You know I ain't messed up about being here."

She shook her head, her eyes on my lips. "We can't do that. We just got here, and Zo bought a good table. We're damn near on the stage, and you know you wanna see Mint Condition. You used to love them."

"Your ass just wanna see Stokley 'cause you used to have a crush on him."

"Still do," she mumbled.

"I heard that."

"Heard what?"

"You know what? I bet his ass can't even sing no more. Let's go home and I'll play *Pretty Brown Eyes* on YouTube while I got my face between your legs, making you scream my name right when they hit the chorus."

Her eyelids were heavy as she licked her lips, and murmured, "*Or we could find somewhere to do that here.*"

"Nah, these stuck-up folks'll be calling the police on me, 'cause I promise I'ma pummel your ass…*mercilessly.*"

"Shit," she whispered, and the next thing I knew, her tongue was down my throat and she was trying to climb into my lap.

"Damn," Zo said. "I don't know who's worse, y'all two or Ryan and Angie."

We broke apart in time to see Angie and Ryan approaching the table. They'd arrived before us but both quickly excused themselves to the restroom after we made it. As they took their seats, Angie looked flushed and Ryan was wearing a huge grin on his face as he buttoned his tuxedo jacket.

"Y'all been screwing in the bathroom?" Nicky said, rather than asked. "Y'all nasty."

Angie shrugged and stuck her tongue out at Nicky. "Hater."

"I *am* a hater. Damon over here talking about I gotta wait till we go home," Nicky said, giving me a frown.

"Which bathroom y'all use? It's got a lock on it?" Zo asked, with a serious look on his face.

"My pregnant ass is not having sex in a public restroom at an event sponsored by a charitable organization I'm a member of!" Renee said.

"Damn, it ain't like you're *that* pregnant. Shit…" Zo mumbled.

"Your mom is here!"

"At her own table!"

"Okay, but what if I pass out? You gonna carry me all the way back here to our table?" Renee asked.

"You think I won't?" Zo replied.

"Pass out?! Shit!" Nicky and Angie shrieked out of sync, echoing my thoughts.

Zo shrugged with a smirk on his face.

"Y'all have no idea," Renee muttered.

"All right, fine, we'll wait. But I'ma tear your ass up when we get home, so you better get ready," Zo said.

"I *stay* ready," was Renee's rebuttal as she kissed Zo.

"That's why I love your ass," he replied.

I chuckled. "Y'all wild over here. Never thought a charity ball could be this lit."

Angie did a little bounce in her seat. "You know us Stricklands love to entertain."

"All right, keep bouncing and shit and I'ma hem your ass up right here, make use of this long-ass tablecloth. I'm tryna behave since your folks are supposed to be coming, but you know how I roll," Ryan warned.

Angie's eyes widened as she took a sip of her water.

"Daaaaaamn," Nicky said.

Then a sly smile spread across Angie's face, and she bounced again.

Ryan raised an eyebrow. "Keep playing."

"We finally made it!" Mrs. Strickland sang, putting an end to the craziness as everyone at the table greeted her and her husband.

Mr. Strickland pulled out her chair, and as she sat down, kissed her on the lips so long even *I* felt a little uncomfortable. Yeah, the whole damn family was nasty as hell.

We all settled at the table, made small talk until the program began, sat through speeches and presentations, ate dinner, and as we all waited for Mint Condition to perform, I noticed Nicky's attention was on a table across the room. I hoped she wasn't looking at some man, because I didn't mind getting ignorant up in there. I knew it wasn't *Law and Order*, because Nicky had told me he and his family had another event tonight. There was some political thing going on that she would've had to attend, too, if she hadn't left him. But either way, whoever she might've been staring at could get these hands.

I guess Angie noticed too, because she said, "Nicky, what are you staring at?"

"That ho' over there in the Fashion Lova gold dress with that cheap-ass weave," Nicky replied evenly.

"How you know that dress is from Fashion Lova?" Angie asked. My question was: what is a Fashion Lova?

"Because I lost my dignity one time and actually perused their website after Amber Rose advertised it. You know she's my spirit animal. But that shit is just too cheap for my taste."

Angie rolled her eyes. "Well, I kinda like Fashion Lova, and I will never understand how you manage to be broke and bougie at the same time."

"It's a rare and unique talent only a few of us possess," Nicky retorted. "I'll max out ten credit cards before I'll buy cheap shit. I have standards."

"Riiiiight, so you're staring at her because of her dress?" Angie asked.

"And hair?" Renee added.

Nicky shook her head, her eyes still on the woman. "No...I'm tryna figure out what's wrong with her damn eyes."

Angie squinted across the room, and said, "Something's wrong with her eyes? They look normal to me," echoing my thoughts.

"Naw, that bitch got stare-itis or something. She been staring at Damon all night, eye-humping him, and I'm tryna decide if I need to go over there and help her eyes find themselves." She raised an eyebrow. "I mean, what I gotta do? Hang a sign on him that says, 'Property of Nicole Strickland' to keep these thirsty chicks from blatantly eye-hustling my man? I'm beginning to feel disrespected."

"Nicky, they probably don't realize he's your man, and come on, you know my brother, Damon, is a good-looking guy. Women are bound to notice him," Angie said.

Angie had barely finished her statement when I asked, "Huh? She's been looking at me?"

Nicky turned to me, opting to answer me instead of Angie. "Mm-hmm. Her eyes been on you all damn night. You know her?"

Here we go with this shit. "Hell, no."

"Oh, damn. Here she comes," Ryan mumbled.

I closed my eyes for a second, praying this woman wasn't really coming to our table.

She did.

Fuck.

I really didn't know her, but that wouldn't matter to Nicky. She only needed half a reason to act a fool and embarrass the whole table.

"Hey! Damon, right?"

Who the hell is this woman? I slowly nodded, cutting my eyes at Nicky. "Uh, yeah. Do I know you?"

"Yes! Ashley Tatum. We went to high school together. We were in the same graduating class. You don't remember me?"

I shook my head. "I'm sorry. I don't." Turning to Nicky, I added, "You remember her, Nick?"

Nicky shook her head, her skeptical eyes glued to the woman.

"Uh, Ashley, you remember Nicole Strickland, right? She went to school with us, too. She was in our class," I said.

"Nicole Strickland? Little Nicky Strickland? Oh, wow! Of course I remember you! I see you still have that body I always wished I had. I was chubby back then, wore those horrible glasses." She let her eyes settle on me again. "I see I'm not the only one who's changed. Ivy told me you were some kind of handsome now, and she didn't lie," she gushed.

Shit. She had no way of knowing it, but Ivy's name was a major trigger for Nicky. As soon as Ashley said it, I could feel Nicky's eyes burning a hole into the side of my face. Plus, her obvious flirting was not helping the situation at all.

"Is your weave synthetic?" Nicky asked, as if she was inquiring about the weather.

"Weave?" Ashley questioned, sounding genuinely confounded.

"Yeah, *weave.* I mean, that can't be your hair. It looks so..." Nicky's eyes rolled toward the ceiling like she was searching for the right word. "Plasticky."

Ashley's mouth fell open as she reached up and patted her head.

Both Angie and Renee gasped.

Ryan said, "Wow."

Zo shook his head.

I didn't have the heart to look in Mr. and Mrs. Strickland's direction to see their reaction.

"Uh...everyone, this is Ashley, right?" I said, trying to avoid the impending cat fight. Ashley nodded, returning her attention to me and smiling brightly. "Ashley, this is Nicky's family."

Everyone greeted her except Nicky, who was again staring at me, so I said, "Good seeing you, Ashley," as a way of dismissing her before some real shit got started. Nicky didn't mind fighting, actually enjoyed it, but who felt like dealing with that shit?

"Did you know Ivy was here?" Ashley asked.

Before I could say no, Nicky said, "Yeah, did you know that, Damon?"

I turned and gave her a confused look. "How the hell would I know that when I'm up under your ass twenty-four-seven?"

"Oh, there she is! Ivy! Look who I found!" I glanced up to see Ashley waving Ivy over to our table and wondered just how awkward it would look if I snatched Nicky up and left right at that moment. But that wouldn't work. It would make me look guilty of some shit I didn't do, like messing around with Ivy, a woman I hadn't given a single thought to, and Nicky would never let me live it down.

"Hey!" Ivy chirped. "Damon, I haven't heard from you in a while."

"Yep," I said, draping my arm across Nicky's shoulders. "Been busy." If I had to, I'd throw Nicky's ass on the table and screw her in front of everyone to keep the peace.

"Oh," she said, letting her eyes slide from me to Nicky. "Wait! You two? Wooooow. I heard about the wedding being canceled. So, this happened after that?"

I opened my mouth to respond, but Nicky beat me to it.

"No. Before," she said.

"Before?" Ivy asked, her voice raising an octave.

Nicky nodded as she scooted closer to me, conspicuously sliding her hand up my thigh. "Way before. *Years* before." And then her mouth was on mine, kissing me so deeply, my dick damn near jumped out of my pants.

"Damn, y'all," Ryan said.

My eyes were glued to her when she ended the kiss, so I barely noticed Ivy and Ashley leaving our table as the lights began to dim, signaling the beginning of the show. My eyes darted over to where her parents were sitting. Nicky didn't care what anyone thought of her, but I had mad respect for her mom and hoped she didn't think any less of me because of what had just occurred. Thankfully, her parents had disappeared. A quick search of the dimming room put them at another table engrossed in conversation with a couple that looked to be around their age.

As Mint Condition took the stage—Stokley's ass could still sing, by the way—I pushed the fact that Nicky had basically just marked her territory—me—in front of her family out of my mind and buried my face in her neck, whispering, "I'ma wear you out when we get home."

She looked at me and smiled. "You better."

27

Nicole

I was so happy for Damon, deliriously happy for him and extremely proud of both him and Theo. They'd left for LA that morning to meet with Karyn McNooner about her acquiring the rights to their digital comic and adding it to her new online comic platform, Southside Strips. Damon wanted me to travel with him, offering to buy me a plane ticket, but I knew I'd be a distraction he didn't need. And besides, we'd been going strong in our little love bubble for nearly three months, and the mature, rational side of me felt we needed a breather, a little time apart. But the sex-crazed, Damon-crack-fiend, madly-in-love side of me was slowly unraveling without him, and he'd only been gone a few hours.

I dropped him off early that morning, and my stomach jumped hurdles as I walked back into the quiet duplex, his scent permeating the air. It took me a couple of hours to get my mind together enough to send an email to a website designer Angie referred me to as I continued working toward making NLS Social Media Management legit. Then I checked all my clients' accounts for DMs or comments that might've needed to be acknowledged. I ate lunch, watched a movie on Netflix, and spent the better part of the evening lying in bed staring at the ceiling, decided to skip dinner, and was falling asleep when Damon called.

I damn near knocked my phone on the floor trying to snatch it up from the nightstand to answer it with a breathless, "Hello?!"

"Why the hell are you out of breath?" was his greeting.

"Uh, I was trying to catch the phone, almost dropped it."

"Oh…well, I made it. Me and Theo getting ready to have dinner with McNooner and her business partner. The change in time is already messing with me, but it's all good. What you been up to?"

"Not much. Missing you."

"You could've come with me. I wanted you to."

"I know. Just didn't want to get in your way."

"You could never do that, baby. *Ever*. Gotta go. I'll hit you back after dinner."

"Okay. Love you, Dame."

"Love you, too, Nick."

Hearing his voice helped me fall into a peaceful sleep, so peaceful that I woke up in a panic the next morning when I realized I'd missed his promised call. Since I knew his meeting was that morning, I opted to text him.

Me: *Hey. So sorry I missed ur call. Was asleep.*

Damon: *It's alright. I figured u fell asleep. Bout to go in this meeting. Will call later.*

Me: *K*

The day dragged on as I fought the desire to call or text him, confident he'd contact me as soon as time permitted. But I was so anxious, I couldn't concentrate on any tasks that might've made the time pass more quickly. I spent the better part of an hour trying to choose what I'd wear to pick him up from the airport the next day. I wanted to wear a short dress that I could go commando in without him readily knowing it. Once that task was over, I was left with nothing but a profound sense of loneliness as everything in that duplex apartment reminded me of him. I couldn't eat, couldn't stop thinking, and as the day progressed, my thoughts became increasingly worrisome as Travis's ominous warning blared in my mind.

Karma is a bitch.

The only way karma could hurt me was if I lost Damon. Having him after a lifetime of loving and wanting him, then losing him? That would destroy me. Everything else, I could get over, but finally opening my heart and then having it crushed again? That would end me.

I started wondering how long it would be before he found a woman more suitable for him, one who'd never played with his heart, one who didn't have a list a mile long of former lovers, one who didn't almost marry another man right in front of him just to spite him, one who didn't have to reap so much sown shit.

Someone other than me.

Someone *better* than me.

As the day wore on and hours passed with no word from Damon, I told myself to leave the house. Angie and Ryan were predictably out of town being Internet stars, but Renee was home, and visiting Little Zo never got old. Or I could go see my mom, but I'd be running an even bigger risk of catching her and Daddy into something now that they were officially back together. Thanks to my ho' days, I didn't have friends. Maybe I could drop by Aunt

Monda's and kick it with her and Onika, hold baby Tia. I quickly dismissed that thought, because if I stayed there too long, I was going to get high, and marijuana would only enhance the negative feelings I was experiencing. Getting high always made me think deeply, and I was already doing enough of that.

So I crawled into bed and held Damon's pillow to my heart, didn't eat, couldn't sleep. All I could do was watch the phone and lay in bed missing my Damon, hoping he wouldn't stop loving me.

*****

I woke up in the middle of the night with my pearl throbbing—no, it was *pounding,* and my whole body felt warm and tingly. *Did I have a dream so intense and vivid that it affected my body this strongly?* As slurping sounds became evident at the same time as the mouth attached to me down below, I wondered if I was still dreaming. It didn't help that my eyes were closed, so I opened them to see Damon's head between my legs and knew that in his absence, I had completely lost my damn mind.

Then I decided to give in to the fantasy and enjoy it. If I had gone crazy, at least I could get a good orgasm out of it, so I threw my head back and moaned as the imaginary Damon went to work. It wasn't until after I'd hit my peak and he lifted to kiss me that I realized it wasn't a dream or fantasy. Damon was home.

Damon was home!

My heart stuttered at that realization.

"You just let any dude come in here and eat you like this?" he asked, his voice husky.

I shook my head, tried to catch my breath. "I knew it was you." In dreams or reality, I definitely knew his touch.

"How?"

"No one else can do that, or anything else, the way you do. What are—"

"I missed you, couldn't wait until the morning to see you. Took an earlier flight, took an Uber home, and when I came in and saw you sleeping, I felt like I needed to thank you again, and again, and again…"

"For what?" I asked.

He reached over on the nightstand and grabbed his wallet, pulled something out of it, and held it before my face. My mouth dropped open at the six-figure check endorsed to him from Southside, Inc.

"Theo got one, too," he said.

"Damon! You signed a deal with her?"

He nodded with a huge grin on his face. "Yep. This check is for the rights to the chapters that're already up on our site. They're gonna move them to the Southside Strips site. And we also signed a contract to keep creating content for the strip. Those payments will be made quarterly. Baby, these contracts are sweet, too. The lawyer Zo put me in contact with out there says they're among the best rights contracts he's ever seen. We'll still get royalties from any animated or live action series that's developed and a percentage of any money earned from feature-length films. McNooner really believes in *Foreign Son*, says Theo's artistic talent paired with my wit are a winning combination, that she's never seen such potential. Baby, you have no idea how good it felt to be validated like that, to hear those words coming from someone like her."

"Dame, I am so happy for you! And I'm so happy you're home! I was going crazy missing you, waiting for you to call. I was gonna jump your bones in an airport bathroom when I picked you up, but this is even better."

"Yeah, Theo wanted to kick it, celebrate out in LA, but the only thing I wanted to do was get back home to you." He grabbed my face and stared into my eyes. "I love the shit out of you, Nick."

I smiled as every ugly doubt about us melted away. "I love the fuck out of you, Damon."

28

Damon

I'd never seen her laugh and smile so much or seem so happy. She was relaxed, something she seldom was when we weren't home alone, but I guess it was because she didn't feel like she had to be on guard here. I was related to nearly everyone in the room, so she didn't have to worry about anyone eye-humping me, as she'd put it.

But I think part of her contentment was that three months into this new level of love for us, we were closer than ever. Work was going well as Southside Strips prepared to introduce *Foreign Son* to the world, and I was more financially stable, moving closer to giving her the life she really wanted. My goal was to give her what she gave up when she ended things with Travis, and I was willing to work hard to do it.

I smiled as I watched her chatting with a tiny cousin of mine, one of the dozens of kids there for Aunt Monda's annual Christmas party, which doubled as a celebration for me and Theo this year. Nicky was good with kids, an odd trait for someone who could be as mean as she could be, but it was part of why she was so complicated, part of why I loved her, and I wondered if her attraction to kids had anything to do with the one we lost. I wondered how often she thought about our baby. Was it as often as I did?

"Aye, cuz. She's a good look for you," Theo said, as he fell onto the sofa beside me, handing me a beer. He surprisingly wasn't high. No one was, because Aunt Monda was reserving her weed for after the kids cleared out.

"Thanks, man. It was a long time coming, but she was definitely worth the wait."

He took a swig of his beer. "Yeah, I'm glad y'all's dumb asses finally got it together. Been fucking longer than half the married folks I know. I mean, y'all should be on your tenth anniversary or something by now."

I shook my head. "It wouldn't have worked back then. I had to grow up and change so I could handle her. Back then, I just went along with whatever Nicky said. I was like her damn puppy. She didn't respect that. I got her respect now."

Theo nodded. "That's deep, man." He paused, then said, "You gon' marry her?"

"I want to. I mean, that's always been the ultimate goal. Just wanna make sure my money is where I need it to be. It's getting there now, though, thanks to the comic."

"I hear you, man. I think I'm ready to wife Onika now that I got more than ambition in my bank account. I can't thank you enough for bringing me in on this, cuz. Letting me do the art. It was your idea; I know you could've chosen someone else."

I frowned. "Man, I wanted the best. Your lazy ass is the best. Wasn't no other choice, nigga."

He smiled, and I noticed he had on jeans and a white t-shirt. He must've bought some clothes with that check. He'd even shaved. Semi-success was changing my cousin for the better. Before I could tease his ass for looking all clean cut, Onika slid into his lap, which made me wonder where their baby was. A second later, I found her in Nicky's lap and shook my head. She really loved kids.

My eyes wandered around the room and stopped at my mother. Shit, I'd forgotten she was there, but that was probably because I'd been working overtime to ignore her. At least she had the decency not to bring Kyle's ass. I was feeling too good to have to share oxygen with both of them at the same time. I quickly looked away, but it was too late. I felt, rather than saw, her move in my direction.

I sighed when she took a seat on the huge ottoman situated on the floor near my feet.

"Damon?" she said timidly, as if she expected me to hop off the couch and strangle her if she spoke too loudly. I was pissed at her, but I wasn't a monster.

I didn't reply, but I did look at her.

"I-uh-just want to let you know how proud I am of you."

I shifted my eyes to Nicky, who was now staring at me with a look of concern on her face. "You don't think I should…what did you say? Oh, yeah…'Give up my silly businesses and get a real job' anymore?" I settled my eyes on her again.

She dropped hers. "I didn't understand what you were doing. I've never really understood you or the decisions you've made, and I'm sorry for that. I'm-I'm sorry for not being more supportive."

I frowned as I stared at her. "Really?"

"I'm trying, Damon. I want things to get better between us. I talked to Nicky earlier and—"

"Damn, I knew it. For a second there I thought you'd grown a maternal bone or something, but Nicky had to tell you how to act with me, huh? Makes sense since she was the one who took care of me when you refused to."

Her eyes darted around the room, because I was raising my voice. "Damon, please don't do this. I want this tension between us to end. I love you."

"Dame, one of your cousins brought cherry cobbler. It's still your favorite, right?"

I looked up at Nicky standing over me and nodded. She was alone, no kids around her feet or on her hip.

"Well, come on. You better get some before it's gone."

I glanced at my mother before standing and following Nicky into Aunt Monda's kitchen. Sitting at the table crowded with foil pans and casserole dishes, I said, "Thanks for rescuing me."

Nicky scooped some cobbler into a Styrofoam bowl and shook her head. "I didn't rescue you. I rescued your mother."

"My mother? What are you talking about? I was minding my own damn business. She came and started messing with me."

She set the bowl in front of me and handed me a spoon. "No, she tried to talk to you. All she did was attempt to have a conversation with her only child."

"Probably because you told her to. She told me you two been talking tonight."

She sat next to me and rested her elbows on the table. "Yeah, we ran into each other when I was leaving the bathroom earlier. She said she's desperate to make things right with you, asked me what I thought she could do to get through to you since we've been *friends* for so long."

Shit. "Nick, I don't talk to her enough for her to know about us. It's not like I'm keeping it a secret, and you know it."

"That's the problem. You talk to your mother so seldom, she has no idea we've been living together as much more than friends for like three months!"

I sighed, took a bite of the cobbler, and damn near moaned. *Who the hell made this?* "Look, Nick—"

"I told her to stop trying to force you into a relationship with your father and just show some genuine interest in you. She's trying, Dame. You gotta at least meet her half way."

I didn't respond, just kept eating that good-ass cobbler.

"And I did it for myself, too."

I glanced up at her. "You did what for yourself?"

"Brought you in here away from your mom. I didn't want you to blow up and then get me home and take it out on me."

I dropped the spoon. "What? I'd never hurt you and you know it!"

She shook her head. "I'm not talking about you hitting me, Dame. Of course I know you wouldn't do that. But you'd screw me half to death, try to break me in two."

I scoffed as I reclined in my chair. "So now your ass don't like it rough? Okay."

"Oh, I *love* it rough. The rougher the better, but I don't love the idea of rough sex as a result of you having an argument with your mom. That's just creepy."

I tilted my head to the side. "I guess I see your point."

"Good. Look, can you at least *think* about treating her like a human? I mean, the whole anger thing you got going is sexy as hell, but it's not you, and shit, I know all about holding on to stuff and refusing to forgive people. You *know* I do. But it wasn't the healthiest thing for me to do. And I want you healthy and strong and ready to screw—"

I leaned in and kissed her. "Shut up, Nick. I'll try to be nicer to her...I guess."

She wrapped her arms around my neck and grinned. "Thanks."

I smiled at her and thought how if this dream, my dream of being with her, could come true, then anything was possible, even me getting along with my mom.

Maybe.

"What're you thinking about?" she asked.

"You want a baby, Nick?" I don't even know where that question came from, but I guess it had been hovering somewhere in the back of my mind for it to spill out like that.

Her arms slid from me. "What? Why would you ask that?"

I shrugged. "I see how you are with kids, especially how your face lights up when you hold Tia and Little Zo. I just figured you wanted one."

"You wanna give me one or something?" she asked, with a voice full of skepticism.

"If you want one. I mean, I'm scared I'll fuck a kid up, but for you, I'm willing to try."

Her eyes softened, and then she dropped them. "Just because I like babies doesn't mean I want one. I wouldn't be a good mother."

"Yeah, you would. You got the nurturing thing down, baby. Look how you've always taken care of me. I have no doubt you'd do the same for my child."

Her breathing was getting loud as her eyes scanned the kitchen but avoided me. Then a thought hit me. "Are you thinking about our baby, Nick?" I asked softly.

She sighed. "I always think about our baby, Damon. That's one of the reasons why I'm all kinds of fucked up."

I opened my mouth, then closed it. I didn't know what to say.

"Can we go?" she asked, standing from her seat.

I nodded. "Yeah."

*****

"I had picked out names."

I barely heard her voice. We were in bed and I'd almost fallen asleep, so my mind was hazy.

"What, Nick?" I mumbled through a yawn.

"I picked out names...for our baby. Before..."

I searched the darkness of the bedroom with my eyes before finally saying, "You did?"

"Yeah..."

"What names did you pick?"

"I had it narrowed down to two girl names and two boy names—Desiree or Antionette and Jason or Jacob."

"Those are nice names, but damn, no Damon Jr.?" I attempted to lighten the mood and wondered if it would ever get easier for us to talk about this.

"I was pissed at you, remember? But I'd definitely put Damon Jr. on the list now."

"Glad I redeemed myself."

"I'm scared, Damon."

I frowned, searched the room again. "Scared of what, Nick?"

"Of...of getting pregnant. You were right. I do want a baby; I'm just scared I can't have one, that I'll have another miscarriage."

I bent my head to peer down at her in the darkness. "Why-why do you think that? Did your doctor say—"

"No...I'm supposed to be fine physically. I just...I'm afraid it'll happen again, and I don't think I could survive losing another baby. It took me a long time to get over it. I still haven't really moved past it."

"Do you...do you think you'll ever be able to move past it enough to try?"

She sat up and switched the lamp on her side of the bed on. "You want a baby, don't you?"

I nodded hesitantly. "That baby was mine, Nick. Losing him or her is something I've had a hard time dealing with, too. And...I'd like to try for another one."

She gasped softly. "Damon, I never thought about how you...can you give me some time? I—for you, I'm willing to try, but I need more time."

"You can have all the time you need, baby. I'm not going anywhere. I love you."

She rested her head on my chest again, and said, "I love you, too."

29

Nicole

I moaned as I virtually inhaled my youvetsi, shamelessly enjoying every spoonful. "OMG, whose idea was it to come here for girls' night? Because this is the bomb!" I garbled.

"Mine," Renee said, taking a sip of her water.

"Well, you're a damn genius. I'd forgotten about this place. I used to love when Daddy brought us here as kids."

Renee, Angie, and I were at Dukas, a family-owned Greek restaurant that had been serving up culinary goodness for as long as I could remember.

"Girl, anything to get a break. I love my husband and my baby, but they both require so much attention, that sometimes I need a breather," Renee said, taking a bite of her food.

"See, that's my issue. I want kids and I'm not getting any younger, but shit, Ryan is a handful all by himself!" Angie said, eyes wide.

Renee laughed. "See, you get me. What on earth am I gonna do with two babies *and* Zo? Half the time, I can't finish breast feeding before he attacks me. I'm trying to figure out how this man can stay turned on all the time?"

I lifted an eyebrow at Renee. "Shit, you complaining about that? I'm in Heaven having my daily screwathons with Damon. It's been pure-damn-bliss!"

"I know…" Angie mumbled. "Loud asses."

I pursed my lips as I sat back to relieve the pressure on my full belly. I had torn through my appetizer and entrée and had drank enough water to fill a pond. I was feeling right. "We are not that loud. You need to stop exaggerating."

"Hell, I'm not exaggerating! I don't know which of y'all is the loudest. I thought me and Ryan were some nymphos, but we ain't got shit on you and Damon. Y'all woke me up last night!"

I frowned and thought about last night. "Oh, yeah. My bad. Damon got a little carried away, had me in like a handstand position in the living room while we did it. It was good, but I was loopy from all the blood rushing to my head. So—"

"Un-uh. I don't need to hear anymore. I do not want that visual stuck in my brain. I'm just thankful Ryan and I are rarely ever in town. Half the time, I'm sitting over there afraid y'all are gonna break something, and by something, I mean your private parts. I was already concerned about Damon's mental health with him being in a relationship with your crazy ass; now I'm afraid you're gonna give him a damn limp!"

Renee's mouth formed an "O" before she covered it with her hand and started giggling. I threw my middle finger up at Angie, and she grinned.

"Sometimes I really can't stand your ass," I hissed at her.

Angie flapped her hand at me. "Yeah, yeah, whatever."

We chatted about her upcoming trip to Vegas for some hair convention thing. I swear she made me want to go natural every other day, but I was too lazy for that. Having natural hair required a level of commitment I wasn't willing to apply.

"So, Rell and Janine are engaged now?" Angie asked, shifting our conversation.

Renee nodded. "Yes! She is crazy about his big behind. I have never seen her so happy before. And you can just look at him and see how he adores her."

"Go, Janine! She's your age, right, Renee? And he's younger?" I asked.

"Yeah, she's like thirty-nine, and I think he's about twenty-nine or thirty."

"Damn, she's getting it good then! I bet his no-talking ass is tearing that up!"

Angie shook her head. "Well, *Nasty Nicky*, how are things with you and Damon?"

With raised eyebrows, I replied, "Uh, obviously good if what you claim you've been hearing is any indication."

She rolled her eyes. "Besides sex, you nutcase! Like, how are you two getting along?"

I shrugged. "Good—great! I'm happy, happier than I've ever been in my life. He's good to me, treats me like a gift. It feels like I finally have what I was missing all those years I messed around with…shit, *everyone*."

"What's that?" Renee queried.

"Love. Love in its purest form. Damon loves me, and all he wants in return is for me to love him, and I do that without a second thought. It's like…I didn't start really living until we got together for real. I just—I love him so much."

My two sisters stared at me.

"What?" I asked.

"I'm happy for you, baby sis. You seem almost normal since you two have been together. Almost…" Angie said.

I threw my middle finger up at her again and stood from the table. "I gotta hit the restroom before we leave."

After I finished my business, I checked my phone and saw a text from Damon: *When u coming home?*

As I stepped out of the restroom, I texted back: *Why? U miss me?*

Before he could reply, a voice snatched my attention from my phone. "Well, look who we have here."

The voice was familiar, but not welcoming or cordial, and when I looked up, I realized why. I was face to face with Judge McClure. I frowned, my eyes darting behind him in the dimly lit hallway where the bathrooms were located.

"Travis is here, if that's who you're looking for."

"I'm not looking for anyone. I was just heading back to my table." I tried to move around his big, imposing frame, but he blocked me. He was taller and wider than his son, and much less attractive. I'd never felt very comfortable around him, and this instance was no exception.

"Can I help you with something?" I asked, with irritation dripping from my voice. I hoped he wasn't trying to confront me for calling off the wedding. It wasn't like he'd paid for it.

"I chose you, you know?"

I frowned. *What the hell is this man talking about?* "Um, what?"

"I chose you. Travis had been looking for a suitable woman to marry for a couple of years. A few came close to making the cut, but I vetoed them all…until you."

The fuck? "What the hell are you talking about?"

He smiled, his eyes perusing my body in my short red bandage dress. "When he told me about meeting you and taking you out, showed me a picture he'd taken of you during your little date, I knew you were the one. You know why?"

I just stood there, too confused to answer him.

"Because you reeked of sex. Even in that photo, I knew you were just my type of woman—loose."

I leaned my neck back. "Who the fuck are you—"

"And that mouth. He told me it was filthy, *dirty*. Made me wonder just how dirty it could get."

"Have you lost your damn mind talking to me like this?!" I shrieked, paying no mind to the fact that we were in a public place or to the people shooting us curious looks as they passed by.

The volume of my voice didn't seem to faze him at all as he continued like a man on a mission, never raising *his* voice. "Travis and I made a deal. He would marry a woman of my choosing in order to advance his political career, and the woman would be at my…disposal. You see, Travis doesn't really like sex with women, so I'd be doing him a favor. Keeping his wife happy."

"Travis really *is* gay…" I mumbled that more to myself, but he heard it.

He shook his head. "No, I suppose my wording was confusing to you. He doesn't like sex *at all*. He's more or less…asexual. He tells me he can perform when he needs to but prefers not to. Although, he did say he grew to enjoy you..."

My mouth dropped open. What the hell did I almost marry into? "So, you think I would've just slept with you because you wanted me to? You must be out your damn mind!" I hissed.

"Oh, I know your type. You would've let me have you for the right price, and I planned to be very generous to you. Still will, if you'd like to enter into an arrangement with me now." He spoke so softly, gently, as he insulted me.

I opened my mouth to curse him out in at least three different languages, not including English, but was interrupted by Travis-the-conniving-asexual. And to think, I still felt guilty about calling the wedding off!

"Judge, Mom is ready to—" He looked up, and noticing me, muted himself.

"You expected me to screw your father after I married you?!" I yelled.

Travis jumped a little. "That was you yelling back here? We were wondering what was going on. Couldn't make out what you were saying over the godawful Mediterranean music they play here..."

"Answer my question, asshole! You thought I was gonna have sex with-with *this*?!" I pointed at the judge.

Travis's eyes darted between me and his father, and then he clutched his forehead. "Uh, Judge..."

"You sonofabitch! You did! I can't believe this!"

"Well, I can't believe you left me for your best friend!" Travis gritted.

"Thank God I did instead of falling into this nasty-ass sex cult of yours!"

"The hell is going on?" That voice made my heart jump in my chest. Behind the judge stood Damon with his eyes glued to me. "Why do you look upset, Nick?"

"Nick," Travis scoffed.

Damon's eyes shot to Travis. "Excuse me?"

Travis cleared his throat and with a nod of acknowledgement, said, "Damon."

Damon returned his nod, and said, "Ben Stone."

Travis looked confused and opened his mouth to respond, then quickly closed it.

"Damon?" I said weakly, relief flooding me as his silly ass stepped beside me and wrapped his arm around my shoulder.

"Oh!" said Judge McClure. "You're the fellow she left my boy for. Lucky man, from what I hear. Travis says she's a tiger in bed. I would love to experience it for myself." He winked at Damon, who lunged for him.

I grabbed him, and so did Angie and Renee, who'd appeared out of nowhere. All three of us struggled to keep his big strong ass off the judge. "Damon, don't! He's a judge. You don't need that kind of trouble. Not now. Not when things are going so good for you. You've worked too hard to mess it up over him," I begged.

"Listen to her, young man. You don't want the trouble I can give you. She isn't worth it." The judge turned to leave with Travis on his heels.

"Oh, but I ain't got *shit* to lose!" I kicked at him, and felt arms grabbing *me* now, heard my sisters yelling something, then felt my feet lift from the floor as Damon hoisted me up and began carrying me out of the restaurant.

*****

My mind raced as I sat in the passenger's seat of Damon's car with an array of emotions crowding me. I was relieved, freaking elated that I'd dodged that bullet, not that I would have ever slept with Judge McClure's old crusty ass, but shit! The thought of him even *thinking* he could have some was nauseating. I might have been a ho', but I was a selective one. I did *not* screw old men. And knowing that Travis went along with this disgusting plan? Now *that* pissed me off.

"What the hell was that back there, Nick?" Damon asked, his voice low, shaky. He was obviously still upset.

"Travis's father cornered me when I was leaving the restroom, started saying all kinds of crazy stuff. Sexual stuff. You heard what he said right in front of you!"

His eyes shot from the road to me and back, but he didn't respond.

"Evidently, he and Travis had a plan for him to keep me 'satisfied,'" I said, making air quotes. "Because Travis is asexual."

"I knew his ass wasn't straight! I knew it!"

"He's not gay either. He's—shit, I don't know or care, but I'm creeped the hell out by this plan they had, and I can't believe he'd confront me in public like that. They're so big on protecting their name."

"You heard him. Asexual or not, A.D.A. Barba's ass recognized you got that good-good and told his father, got him feenin' for it. Nick, good pussy, or the prospect of some, can make a man forget how to think rationally. Believe me, I know."

"I guess, but…"

"But what?"

I blinked back tears. "He basically said he knew I was a ho'. Like, he could just tell. What have I done? How could I put myself out there like that to the point that it was so obvious? I mean, I couldn't even get mad about him saying it, because I *was* a ho'. A huge one." My voice broke, and so did the damn. There my ass was, crying again.

Damon pulled the car over and reached toward me, wiping my wet cheeks with his hands. "That's not who you are, Nick. It might've been what you did, *but it's not who you are.* You're beautiful, maybe a little crazy, but a good woman who has always been good to me…even when you were bad. Shit, *especially* when you were bad."

I looked up to see him wearing a sly grin. "Stop playing," I whined.

He pulled me as close to him as he could with the console between us. "Hey, I love you for who you are, no matter your past. I'll always love you, Nick."

"I love you, too."

"Now, stop crying before I turn around and kick his old ass and end up in jail."

I sighed and smiled at his crazy butt. "Okay…Hey, why'd you come to the restaurant?"

"I missed you, knew you rode with Angie, so I thought I'd surprise you and pick you up. Maybe do something nasty in the car on the parking lot, but that didn't happen."

"You were on the lot when you texted me?"

"Yeah, I didn't see Angie's car at first. Wanted to make sure you were still there."

I looked down at my phone to find I'd missed his reply to my last text in the restaurant asking if he missed me. It read: *I always miss ur ass.*

I peered over at him, and said, "You're everything, you know that?"

He grasped my hand and squeezed it. "So are you, baby."

30

Nicole

He kissed my forehead and frowned down at me. "You're still warm. Fever hasn't broken. I don't wanna leave you, Nick. Maybe Theo can go by himself and—"

I shook my head and covered my mouth as I coughed. "You can't do that. You're the brains of the operation. He can't do the interviews alone. They'll want to discuss the story, not just the artwork, and no one can explain the story like you. Go. I'll be okay. I promise."

With a creased brow, he remained in place, squatting next to where I lay on his sofa. "I really wanted you to come with me this time."

"I know, and I wanted to come, too, but I can't, Dame. I can barely hold my head up. Just my dumb luck to get sick right before this trip."

He sighed and nodded. "You sure you don't wanna go to your mom's or one of your sister's? I don't want you here alone. Who's gonna take care of you?"

I smiled weakly. "I'ma take care of myself. I'm okay, and if I need anything, Angie and Ryan are right next door, since they're home for once. Plus, I can call my mom for help, too. But I won't need it."

He finally stood, giving me a full view of his tall, beautiful body covered in black jeans, a Black Panther t-shirt, and black—you guessed it—Chucks. He walked across the room and pulled his jacket on, his concerned eyes never leaving me. "You got juice, that soup Angie made, your medicine..." His eyes roamed the room. "Kleenex! You got enough Kleenex? Anything you want me to get you before I go? I can run to the store—"

"No, you can't. Bye, Damon. Leave before you're late getting to the airport."

He sighed before leaning over to kiss my hot forehead again.

"Stop touching me before you get sick, too!"

"I don't care about that. I'll be checking on you. Love you."

"Love you more."

Then he left, and my heart twisted in my chest. It was just a quick turnaround trip to LA—two days of promo work for the comic, which was scheduled to launch on the Southside Strips site later that month. Damon and Theo were to do a couple of videos for McNooner's YouTube channel and her comic website, as well as some interviews with a few popular YouTubers whose content was centered around the world of comics. Their itinerary was packed, and I was sad to miss this trip with him but couldn't help it. I was sick, felt horrible, and didn't have the energy to make the trip. Plus, if I did muster up the energy to accompany him, I knew I'd be a drag, more of a concern and a liability to him than anything else, and he needed to be able to focus.

I stayed at his place, honestly not wanting to share my germs with my family, but was grateful for Angie checking on me a few times after Damon left. And poor Damon must've texted and called me twenty times, feeling guilty about leaving me in this state, but I didn't mind. My pride over his success overrode the emptiness I felt over his absence.

*****

"You sound tired," I said, upon hearing the strain in Damon's voice the next morning. "Long day yesterday, huh?"

"Yeah. That and the time change…and I didn't sleep well."

I turned over on my side in the bed, where I had migrated from the couch last night. "Why?"

"Worried about you."

"Don't be. I'm much better. I'm good, really. Fever broke. I even feel like eating again."

"Really? That's great, baby! Can't wait to see you tomorrow. I miss the hell out of you."

"I miss you, too. So, what's on your agenda for today?"

"Uh, a meeting with Karyn McNooner and her staff, a couple more interviews, and some event tonight. A party, I think."

"Hmm…well, be sure to post some pics from the event on IG. I'll add some hashtags in the comments."

"Nick, you're sick. Don't worry about Instagra—"

"I'm fine. Now, do what I said or I will screw you numb when you get home."

He laughed for a good minute, causing a smile to spread across my dry face.

"That's supposed to be a threat? You're a damn lunatic, Nick."

"I know."

After our call ended, I dragged myself from the bed to the shower, dressed, ate some of Angie's soup—our grandmother's special recipe—and drank a ton of orange juice as I watched TV before drifting off to sleep.

I awoke several hours later to the TV watching me and shut it off. I smiled when I saw the bottle of water and unopened package of cough drops sitting on the coffee table, indicating Angie had been over to check on me while I slept. Checking my phone, I noticed two missed calls from Damon. I must've been damn near comatose to miss a visit *and* two phone calls!

Sitting up, I navigated to my text messages to find one from Damon:

I tried to call. Talked to Angie and she said u were sleep. Heading to this party but wishing I was with u. Text me when u get this and let me know how ur feeling. Love u.

It was after midnight in Romey, but not too late in LA, so I replied: *Sorry I missed ur calls baby. Feeling good enough to climb ur fine ass.* (Water droplets emoji) *Call me when u can. Love u.*

I was grinning as I clicked on the Instagram icon on my way to the bathroom. I checked my account first, then Angie's, Genesis's, Zo's two accounts, and finally, Damon's. I hadn't had the strength to check on them over the past couple of days. I frowned when I saw all the notifications he had. Tons of them. What the hell had he posted?

I went to his page, saw a pic of him in his hotel room wearing his usual attire of jeans and a t-shirt. You could see the tattoos on his arms, mostly Korean alphabetical characters, and yeah, he was handsome and sexy as hell, but he didn't even hashtag it and the pic only had twenty likes. I kept checking his account and found that he'd been tagged in three or four photos. After I clicked on them, the air seemed to vacuum from the bathroom. I finished my business, washed my hands, and quickly headed to the bedroom, plopping down on the side of the bed, my eyes glued to the phone.

Missy Mae, his ex, the only woman other than me he'd ever cohabitated with, had tagged him in four pictures. The first was a picture of him taken from a distance in what looked like a night club. The caption read: *Look who I found! Be still my heart! #hemakesmyheartrace*

Then another pic taken from a distance. Damon was smiling, engaged in a conversation with some guy. This time, the caption read: *Should I say something to him? #helpme #yesorno #damhesfine*

My eyes blew the hell up as I scrolled down to see the comments encouraging her stalking ass to approach my man. And this ho' knew he was mine, because she still followed him on IG, as evidenced by her tagging him. She'd seen the pics of us he'd posted. Hell, her thirsty ass had even liked some of them.

The third picture was a selfie of her biting her bottom lip with her eyes wide. Damon could be seen in the background, still in the distance, unaware of her creepy ass. The caption read: *Here goes! Why am I so nervous?! #damonisbae #stillinlovewithhim*

The fourth picture made my blood run cold and my head begin to throb. My entire body trembled as I held my phone and stared at it. It was a photo of her snuggled up close to Damon. They were both smiling widely, her head resting on his shoulder contentedly. I could tell they were sitting down. They looked…happy. Hell, they looked like they were in love. She captioned this picture: *Together again. Feels like we were never apart. #reunited #trueloveneverdies #newbeginnings #imgettingsometonight*

The comment section was full of fuckers cheering this bullshit on.

And the tons of notifications? They were from other people reposting the pics and tagging him in them.

My first thought was to catch the first flight to LA and beat both their asses then come back here and fuck up everything Damon owned, pour bleach on his laptop *and* his clothes. In pajama pants and a thin tank top, I shoved my feet into a pair of sneakers and stomped into the living room, stopping to send a text to Damon: *Ima make you wish you never met my ass! I hope that bitch is worth it!*

Then I snatched my keys up from the coffee table and raced out into the frigid January air. I paid no mind to the fact that I was recovering from an illness, had on no coat, and my hair was all over my head. I had some emergency ass-kicking to do. Once in my car, I realized I didn't have my purse, and that's when I broke down, laying my head on the steering wheel and crying like a baby. How could he do this to me after I gave him my damn heart? How could he betray me, hurt me *again*?

The rational part of my brain tried to reassure me that it was just a photo. Probably harmless, but I had to wonder what made her bold enough to tag him in that shit and put those captions under those pictures. The bitch alluded to screwing him tonight, and she tagged him in it! So that meant he knew about it. How could he let her do that when he had my face plastered all over his page? This shit was embarrassing and hurtful as hell. He hadn't even called or texted to explain. I guessed he was…busy.

With her ass.

Was this my karma? Was I finally getting my payback for all the shit I'd done?

My heart felt like it was going to split in half, the pain unbearable as I wailed loudly in the confines of my car. I'm not sure how long I was out there. I just remember Angie appearing at the driver's side door, opening it, and coaxing me outside. As she wrapped her arm around me and led me to her side of the duplex, I ignored the continuous calls that finally came from Damon.

31

Damon

I was wound so tight, I could've run home from the airport. That shit Missy pulled was foul. All up in my face, grinning, saying she missed me and hated we weren't at least friends. I was cordial, smiled, spoke to her, and moved on. I had no idea she'd been posting pictures of me all night with those captions and hashtags, because my phone died while I was at the party. I'd forgotten to charge it, but didn't plan on being there long enough for it to matter.

After leaving the event McNooner wanted me and Theo to attend, a small mixer for her employees, Theo asked if we could drop in at a party one of the chicks who worked at Southside Inc. told him about, some chick he was trying to bone behind Onika's back. I honestly didn't want to do anything but head back to the hotel and call Nicky, then crash. But I agreed for some stupid-ass reason.

Once there, I met some cool people. It was a birthday party for a popular YouTuber. Missy was also a YouTuber, but since we had lost touch, I had no idea she was in the states, or in LA, or would be at the party. Hell, I didn't know she'd followed me to a couch until I felt her body heat damn near on top of me, and even then, I tried to ignore her. I didn't realize she was taking a selfie with me at first, because I was laughing at something Theo said. When I realized what was going on, she was posting the pic, and when I asked to see what she was doing, her childish ass started giggling and holding her phone behind her back. I had to use Theo's phone to see what she'd done, and I knew if Nicky saw those pics, my ass was grass.

So I cursed Missy out.

I mean, I know it was messed up how we broke up, and I was sure this was her revenge or whatever, because when I returned to Korea after that visit to Romey, I was no good to Missy, barely touched her. When she asked what had changed, I admitted to her the reason was Nicky. Maybe I was too honest with her, letting her know if there was ever a time I had to make a choice, I would choose Nicky. Always. I thought I was doing the honorable thing but didn't account for the fact that while my relationship with Missy didn't mean much to me, just like any interaction I had with women who weren't named Nicky Strickland over the years, Missy was actually in love with me. And she knew about me and Nicky, because she asked about us at the club, asked me how we were doing together. I told her we were good. So yeah, she did what she did on purpose.

After I cursed her ass out, I left. Didn't even tell Theo, who'd disappeared on me, that I was leaving. Went back to the room, charged my phone enough to turn it on, saw the text from Nicky, and tried to call her about twenty times, texted her, too, but she wouldn't answer or reply. And my ass panicked. My flight was scheduled to leave at ten the next morning, but I headed to the airport that night, tried unsuccessfully to get an earlier flight out, and ended up spending the rest of the night in the airport.

And now, as I pulled up to my place, I felt like I was going to throw the hell up. I couldn't lose Nicky, not over some bullshit like this, not after the shit I went through to get her.

I hopped out of my car and ran inside my place to find it empty, tried to call Nicky again only to get her voicemail. I snatched the closet door open, and closed my eyes, collapsing my shoulders in relief when I saw her clothes were still in there. Then I remembered her car was still outside and rushed over to Angie's side of the duplex, knocked on the door, waited two seconds, and knocked again. Ryan answered.

Before he could say anything, I looked around him, and asked, "Hey, man, Nicky in there?"

He nodded, stepping outside and closing the door behind him. "Yeah, uh…look, man. You probably should give her some time. You don't wanna go in there right now."

I shook my head. "I can't give her time. Nicky'll be done backslid or something."

"Backslid?"

"You know…*backslid*."

Ryan's eyes lit up with recognition. "Ooooooh, I got you."

"Look, I just need to explain this shit to her, make her understand I didn't do anything wrong!" I didn't mean to yell at him, but I couldn't help it. I was past frustrated.

He sighed as he glanced back at his front door and shook his head. "Man…"

I jiggled my keys in my hand. "Can you just tell her I'm here, that I wanna see her?"

He seemed to think about that for a moment, then nodded and disappeared into his apartment, leaving the front door slightly ajar. I started to go in there, but heard her shrieking, and changed my mind. She was pissed the hell off.

Ryan reappeared. "Yeah…you should definitely give her some time."

"What did she say?" I asked.

"Uh…that she didn't wanna hear a word you had to say and that you and your bitch could go straight to hell."

I dropped my head and my shoulders. "Is she, is she still feeling sick? I mean, is she feeling any better? Fever?"

"She's better. Look, I'm sorry, man. I'd let you in, but I ain't tryna have Angie up my ass. She's pissed at you, too."

"It's all right. Just let Nicky know I'll be next door. I—thanks, Ryan."

"Yeah, man."

I went home and texted Angie, explaining my side of things. It took five hours for her to reply that she believed me, but that I needed to give Nicky time to calm down. I knew that was sound advice, but it didn't change the fact that I missed her and needed to talk to her. But something told me to chill and wait.

*****

A whole day passed with no word from Nicky. She was still ignoring my texts and calls, and Missy's posts were damn near going viral with likes. I couldn't eat or sleep; I was so wound up. I just didn't know what to do to make this shit right.

After the second day, I called Angie trying to plead my case again. She reassured me that she was on my side, but reiterated that Nicky was still too upset to listen to reason. I needed to give her more time. The only positive thing was she hadn't left Angie's. At least I knew she was safe and getting better and wasn't out screwing some random dude, since that was her go-to coping mechanism.

Day three came with more of the same, and I was about to lose my mind. At this point, didn't she need clothes or something? Underwear? Shouldn't she have come home for those things? *Maybe I could take some of her stuff to her.* I shook that thought off just as quickly as it hit my mind. Shit, I wasn't going to help her leave me.

Day four arrived, and by then, I was mad as hell that her ass left me and refused to hear me out. Didn't what we had at least deserve a conversation? If she loved me like she claimed to, shouldn't she want to hear my side?

Maybe she didn't love me. Maybe this was just as one-sided as it felt back in high school. Maybe what we had was never real in the first place.

Maybe I should pack her shit and take it to her.

Maybe I should be done with her.

Yeah, right.

One thing was for sure: I needed to get up out of that apartment before I totally lost my damn mind.

I sat in there staring at nothing for ten minutes before I grabbed my keys and left with no destination in mind. I drove past Aunt Monda's, knowing I needed a clear mind in case Nicky came home, and if I stepped foot in my aunt's house in my current state of mind, I was going to get high. No doubt about that. So I kept riding, wishing my ass had more friends, someone to talk to about the shit I was dealing with. I hadn't spoken to my Navy buddies in so long, their numbers had probably changed. So all I had was Theo, who still lived with Aunt Monda…and Nicky.

I kept driving, thought about dropping in on Nicky's mom since she'd always been kind to me, but she was *Nicky's* mom, and being there would only remind me of Nicky. Zo and Renee? I was never as close to Renee as I was to Angie, because she was so much older than me and Nicky. Damn, I had no life in Romey that wasn't connected to Nicky. This shit was pathetic.

I eventually made my way to my mom's house, of all places. I guess home is home no matter how jacked up it is. I didn't expect her to be there before five in the evening, but her car was in the driveway, so I parked, took a deep breath, stepped out of my car, and found myself at her door. I stood there for a minute or two before I knocked. Another minute passed before I heard her ask who it was, even though there was a peephole on the door.

"Damon," I said, almost as if I was unsure if that was my name.

The door swung open, and my mother didn't even try to hide her surprise at me being there without her requesting it. Her eyes, the ones she gave me, were wide, and her mouth hung open before she finally stuttered my name and invited me in.

I stepped inside my childhood home and stood by the front door, thinking to myself that this was probably a mistake, but I needed something and I guess I thought I could find it there.

"Uh…" she said, nervously rubbing the thighs of her jeans then fiddling with the collar of her yellow oxford shirt. "Are you hungry?"

I should've been, since it'd been a couple of days since I'd eaten, but I wasn't. Nevertheless, I said, "Yeah."

She nodded, her eyes avoiding mine. "Uh, I haven't cooked today, but I could warm up some leftovers. I've got spaghetti. And I could make a salad to go with it."

I nodded.

"Wanna have a seat?"

I hesitated. "Is Kyle here?"

She had turned to leave the living room, where the front door led into, but froze. "Uh...yes. He lives here now."

I stood there, trying to decide what to do. I didn't want to see him, but the thought of being alone at my place with nothing but my thoughts was even less desirable to me, so I said, "Okay," and sat on the sofa.

"Should-should I tell him you're here?"

I shrugged.

She nodded and left the room.

I sat there and looked around. All the times I'd come over for those ambush dinners, I hadn't noticed that not much had changed. My school pictures still hung on the walls along with my academic awards. I was smart in school, so smart my decision to join the service rather than go to college had been a point of contention with my ambitious mother. But more school was the last thing I wanted. It bored me. I wanted the adventure and travel I believed the Navy could afford me, and I got it, too. The Navy transformed me from a boy to a man, gave me experiences that changed and molded me. So did living in South Korea and being an entrepreneur here in the states. My parents never understood me, from my hanging with a pretty little girl all through school, to my decision to struggle rather than get a regular job. Nicky was honestly the only person who'd always understood me. That was why she meant so much to me. It was also why losing her again was driving me nuts. No matter her crazy ways, slick mouth, or loose past, I needed her like I needed air to breathe.

"Hey, son."

I closed my eyes and took a deep breath, told myself not to get upset about him calling me that. Biologically, the word was correct. I *was* his son. My height, skin tone, build, and even my damn nose and teeth were proof of it, whether I liked it or not. Plus, this was evidently his home now, and I'd shown up uninvited. The least I could do was act like I had some damn sense.

"'Sup," I replied, giving him a reverse nod of my head.

His eyebrows lifted, and I could see the smile in his eyes. He was happy I didn't curse him out. Damn, had I been acting that crazy with him?

"Glad to see you. When Wanda said you were here, I was surprised."

"Yeah, so am I," I mumbled. "Just needed to come home…I guess."

He was silent, and although my eyes were on the floor, I could feel his eyes on me. Finally, he said, "You feel like talking about it?"

I looked up at him. No, I didn't want to talk about it, but I needed to. As messed up as my head was, I knew I needed to talk to someone who wasn't related to Nicky or high on marijuana. So I shrugged, and said, "Relationship problems."

"With Nicole Strickland or Missy Mae?"

I frowned, my eyes glued to him.

"I follow you on Instagram," he said, answering my unspoken question.

My father is on Instagram?

"I've seen all the pictures of you and Nicky," he continued.

"Mama know?"

It was his turn to shrug. "She's not on social media, and I haven't mentioned it to her. We don't talk about you much. You're a sensitive subject for her. She blames me for...how things are between all of us."

I nodded.

"So which one are you having trouble with?"

"I'm only in a relationship with one woman. I only love one woman. I'm not like you," I shot at him.

He raised his hands. "Okay, I guess that's fair, but it doesn't answer my question. There are pictures of you with two women."

Damn, if this was how my father and the rest of the world saw things, no wonder Nicky was so upset.

"Nicky! I didn't post that shit with Missy! Why are you acting like I did? How'd you even see those pictures she posted? You follow her, too?"

He shook his head. "Those pictures were on my explore page, probably because I follow you."

I sighed, leaned forward, and rubbed the back of my head. Then I sat up and began gnawing on my thumbnail. "Shit," I muttered.

"Yeah…"

I looked up at him. "She won't talk to me. I need to fix this, but I don't know how when she won't talk to me."

"Well, in my experience—and you know I have plenty experience when it comes to messing up with the woman you love—you're just gonna have to be patient and wait her out. Give her a little time. You say you love her, right?"

"More than anything in this world."

He smiled. "And she loves you?"

"I believe she does."

"Then she'll hear you out eventually."

I shook my head. "You don't know her. I can't wait her out. No telling what she'll get into in the meantime."

He was silent for a moment or two before saying, "Okay, I'll give you that. I don't know her, not like you. You've known her since you two were kids, so tell me about her."

I sighed, staring at the wall across the room. "She's headstrong, rude, loud, impulsive, protective, always been there when I needed her. Jealous as hell when it comes to me. I actually like that about her, but it's working against me right now."

"Okay, knowing all of that, what do you think you should do?"

"I *know* I need to make her listen to me, but I don't know how when she refuses to see me."

"Then I guess you need to figure out a way to get her to see you."

"Yeah, I know."

I didn't solve anything during that visit. I had dinner with my parents, a peaceful dinner, and then I left, but not before my mom pulled me into a hug, and whispered, "I know about you and Nicky, and I hope you two work things out."

I had no idea how she knew, and I really didn't care. I gave her a smile and have to admit it felt good to hear something so motherly coming from her. Nicky still wasn't home when I returned, but my heart didn't feel as heavy. I'd been able to offload some of the weight of what was going on, and I felt better because of it.

*****

Eight days passed and still no Nicky. I had dinner with my parents three or four more times, somehow finding comfort in being with them. We talked about a lot of things, including my relationship with Nicky. Little by little, I saw them for what they were, two human beings who'd made mistakes they regretted, just like I had. I regretted hurting Nicky, regretted ever leading Missy on, regretted letting Nicky be with Travis for so long. My family hadn't morphed into the Huxtables, but things were better between us, and that was a welcome change considering how screwed up other parts of my life were.

Things with *Foreign Son* were still going well, with the launching of it and the other comics on the Southside Strips site still on schedule. There was a huge launch party Theo and I were supposed to attend in LA in a couple of weeks, but I knew there was no way I could go with things between me and Nicky still up in the air.

The thing was, although she hadn't returned home, I kept seeing signs of her having been there. On those evenings when I had dinner with my parents, I would return home to find some of her clothes missing from the closet, or that her toiletries had disappeared from the bathroom. She was moving out little by little while I was away from the apartment. That shit made my stomach twist into a knot. She was actually leaving me. For good.

Hell, no! That shit was *not* happening.

I searched my mind for a plan, some way I could make her talk to me, and finally, one came to me. I left like I had many nights that I had dinner with my folks, but this time, I parked my car down the street and walked back home, quietly entering my apartment, trying to be undetected.

I sat in my bedroom, no TV or stereo on, and waited. I texted Nicky a couple of times, like I did every day, sent her a link to DeJ Loaf's *No Fear* in one of them, hoping she'd pay attention to the lyrics. She still didn't reply, and after an hour passed, I thought my plan was a bust. Then I heard a key in the front door, and my damn heart shimmied in my chest.

I stood from the bed, listening to her move around in my apartment, and when she finally appeared in the bedroom doorway with her eyes downcast, my heart dropped. She'd lost weight, and Nicky was already tiny. There were dark circles around her drooping eyes, and she just looked so…sad.

"Nicky…" I said.

She jumped, startled by my presence, mumbled, "Shit," then

turned to leave.

"Don't," I said softly. "If you have ever loved me, then don't leave."

Her back was still to me as she said, "The way I feel doesn't have anything to do with it. I'm not staying, Damon."

"You ain't leaving, either. The fuck you thought this was? This is forever, Nick. You don't get to leave me. Not today or tomorrow. Not ever."

She turned to face me, mouth hanging open. "What you gonna do? *Make* me stay? Tie my ass up and screw me into submission like you did in high school?"

"You asked me to do that!" Damn, I was yelling already. I calmed myself. "Nicky, I don't give a damn what you say, you don't get to leave me over some shit I didn't do. I know you. This is about more than just some pictures. That overactive brain of yours got you thinking I screwed that girl, but I didn't. I did *not* mess with Missy's ass, and if you know me like I know you do, you know I'm not lying."

She moved a little closer to me, the strap of her thin tank top slipping from her shoulder. "What I know is, another woman, some fake Korean skank, declared on social media that she was gonna fuck you while posting a pic sitting up under you, and your ass hasn't said shit about it in response. You haven't addressed it *at all*. No posts, nothing!"

"I've been too busy tryna get my damn woman back to worry about posting on IG, and I *did* address it! I cursed her ass out for it!"

She rolled her eyes. "I'm sure you did."

"I did! You want me to make a post cursing her out? I will! What do you want me to do? Tell me and I'll do it!"

"I want you to stop breaking my heart! And the only way for that to happen is for me to take it back from you!"

"I didn't do shit!"

She was in my face in seconds, smelling like she always smelled, making me want to throw her on the bed and screw her beyond reason. "I *saw* the pictures. Yeah, the first few were stalkerish as hell, but the last one, the one of your dumb ass sitting there with her grinning and shit? That one showed me just how much you love me! How could you let her post some mess like that?! Did you screw her, Damon?"

"Hell, no! I already told you I didn't! And I didn't *let* that motherfucker do shit! I didn't even know she was taking the picture at first, and when I realized what was going on, she'd already posted it! My damn phone was dead so I had to see what she did on Theo's phone. And that's when I cursed her out, because right or wrong, Missy don't mean shit to me, never really has and never will. Hell, she means less than *not shit* to me now. It's always been you. I ain't the best man in the world and I know it, but I love you, Nick, and I wouldn't do anything to hurt you. Not again."

She stared at me, but she didn't reply. I could tell she was considering what I said.

"Baby, did you really pay attention to that picture?"

"Yeah, I did, and I saw your stupid ass smiling at that bitch!"

"Did you really? I was smiling at Theo. I wasn't even looking at her."

Boom! Boom! Boom!

Fuck! Not now! Who the hell is at the door?!

"Y'all okay in there?!" Angie yelled through the door.

"Yes!" Nicky and I shouted at the same time.

"Okay!" she replied.

With a lowered voice, I said, "Nicky, I know I messed up in the past, but I owned it. I never denied it. If I had messed up this time, if there was anything going on between me and Missy, I'd admit it and then beg for your forgiveness, but nothing happened. I don't want her, never really did. If I'm honest about it, I was only with her because I couldn't be with you."

Nicky dropped her eyes, but remained silent.

"I can't lose you again. My ass won't make it this time. I can't sleep, don't wanna eat. I need you, baby."

Her eyes slowly found mine. "Why does it have to hurt so bad? I don't like feeling like this, Damon."

"Then stop feeling that shit. I did nothing wrong. You're pissed at me over Missy trying to get some revenge. She was trying to break us up and you fell for it."

She frowned and leaned her neck back. "Are you calling me stupid?"

I shook my head. "No, baby. You're anything but stupid. Hell, you're the smartest person I know. But I think you have tunnel vision when it comes to me. You're so convinced something is gonna happen, you jumped on Missy's fake evidence without really thinking it through. I do not want her. I. Only. Want. You."

Her head dropped.

"Please, Nicky. Don't leave." I moved closer to her, placing a hand on her cheek. "This is killing us both, baby. You need to believe me and let it go so we can be together again. *Please.*"

She shoved me in the chest, knocking me off balance a little. I stumbled but didn't fall. Standing there and staring at her, I prepared myself for whatever else she was going to do to me. This was Nicky, so violence was expected. Hell, she could've kicked my ass to a bloody pulp and I wouldn't have cared as long as she didn't leave me.

With her chest heaving, she swiped at her nose, and asked, "Why did you bring Ivy to my rehearsal dinner? You had to know that would upset me."

Damn, that threw me for a loop. "Uh…I don't know." I shrugged. "Because you hurt my feelings?"

"With Travis?"

I opened my mouth, closed it, and nodded.

"Damon…I'm sorry about the Travis thing. I'm sorry for taking so long to move past what happened in high school. I feel like this is my punishment, my karma, and—"

"I lied," I interrupted her. "Back when we were in high school and I said the reason I missed your appointment was because I was with Ivy? I lied. The truth is, I'd already broken up with her right after you told me you were pregnant. I lied because I was scared, but I didn't want you to know I was scared. I was tired of being weak and scared around you. I've regretted it every day since. Ivy didn't mean shit to me. Still doesn't. Missy, either. It's you. Always been you. And even if…even if you leave me, it'll always be you."

She didn't move for a full five minutes, just stood there with her eyes glued to me, and then she collapsed against my chest, her body shaking as she cried. I held her close to me, gripped her tightly, and whispered, "Thank you, baby. Thank you."

She wrapped her arms around me, and whimpered, "I love you so much."

"I love you, too, and from now on, you're traveling with me no matter what, so we can avoid shit like this. I can't go through this again."

She looked up at me with wet eyes. "What if I get sick again?"

"Then my ass is staying with you. No more being apart."

She nodded and leaned into me again.

Later that night, I took a picture of us with Nicky lying asleep in my arms, being sure to angle it to hide our nakedness, and posted it on Instagram with the caption: *This is my Heaven, my everything. Always has been and always will be. We know the truth and that's all that matters. #mygirlforever #andever #andever*

By the following afternoon, Missy had deleted all the pictures from that night. There were still copies floating around the Internet, but I was glad she got the message.

32

Nicole

One thing the whole Missy Mae picturegate taught me was that maybe I was too attached to Damon. Like, in an unhealthy, "he's my world" type of way. It felt good to be immersed in that type of relationship when things were good, but the moment I saw that picture, I lost it, and by *it*, I mean everything—my identity, my mind, my desire to take care of myself. And even before then, my every waking desire was to be pasted to Damon's side. The problem was, I'd never been in a real relationship...ever. I didn't know the proper way to behave. I just knew I loved him, and didn't mind getting lost in him.

So after I recovered from our steamy reconciliation, I decided to find myself again. It wasn't like I was going to move out, because neither of us wanted that, but I knew I needed to do a better job of taking care of myself. The first order of business was for me to hit the massage parlor, the nail salon, and the beauty shop, because I couldn't remember the last time I'd gotten my hair done, and pre-Damon relationship Nicky would've never missed a week of getting her hair laid. I went on a Saturday with Angie and Renee tagging along to the massage parlor and nail salon, and only Renee indulging at the beauty shop with me, since Angie was a natural hair guru who didn't let anyone but Ryan touch her hair. We met back up with

Angie later so we could all three have dinner together, ending a long day of pampering and sisterly bonding. We had so much fun, and I felt more like myself than I had in a long time when I returned home with my hair smelling good and laying on my back and neon orange polish glossing my fingernails. You couldn't tell me I wasn't looking hot!

Although I was trying to do more than be up under Damon all the time, I was disappointed when I returned home to find it empty. No Damon. And shit, if I was real about it, I was horny as hell. Well, I was always horny, but that's beside the point. Anyway, I sighed as I locked the door behind me and texted him: *I'm home. Where r u?*

Damon: *I'll be home in about an hour. Go to the bedroom.*

I frowned. Was he trying to initiate some freaky sexting, or did he just want me waiting in the bedroom for him? Either way, I was down.

Me: *K...*

I walked into the room to find a big gift box on the bed, and on top of it, a smaller gift box.

Damon: *U in the bedroom?*

Me: *Yeah. What's this? A gift? For what?*

Damon: *Damn u ask a lot of questions! Open them.*

I rolled my eyes as if he could see me and ripped into the boxes. The first held a bottle of Versace *Bright Crystal* perfume. The bottle was so pretty, I almost didn't care what the perfume, which I'd never owned before, smelled like. But it smelled good, really good. In the larger box was a dress similar to one I'd seen Kim Kardashian rock the hell out of—a white, crew neck, tea length, long-sleeve bodycon dress in my favorite size, a size too small. I was going to have to grease myself to get into it, and Damon would have to peel it off of me whenever I wore it. And it wasn't cheap. I could tell. Damn, Damon had dropped some of that *Foreign Son* money on me!

Me: *OMG! I love it! I love both! What's the occasion?*

Damon: *I wanna take my girl out and I want her to look sexy as hell when I do it. Wrapping up some stuff with Theo for the comic. I'll be home by 10. Be ready to jet.*

Me: *K. Thanks, baby!*

Damon: *Nah, Ima be thanking u when I see u in it. Love u.*

Me: *Love u 2.*

Damon: *But I'm not playing. Be ready Nick!*

Me: *I will! Dang!*

So…I wasn't ready when he made it home, but he knew I wouldn't be, so whatever.

He took me to Club Trio, my favorite, most ratchet night club. It sold cheap liquor and held weekly twerking contests. You know, the type of club that allows entry for one guy for every ten girls—an intense ho' training ground. It was the one place in Romey where you could let your hair down and flat-foot kick it without worrying about being judged, and I loved it. Back in the day, I *stayed* up in Club Trio. And tonight, I was in the spot with my guy, the sexiest man in the building. That was proven by the gawks he got from the overflow of women. But I told myself I wouldn't act a fool. He was mine and he was with me, and if I didn't know anything else, I knew he loved him some Nicole Strickland.

We found a table, ordered drinks from a waitress in a tight black romper (I had never seen a romper so tight before in my life), and just enjoyed the atmosphere. The place was packed, and the DJ was killing it with a good mixture of old school and current hip hop. I bounced in my seat and Damon was chill, nodding to the music while nursing his beer. This wasn't really his scene, but he knew it was mine, and he knew I hadn't been to a club since before we got together. So I appreciated him for bringing me.

"Wanna dance?" he asked.

"Yeah. You wanna dance?" I asked.

He tilted his head to the side and lifted an eyebrow. "I damn sure ain't letting you dance with no one else." Standing from his seat looking gorgeous in a black *Fullmetal Alchemist Brotherhood* t-shirt, jeans, black Chucks, and a vintage Oakland Raiders baseball cap, he reached for my hand. "Come on."

We danced to a Cardi B song. Well, I danced and Damon just stood there cool as hell, grinning and grabbing my hips from time to time, but I could tell he was enjoying the show I put on for him in that tight dress. We drank and danced a little more, and the few guys who approached our table didn't hit on me, but rather gave Damon dap and said things like, "This you?" or "Man, she bad," while nodding toward me. Damon would grin, nod, and say, "Yeah, all me."

After one of the guys left, Damon leaned across the table, and said, "I'ma tear your little sexy ass up when we get home."

And that's when I realized something. While Travis didn't like my attention-seeking behavior, Damon loved it. He liked my ho-ish way of dressing, the way I twerked on him on the dancefloor, the attention I got from other men as long as all they did was look. He accepted me for who I was, every bit of me. Hell, it turned him on for other men to want me, because he knew they could never have me. And the fact that it turned him on turned *me* on, made me once again feel like he saw me as a prize, and by the time he was ready to leave, I was close to overheating. After I made a quick trip to the ladies' room, we headed to the car, and before Damon could get in the driver's seat good, I was yanking on his belt, trying to open it, my breathing so loud I was sure I was going to fog up the windows.

We worked together to get his pants open and down, and with much effort, I pulled my tight-ass dress up around my waist and straddled him as he let the seat back, giving me room to move freely.

"You just determined to screw me in this car, huh?" he asked.

"Uh-huh."

He reached between my thighs. "No panties?"

I leaned in and nipped his neck. "Nope."

"Shit," he murmured, as he gripped my ass.

As I took my hand to guide him inside me, he said, "You gonna get us arrested."

I smiled, but it quickly disappeared as I eased down onto him with a moan.

He bit his bottom lip and closed his eyes, his brow furrowed as I grabbed the headrest, buried my face in his neck, and slid up and down his erection.

"Damn, Nick!" He raised his head and captured my mouth, his tongue searching for mine, sending me to another plane of arousal. He used his hands to orchestrate my movements, making me ride him faster and faster, our breathing labored as we kissed, broke apart, and kissed again.

"Oh, shit!" I yelled. "Damn, baby!" He felt indescribably good, like something from a really nasty dream.

He tightened his grip on my butt as he thrusted upward, filling me beyond capacity and hitting my spot repeatedly until pleasure swarmed me, collected in my core, and then erupted, causing me to buck and jerk violently in his lap. "Ahhhhhh!" I screamed. "Damon!"

His eyes were glued to me as he thrusted two more times before throwing his head back with his mouth hung open, emptying himself into me. I collapsed onto him, my head against his as his heaving breaths disturbed my hair.

Once we'd both settled down, he said, "And I'ma still tear your little sexy ass up when we get home."

*****

The place was nice. And when I say nice, I mean posh, expensive, decadent. We were at the Southside Strips launch party being held at an upscale LA club appropriately named The Launch Pad. The place was huge, gorgeous, and Karyn McNooner had reserved the entire club for the party. Champagne flowed liberally, fancy hors d'oeuvres were served, and everyone in attendance was friendly, especially Karyn McNooner, who seemed very fond of Damon. Petite, beautiful, stylish, appearing much younger than her forty-five years Karyn McNooner stayed in Damon's face, grinning and clutching his arm as she introduced him to some of everybody. Damon never released my hand, keeping me at his side the entire evening. There was no doubt in my mind that he held no interest in her, and shit, she was technically his boss, so I didn't trip. I'm not *that* big of a fool. And besides, it was Damon's night, his and Theo's, and they deserved to be celebrated sans drama, because *Foreign Son* was nothing short of genius work from both of them. I was full to the brim with pride for my man and happy to be on his arm, right where he wanted me, right where I belonged. We danced, drank, ate, kissed, even fondled a little bit, and had a wonderful time. But make no mistake, I kept my eyes on Karyn McNooner and took note of her fondness for *my* man.

33

Nicole

I knew Damon was talented and quick-witted. I knew he was smart, passionate, and dedicated to whatever he put his mind to, including me. I knew if *Foreign Son* got the attention of the right person, it would take off. I knew, was positive even when we were kids, that he'd be successful one day. And I was right. *Foreign Son*, bolstered by Theo's beautiful artwork and Damon's compelling story about a black expat teen trying to find his footing in an unknown land, seemed to resonate with the masses. People loved it! Talks of an animated TV series materialized quickly. Requests for interviews and Comic-Con appearances multiplied. Theo and Damon were even asked to appear on *The Today Show!*

In a few weeks' time, Damon and Theo signed a contract to create another comic, one I didn't even know he'd been developing, about the adventures of two best friends—a feisty African American girl who was smart and complex, who befriends a geeky little African American boy, quickly becoming his protector. The name of the comic was *Nick and Dame*. When he showed me a rough draft of the first chapter, I cried like a newborn baby. There we were, me and him as kids, immortalized in Theo's artwork and framed by Damon's words. And after I cried, I screwed him until both of us passed out.

McNooner loved the premise of *Nick and Dame* and quickly cut Damon and Theo another check, another huge check. Shit, a *huger* check. I was excited and proud but not terribly surprised, because I knew his potential for greatness long before he did. What did surprise me was the fame that surrounded Damon that had nothing to do with his work. Fairly quickly, Damon went from being touted as the creative mind behind *Foreign Son*, to the sexy comic book guy. His social media following exploded. Interviews veered off the path with questions about his love life—which he answered truthfully by saying he was in a relationship. But that did nothing to halt the rampant thirst of the droves of women who commented on his posts and DM'd him. I got it. I mean, shit, Damon was sexy as hell, an anomaly in the world of comic lovers—tall, brown, fine, and tatted, with a smile that could make virtually any coochie cream. Hell, the thought of him alone kept me moist. Still, I'd be lying if their reaction to him didn't piss me off, but what could I do? There were too many of them. I couldn't whoop all their asses. There were so many women after him, I couldn't keep up with the DMs. So, I did something that was totally out of character for me. I ignored them and just let it go. He was mine even before he was mine. His connection to me kept him from loving another woman even when we were apart for years. We were bonded in a divine way. Hell, *we* couldn't even break us apart, so I knew those women were powerless to hurt us.

I was good. That is, as long as no one stepped to him in my presence. I couldn't be responsible for how I'd react if a bitch tried to get to him in my face.

Just saying.

Damon

"Move to LA?" Nicky's eyes were wide with some emotion I couldn't identify—fear? Anxiety? Whatever it was, it was out of character for her. The only time she showed fear was when it involved her heart, and even then, she wasn't that transparent about it.

"Yeah, baby. All this traveling is messing with me, and I don't think it's gonna slow down anytime soon. At least I hope it doesn't."

She nodded. "Uh…yeah. It's been h-hard. The traveling, I mean. But LA? That's a big leap from Romey. You sure you're ready for that?"

I shrugged. "Yeah. It's not like all I know is Romey. I've been around, baby, and at least I can afford it now. Got plenty of money in the bank, and Karyn offered me a job with Southside Strips. A full-time position as a content curator or something like that."

"Karyn? When'd you start calling her that instead of McNooner?"

I frowned. "I don't know. Anyway, I'll be searching for other strips for the site. The pay is crazy good and the work is easy, so I couldn't turn it down. With that and everything I'm having to do for *Foreign Son*, and soon, *Nick and Dame*, I think it makes sense to just move out there. Doesn't have to be permanent, but I feel like it's a move I need to make right now."

We were sitting on the couch in our living room, her eyes now searching the room as if she was deciding what to say next. Finally, she said, "Everything is changing and I don't know how I feel about it." Then her eyes met mine. "You're changing, becoming famous, moving away. Where does that leave me? What am I supposed to do here without you?"

My eyes widened as I stared at her like she'd lost her mind. "You think I'm moving without you?"

With a furrowed brow and upturned palms, she said, "You said you were 'seriously thinking about' moving, then gave me all the reasons why. You never mentioned me going with you."

"Shit, that goes without saying! I'm not leaving you here, Nick. What the hell would I do without you? You're my muse, my-my *everything*. Of course your ass is moving with me!"

She tried not to smile, but I could see her lips twitching. "So we're moving to LA? *I'm* moving to LA?"

"Your ass ain't staying here for me to have to kill a motherfucker."

She grinned. "LA. Wow…wait until I tell my sisters." She frowned. "My sisters…we'll come back to visit, right? And Renee's having the new baby in a few months. I have to come back for that, and my mom. I have to visit my mom…" Her voice trailed off as her eyes fell to the floor.

I reached for her hands, tightly grasping them in mine. "Yeah, baby. We'll come back whenever you want to. Theo and Onika are moving to LA, too, but I got my parents to visit now, since we're halfway getting along these days."

"I still can't believe that, although I'm thrilled about it," she mumbled.

"Hell, I can't believe it, either. But listen, your family can come visit us, too. I'm not tryna separate you from them, just tryna do what makes sense."

She nodded and sighed. "Okay. Let's do this, then."

"You sure? You're really okay with it?"

"Dame, as long as we're together, I'm okay with just about anything."

34

Nicole

"So you're quitting? You're not going to be a midwife anymore?" I asked, before shoving a spoonful of Angie's banana pudding into my mouth.

Renee smiled at Little Zo as he toddled into the kitchen. Reaching for him and pulling him into her lap, she said, "For now. Little Man here is ten months old now, and I still can't see myself leaving him to go to work in the foreseeable future; plus, I'm due to have baby number two in a couple of months. I'll have my hands full. And honestly, I don't miss it. Not at all. I'm actually thinking about selling my half of the clinic to Cass, but we'll see."

"I can't believe you're having another boy!" Angie gushed.

"This'll be Zo's fifth son. I swear that's all he makes!" Renee said.

With a frown, I asked, "I thought he had a daughter, too?"

Renee gave me a smirk. "An *alleged* daughter. I actually met her at a book event we attended in Chicago a few months before Little Zo was born. Child, if her daddy ain't white…"

I laughed. "Oh, yeah. I forgot you had doubts."

"I do. But Zo still claims her, so I keep my mouth shut. His heart is just too big."

"Yours, too. You guys were made for each other," Angie said.

"Yeah." Little Zo wiggled out of her lap and left the kitchen. "Incoming, Zo!" she shouted.

"I got him!" Zo yelled in response.

"It's a wonder y'all don't lose that baby in this big-ass house," I observed.

"It's a struggle. Zo wants to hire a nanny to help out, but both our mothers help us, so I think it's an unnecessary expense." Renee said.

I stared at Renee for a second, and said, "You are crazy as hell. I'd be all over that nanny offer."

Renee rolled her eyes. "Anyway, are you excited about moving to LA? Man, I'm gonna miss your loony ass!"

"Oh, me too! Where will I get my doses of crazy from with you gone?" Angie asked.

This was our last girls' night before Damon and I moved. I guess it was a guys' night, too, since our men were hanging out in the living room. Damon and I had had an awkward, but calm, dinner with his parents earlier that week, and shortly after that, a dinner with my parents during which I'd cried all in my plate of food. I was fighting not to get emotional tonight.

I sighed. "Um, we all have phones, *duh*."

Angie smirked at me.

"Okay...so, I'll miss you guys, too. But I think I'm ready. I want to support Damon in any way I can. The traveling back and forth was getting to him, and now that he has an actual job at Southside Strips, the move makes sense." Then I rolled my eyes at Angie. "And I'm not crazy or loony, you skanches."

"Crazy people never think they're crazy." Angie shrugged. "Go figure."

I wrinkled my nose at her before dipping my finger in my glass of water and flicking it at her.

"Stop! Always trying to throw shit at me!" Angie yelled through a giggle.

I smiled. "Tryna be like you!"

We both laughed.

"But hey," I said, "we're coming back to visit. And you all have to come see us." My voice cracked a little. I'd lived in Romey my entire life. Had never lived away from my family. This was hard, but I knew it was the right thing to do. I loved Damon and had his back no matter what. I took care of him and supported him. It was what I'd always done. It was my role in our relationship, and I was fine with that.

Both my sisters stood from their chairs and hugged me, reassuring me we'd all stay in touch.

The doorbell rang, breaking into our moment, then Zo yelled, "I got it, baby!"

A second or so later, we were all in our seats wiping tears and laughing at our emotional selves when a loud wailing sound filled the humongous house.

"What in the world?" Renee murmured, as she shot out of her chair.

Me and Angie were close on her heels as she left the kitchen and entered the living room. We all halted our steps at the sight before us—our father shirtless in an open robe, brown dress pants and black house slippers, slumped against a bewildered-looking Zo, crying his eyes out.

*****

"She put me out!" Daddy howled, his breaths coming in short spurts as he fought to control his emotions. Everyone had migrated to the kitchen, and we all looked confused as hell.

"Who? Mama?" Angie asked.

He nodded vigorously. "She-she put me out againnnn. Oh, Lord! I'm gonna die this time! I need my Lisa! I want my Lisa! Lisaaaaaa!"

Renee and Angie and I looked at each other, and I mouthed, "Should we call Mama?"

My sisters both shrugged in response.

"Uh, Pops, what happened? I mean, did y'all have a fight?" Zo asked.

Daddy's head snapped in Zo's direction. "Can I hold my little buddy? I need to hold my little buddy."

Zo pulled my now-sleeping nephew from Angie's lap and handed him to my father. Daddy hugged the baby to his body and kissed his forehead as tears streamed down his face. I'd never seen my father so distraught, so completely bereft. My heart actually ached for him, while simultaneously, I wondered how he'd fucked things up this time.

Renee left the kitchen and returned less than a minute later with some tissues she handed to Daddy. He took them and mopped his face. With a sigh, he began to speak. "One of my—" His eyes rounded the room. "—former acquaintances came by the house asking for me, a woman I haven't spoken to in years. She told your mother we were still seeing each other. She lied! I have not been with another woman since shortly after your mother kicked me out the first time, since right after I showed up at your house asking for help, baby girl." His eyes were on Angie, baby girl number two. "I don't want anyone but my Lisa. I worked hard to get her back, and all it took was a lie to ruin us this time." He started wailing again, causing Little Zo to stir. When Renee reached for her son, Daddy tightened his grip on him. "Please don't take him! I need him!"

"Daddy, you've got to calm down before you wake him up and scare him," Renee said.

He nodded, wiping his face with his hand this time.

"Uh, Daddy, if you're telling the truth, just give Mama some time. Maybe she'll be willing to talk rationally once she calms down some," I said softly.

"If I'm telling the truth? I *am* telling the truth, baby girl! I have not been seeing anyone else. Ivy lied on me!"

My head jerked toward Damon, who looked equally as shocked. Surely he didn't mean… "Ivy? Ivy, who?" I asked, leaning forward and giving Daddy my full attention.

He frowned slightly as his eyes found me. "Amato. Ivy Amato."

My mouth fell open. My first thought was: *I knew that ho' was not to be trusted!* My second thought was: *Evidently, she likes old men now—which, by the way, ew—so I don't have to worry about her coming after Damon.*

Sad, I know.

"She started trying to contact me again after seeing me at your rehearsal dinner, really ramped up her efforts after seeing me at the benefit. I told her we were not starting back up, *ever*, and she just won't take no for an answer." He shook his head and dropped his eyes.

"Daddy, she's my age!" I shrieked.

Then again, Mama had once screwed a guy who was younger than me. My parents were just…wrong.

"I know, I know," he groaned. "I've done some stupid stuff, but I've changed. I promise I have."

"Daddy, is her little girl yours?" I asked, ready to beat my daddy's ass if the answer was yes.

"No! Look, I messed up. I've done my dirt, but I only have three daughters. I only have three children, period. I made sure of that!"

Out of the corner of my eye, I could see Renee and Angie recline in their seats, both releasing relieved breaths. The doorbell rang again, and when no one moved, Ryan hopped up, advising the room that he'd answer it.

When he returned, my mother was with him. Before anyone could address her, she rushed over to Daddy. "Are you over here bothering our children with your foolishness?"

"I-I needed to see my little buddy," Daddy whined, almost cowering at the sight of Mama.

Wow.

"And you could've put a damn shirt on before you left!"

"You told me to get my ass out before you kicked it! Then you threatened to cut my thing off!" Daddy shrieked.

"I know that, but I would've given you time to put on a shirt, Angelo! You're over here looking crazy in front of our daughters."

He really did look crazy.

"Lisa, baby, she's lying! I swear to God she's lying! You've got to believe me!" he begged.

Mama sighed. "I know that little heifer was lying. She came back after you left and talked too much, said she was with you last night and I know that's a lie. I just…I could kick your ass for *ever* cheating on me, for there being a possibility of women like that coming around starting mess."

"I know, baby. I'm sorry. I'm so sorry. If you want a divorce, I'll understand. I won't fight it." The tears started up again. "I don't deserve you…I don't deserve youuuuuuu! Oh, God! Help me please! I just want my wife!"

Mama took Little Zo, receiving no resistance from Daddy, and gave him to Big Zo. Then she slid into Daddy's lap, wrapped her arms around him, and said, "I'm not divorcing you, Angelo. But I *am* going to punish you."

Daddy stopped crying almost instantly, his eyes lighting up as he gazed at Mama. "What you gonna do? Spank me?" He smiled.

Mama tilted her head to the side. "That's what you want me to do?"

Daddy's ass started giggling like a teenage girl. My stomach gurgled in response.

"I'll even use one of my wooden spoons. You'd like that, huh?"

Mama's voice was low but not low enough.

"Nope. That's it. I'm out of here," Renee said, hopping to her feet, belly and all, and ambling out of the kitchen. She was followed by a medley of murmurs in agreement as the rest of us cleared out of the kitchen, leaving Mama and Daddy alone.

The only thought in my head was: *double ew.*

35

Nicole

Our LA home was a property belonging to one of Karyn McNooner's close friends, a gorgeous loft apartment, a small but luxurious space located in a Hollywood high rise that boasted half-wall windows that spanned the entire width of the place, giving a breathtaking view of the city.

The friend owned a home in New York, where he spent the bulk of his time, freeing up the apartment—which Damon would only say he was paying a reasonable price for, but I knew better—for us to live in. It held sleek, expensive modern furniture with beautiful abstract artwork on the stark white walls, and we spent every night our first couple of weeks living there christening every inch of the place, including the huge bathroom and its glass-enclosed shower.

I continued to work from home. NLS still had the same clients, my family members, Genesis Birthing Center, and Damon, because I honestly no longer cared about expanding the company. Expansion would necessitate hiring help, something I was unwilling to tackle, since I was already dealing with having moved all the way across the country from my family and the only home I'd ever known, not to mention the separation anxiety I was experiencing with Damon working outside our home. I missed him from the time he left in the morning to the time he made it back. Could do little else but think about him in between, and it didn't help that he worked for and with Karyn McNooner, who, if my ho' senses were correct, had the hots for him. I was feeling insecure like a motherfucker.

My t-shirt, jeans, and Chucks-wearing man was becoming a real adult, a businessman, and I was having one hell of a time adjusting.

I managed to get my work done, and I was good at it. My efforts had spawned growing followings for all my clients, including Damon, but I was pretty much on autopilot. I'd been managing their social media accounts for months, so it required little to no thought for me to get my tasks done. The same wouldn't be true if I took on new clients.

So for about the first month of us living in LA, I was stuck in this weird limbo, between being with Damon and being alone…and lonely. With him gone all day, sometimes working late hours, I felt extreme loneliness. And when I had to attend events with him, the same feelings would creep up on me, because those events were business-related. He was not totally mine then, either. Sure, he showered me with the gifts he could now afford—purses, perfume, dresses, trips to spas, lingerie—but as much as I loved being pampered and living the fantasy life I'd dreamt of for years, I missed living in my sister's duplex, sitting beside him on the sofa as we both worked to make ends meet. I missed the bond we shared as we struggled to fuel our dreams. I missed lazy days of sex, watching him play video games, and laughter.

I missed Damon.

*****

Onika was loud, silly, and ghetto as hell, all reasons I loved hanging around her. Well, I also loved playing with little Tia, who was getting bigger by the day. Onika had picked me up so that I could go shopping with her, and I was glad she'd driven, because that damn LA traffic made me nervous as hell. Damon had had both our cars shipped to us, but I usually caught an Uber when I wanted to explore the city.

Onika loved buying make-up and had a knack for finding stores that sold ho' clothes—a chick after my own heart. Then again, she did have cousins who lived in LA, so I was sure they were pointing her in the right direction when it came to shopping. The stuff in the store we visited that day was cheap, but some of it was cute, so I bought a couple of pieces just because. When I needed something for one of the many events Damon was invited to that seemed to pop up at least once a week, I'd opt for something of better quality. What I bought with Onika would work for a night at the club.

As I climbed out of her Tahoe in front of my building, she gave me a big smile and a wave as I thanked her again for driving.

"Ain't nothing, girl. Just glad you came with me so I wouldn't be alone with Tia's spoiled ass."

I laughed. "You need to leave my girl alone."

She rolled her eyes. "Whatever, See you later, Nicky."

"Bye." As she waved again, I tried to act like I didn't notice the rock Theo had put on her finger, but I was salty as hell about it. Those two argued all the time, and he still proposed.

I realized we'd only been together a few months, and that I'd just been seconds away from marrying another man, but shit, this was us.

This was Damon and Nicole. We had history. We'd been in love for decades. It wasn't like this was new. What the hell was he waiting on? Why hadn't he proposed? Was he ever going to propose? I mean, it really fucked with my head that lazy-ass, slacking-ass Theo had proposed to Onika and I had yet to receive a ring from the man who had declared I was the love of his life.

The mature thing to do would've been for me to just come on out and ask him about it. It wasn't like we'd talked about marriage or anything like that. He'd made it clear what we had was a forever thing, but did forever to him mean us just shacking up? He'd said he wanted a baby, but did he want marriage to go along with that? Yeah, I should've asked him, but in my mind, asking was akin to begging, and I couldn't bring myself to beg Damon to marry me, so I just drove myself half-crazy speculating about our future and tried to convince myself it didn't matter if he ever proposed when I knew it did. At least it mattered to me.

Times like these, I thought about calling my sisters to vent, but they were busy with their own lives. So was my mother. So I just worried in silence.

I walked inside our apartment and dropped my purse and shopping bags on the sofa before heading over to the windows to look at the city. It was nearing time for Damon to get home, and I silently hoped he wouldn't call or text saying he'd be late. If he came home on time, I had plans of jumping his bones before he got in the door good.

I let my eyes roam from the windows to the bed at the far end of the open space where my laptop sat on top of the comforter and decided to check my email, because Damon would sometimes send one instead of calling or texting. When I saw there was no email, I breathed a sigh of relief. *He would've contacted me by now. He must be coming home on time.*

I shook my head at the fact that my damn moods depended on his arrival time. I really needed to get myself together, but hell, I loved the man.

Mindlessly perusing my inbox, I damn near fell from my perch on the bed when I saw Travis's name.

What the hell?

I let my hand hover over the screen of the laptop before tapping the line that held his email.

Hey, Nicky,

I don't have your new phone number, and I'm sure that's by design, but I need to talk to you. I'd like to apologize, and it would be nice to hear your voice. My number hasn't changed. Please call me when you get a chance.

Travis

I stared at the email for ten minutes, and then for some insane, arbitrary, stupid-ass reason, lifted from the bed to grab my phone.

*****

"Hello?" He sounded uncertain, probably wondered who was calling him from a blocked number.

"What do you want to apologize for? Trying to marry me into screwing your father?" was my response.

"Uh…that wasn't my plan; it was his," Travis replied, sounding a little taken aback, but how'd he think this would go? Surely he wasn't expecting a little benign, pleasant chit-chat.

"A plan your ass was going along with."

"No, I wasn't."

"Well, I sure as hell didn't hear you denying it at Dukas."

He sighed into the phone. "I'm not good at directly defying my father, but I would never have let him touch you, Nicky."

"Yeah, well, I don't believe you."

"I don't blame you for being skeptical. But I do care about you. I wouldn't have let it get that far."

"Get that far? What the hell does that mean? How far would you have let it get? To him touching me? Almost, but not quite, screwing me? I mean, was I gonna have to cut off his hand or his dick? Huh?!"

"What I meant—I wouldn't have let him come near you, Nicky." He was whining. He was actually whining into the phone.

"Your father is a disgusting, nasty, old-ass predator. And you're not much better than him. He said he chose me for you like I was a damn puppy or something, and you let him.

"He approved you. There's a difference."

"You mother—"

"He got arrested last night. My mother bailed him out this morning."

My eyes almost popped out of my head. "What?! Who'd he

molest?"

"He didn't molest *anyone*. He got caught in his car with his mistress's head in his lap, and there was marijuana in the car."

"What?!"

"It's in all the papers and online. He's a federal judge, so it's big news. Embarrassingly big news."

I thought back to when Travis was worried about my way of dressing embarrassing him. I bet he wished that was the only thing he had to worry about now.

"Guess I just made your day, huh?" he asked, breaking into my thoughts.

"Well, I'm not planning on popping any corks, but I won't be losing any sleep over it, either."

"Yeah, well, the only good thing to come out of this is his mistress was arrested, too. He's been seeing that woman for years, since I was a baby. He has a son with her. I hate her…"

I rolled my eyes, finding it hard to conjure up an ounce of sympathy for him and his family drama. "I bet you do."

"But nothing will come of this. He'll probably bury it under a rug and be back at it with her soon. I hope he loses his job…"

"Uh, yeah."

Silence.

"Um, Travis, I should probably go now…"

"Damon's on his way home?" It was more of a statement than a question.

I held the phone.

"I'm sure you wouldn't have called me if he was with you right now. He's, uh...very territorial with you. I can tell."

"He loves me."

"And you love him?"

Fuck it. Why lie? "Yes, I do. Have for a long time."

"Are you happy?"

I hesitated. Was I happy? Finally, I said, "Yes, I am."

"Good."

More silence.

"Um, I guess...bye, Nicky. Thanks for calling. It was good to hear your voice."

"Bye, Travis."

I pulled the phone from my ear and kind of just stared into space, trying to process my conversation with Travis. When a text from Damon came through, it startled me.

It read: *Get ready.*

Included in the text was a YouTube link that I quickly clicked on. My ass was grinning from ear to ear when *OTW* by DJ Luke Nasty began to play. I hopped my butt up from that bed and raced into the shower.

"Damn, baby!" Damon moaned.

I smiled. "I know, right? It's good, huh? Got the recipe from Pinterest. Who knew I could cook?"

"Shit, I have no doubt you can do anything you put your mind to. That brain of yours is incredible."

I loved when he said stuff like that, but never really knew how to respond to it, so I took another bite of my maple salmon, and said, "I really did cook the shit out of this, didn't I?"

Damon grinned. "Yeah, Nick, you did."

We were at the small kitchen table half-naked, enjoying dinner together, both sated from some bomb-ass sex.

"I can't believe your scared-to-drive ass went grocery shopping, though," Damon quipped.

"Oh, I had them delivered before Onika picked me up. I ain't driving in this traffic out here."

He chuckled and pointed his fork at me. "I almost forgot. Aunt Monda got arrested last night. Theo had to wire some money to bail her out."

My eyes widened. "What?! Is she selling weed again or something? I thought she stopped doing that years ago."

He shook his head. "No, get this, she was arrested for public sex or some shit like that, plus possession of a controlled substance."

I damn near dropped my fork, but didn't say a word.

"And guess who she got arrested with?"

Not—

"H-who?"

"Judge McClure."

I still couldn't speak. Hell, I didn't want to give away the fact that I already knew about his arrest or how I'd come across the information. I'd be damned if I told Damon I'd called Travis. Hell, no!

With raised eyebrows, he said, "Crazy, right?"

I nodded. "That really *is* crazy."

"Man, Theo was so pissed, he started talking all over himself, told me the judge is his dad. I think he hates him more than you do."

"Theo is Travis's brother?" That fact was mind-boggling to me. Could they be any more different?

Damon nodded as he forked up more salmon. "Yeah, ain't that some shit?"

That truly *was* some shit.

Damn!

36

Damon

Something was off.

Nicky had been too quiet lately, reserved even.

Nicky Strickland—*reserved.*

Hell, if we weren't still having sex virtually every second we were together, I'd be in a panic. We'd been in LA for nearly two months and were getting ready to return to Romey for the first time since the move, because Renee's baby was due in a week or so. I had to figure out what was going on before we left. I didn't want Nicky to get to Romey and decide she wanted to stay. We were going to have one hell of a fight if she did, because that shit was *not* happening.

I finally decided to come on out and ask her what was going on after she showed her ass at Karyn McNooner's birthday party, a party packed with celebrities. I thought Nicky would be thrilled about being there, since she loved clubbing and celebrity-watching. But instead, she stayed in her seat the whole night sulking, didn't dance, and rolled her eyes every time they landed on Karyn. She kept mumbling stuff under her breath, and when different people—famous people—came to me, congratulating me on the monster success of both *Foreign Son* and *Nick and Dame*, she would smirk or roll her eyes dramatically. Now, that shit hurt my feelings. *Nick and*

Dame was for her. In my mind, it was more of a love letter than anything, a chronicling of the most important relationship in my life, and there she sat, acting like it didn't mean anything to her.

We ended up leaving early, and once in the car outside the club, I asked, "The hell is wrong with your ass tonight?"

She rolled her eyes a-damn-gain.

"Keep rolling them motherfuckers and I swear…"

There she went smirking once again. "You swear what? You ain't gon' do shit but screw me. That's all you do with me anyway!"

I turned in my seat to fully face this lunatic I was hopelessly in love with. "And that's a problem? Since when?"

"No, Damon, *you're* a problem!"

"What the hell does that mean?!"

"It means you're never-the-hell home! All you do is work, and when you're not working, you're dragging me to some bullshit-ass party or something! And are you fucking Karyn McNooner? I can tell she likes you."

"Nick, are you on crack? What kind of shit is that to ask me?"

"Are you?!"

My mouth hung open for a second. "Hell-no I'm not fucking her! Have you lost your mind?! She's my boss and a mentor. Got-damn, Nick! Really? I mean, even if she *does* like me, that means I gotta be fucking her? Like my ass is brainless or something? A damn pussy drone? Shit, how many niggas want you? Are you screwing them?"

"No."

"Exactly. And believe me, I got more than I can handle with just you."

"Then why are you always working and stuff? You're barely ever home!"

"For the same reason I worked all the time back in Romey. For you! The job, moving out here? All of that is for you! I'm tryna take care of your ass!"

I could tell she'd been prepared to shoot something back at me, but wasn't expecting me to say what I said, so she closed her mouth, frowned, and softly said, "W-what?"

I nodded. "Yeah, crazy-ass woman, I took this job and have been working my ass off for you! Hell, you know I don't like working real jobs, but I know how you grew up and I realize you picked Paul Robinette because of his money. I'm trying to give you what you want. Damn!"

Nicky's back fell against the passenger's seat of my car. "Damon…I'm sorry if I gave you the impression that I wanted you to be rich or something…"

I shook my head. "No, you didn't just give me the impression, you said you wanted a man with money. You told me that years ago. Then you admitted that's why you were with old dude you were gonna marry."

"You just refuse to say his name, don't you?"

"Yep."

She shook her head and turned to face me again. "Look, Damon, I-I just want *you*. I don't care if you don't have a damn penny to your name. I couldn't care less about how many commas and zeros are in your bank account. Not anymore. I just want you, Damon. I-I miss you." I watched the first tear trickle down her cheek.

I reached over and wiped her face. "You don't like the gifts? The apartment? None of it."

"The apartment? That was for me, too?"

"Who else? You know I don't care about shit like that."

She was on me in seconds flat, hugging me tightly across the center console. "Oh, Damon! You were just—"

"Trying to make you happy, Nick. That's all," I said, as I closed my eyes and wrapped my arms around her.

"But you were already doing that. Just being with you makes me happy. Don't get me wrong, I love the gifts, like really, really love them, but I need more of you. I'm not saying you have to quit your job, because I can tell you actually like it."

"I really do, baby."

"Yeah, I don't think you'd spend that much time there if you hated it, even for me. So I want you to keep working there, because I want you to do what makes you happy, but can you stop working late? And can we go to fewer parties and let it just be us together at home more often?" She released me and looked me in the eye.

I nodded. "Yeah, baby. Anything you want. If it'll mean I get my Nick back, I'll do anything."

She smiled widely and kissed me before settling in her seat again.

"Is that it? Anything else bothering you?" I asked.

Her smile faltered, and her gaze shifted to the windshield. "No."

"You're lying. Just tell me."

She shook her head. "Nothing else is wrong."

"Nick, you know I can see through your ass."

"Fine." She faced me again. "What do you see in our future?"

I shrugged. "More of this, us being together, having kids when you're ready, traveling, just being happy."

She sighed. "Okay."

"You don't want that?"

"Yes, but…"

"What?"

"Nothing."

"Nick, what is it? Is there something more you want? Did I answer wrong?"

"Let's just go, Damon."

"No, tell me—"

"WHY DON'T YOU WANT TO MARRY ME?!"

I jumped at the volume of her voice, but kept my cool as I said, "Is that all?"

"Is that all? What the hell is that supposed to mean? Theo's sorry ass already gave Onika a ring! What're you waiting for?!"

"Theo is also a serial cheater. Not a good comparison, Nick."

She closed her eyes and turned from me. "You're avoiding my question. So that must mean you *don't* wanna marry me."

"How'd you come to that conclusion? I mean, that's a stretch, Nick."

"Well, do you?!"

I sighed. "Nick—"

"Don't *Nick* me! Answer me!"

"You know what? Fuck it!" I opened the glove compartment, reached inside, and pulled out the small black box. Her eyes blew the hell up when she saw it.

"I was tryna wait until we got back to Romey so I could do this in front of your family, but your impatient ass just fucked that up."

"Dame, I—"

"No, be quiet and listen. Nick, you are jealous as hell—"

"I'm jealous, because I know I don't deserve you and—"

"Nick, didn't I just tell you to be quiet and listen?"

"My bad. Continue."

"You're jealous, bossy, too impulsive, downright mean sometimes, crazy most times, beautiful, sexy, smart, and I love all of that about you. I love that we've got this history between us and that our love is so volatile and unconventional. I love that we were friends before we were lovers. I love that you let your walls down and gave me a second chance, a *real* chance to be your man. But most of all, I love how you love me and have always taken care of me. I've been working like a mad man to provide for you, because I've always felt like our relationship was lopsided. I always felt like you gave me more than I gave you."

She shook her head as tears raced down her cheeks. "That's not true. You were my only friend, Dame. You listened to the stupid stuff I'd tell you back when I thought I was so smart. You were my escape, the way I coped when my doting father started being an absent one. You loved me unconditionally. And even now, you love me like no one else. You don't hold my past against me. You've never used it as leverage in an argument when I know I would've. You accepted me even after the Travis bullshit and I know I hurt you—"

"I was speaking, Nick. How many times I gotta tell you to be quiet?" She was about to make me cry, and I wasn't trying to go out like that.

"Okay, I'm sorry," she almost whispered. "Go ahead."

"You cared about me when I was unattractive as hell—"

"No, you weren't—"

"Nick, damn! Let me finish!"

"Okay! Shit! You ain't gotta yell!"

I blew out a breath. "Man…I'm nervous as hell over here."

She reached over and traced the scar on my forehead with her thumb. "Why? We're just us. Nick and Dame."

I closed my eyes, trying to ignore the fact that her messing with my scar was turning me on and breaking my concentration. "I know…"

"Then just ask me, baby."

Opening my eyes and fixing them on her, I thought, *screw it.* "Will you marry me, Nick?"

"Hell, yes. Right now. Today. Yesterday. Last year. Tomorrow. Yes, I will marry your fine ass!"

My chest swelled up as I grabbed her at the back of the neck and stuck my tongue down her throat. By then, my ass was crying, but I didn't care. After all those years of wanting her, she was going to be mine—legally and spiritually.

I ended the kiss, opened the box, and slid the ring on her finger, grinning as she stared down at it with her mouth hung open.

"Damon! It's beautiful!"

Before I could respond, her mouth was on mine, and we kissed so long and savagely, I almost passed the hell out. When I finally backed away from her, we were both breathing hard. "Get that Wonder Woman costume ready, baby. And call your mom to reserve True Vine. We're doing this as soon as we get to Romey," I said.

"Nope." She shook her head.

Aw, hell. "What? Nick, I'm not waiting to plan some big wedding. Screw that. We gotta do this as soon as we can. I've waited long enough."

"Can I speak now?"

I nodded, hoping she wasn't on some bullshit.

"First of all, you've got to stop holding me to stuff I said as a kid. I like Wonder Woman and all—less now, because I hated that new movie—but I'm not getting married in a costume. I'm too grown for that now. Second, I'm not waiting until we go to Romey to get married. You're taking my pregnant ass to the courthouse in the morning. Call McNooner and tell her you need a few days off, because after we leave the courthouse, I'ma close you up in that apartment and screw you until my coochie locks up multiple times."

"Did you—Nick, you're—are you—"

"Pregnant. About two months now." She stared at me, obviously waiting for a reaction.

"I thought-I thought you were going to wait until you were ready."

"I *am* ready. I decided I was ready after I realized you wanted a baby, so I stopped taking my pills. I didn't tell you because I wasn't sure it would happen, but it did happen. Are you...are you okay with this?" she asked timidly, a word I'd rarely associated with her.

I stared at her for a second before saying, "I love you so much.

I've always loved you so much, to the point that the shit is actually painful sometimes. It's probably unhealthy to love a person the way I love you, and now…now? Nick, I…" My voice broke and I took a deep breath, placing my hand on her flat stomach. "Thank you for this, baby. Thank you so much."

She reached over and hugged me again as my mind raced.

I pulled away from her. "Are you—is everything okay?"

She smiled and nodded. "Everything is perfect, according to the doctor I saw."

"Good—Wait. No more rough sex, then, right? How you let me do all that shit last night?!"

"The doctor says everything will be fine as long as we don't go overboard."

"You sure?"

"Yeah. Now take me home and do some more of what you did last night."

I grinned. "I love the shit out of you, Nicole Strickland. You know that?"

"Mm-hmm, and I love the fuck out of you, Damon Davis."

As I started the car, I asked, "Hey, if it's a boy, can we name him T'Challa?"

"Hell, no."

37

Nicole

Two years later…

"I'm so glad you could join us today. I know you're a busy man. I can see you have your hands full right now," the interviewer said, with a bright smile spread across her face.

Damon grinned and nodded as he bounced his namesake—who was a carbon copy of me—in his lap. "Yeah, he's a little attached to me, aren't you, big boy?"

Damon Jr. smiled up at his daddy and giggled while clumsily clapping his chubby little hands.

"Well," Gail, the interviewer, continued, "let's talk about how you juggle all the roles you play in your life. You're Karyn McNooner's right hand man, creator and author of two successful comic strips along with your partner, Theo Winters, you're gearing up for the premiere of the *Nick and Dame* animated series on Netflix, the *Foreign Son* animated film was a wild success, and I hear you're launching your own comic site, and all of that on top of being a husband and a father. How do you manage it all?"

Damon shrugged. "What can I say? I'm just that guy, you know?"

Gail threw her head back and laughed hard, *too* hard. She was obviously attracted to Damon, but shit, most women were. Now I fully understood what Angie went through with Ryan, only on a much larger scale. Damon was world famous now—and rich. *Hallelujah!* His *Fake for Bae* days were far behind him. I'd learned to take it all in stride and to stop pulling my clown suit out all the time, because if I didn't know anything else, I knew that man loved me and that his devotion to me was exclusive despite me being, well…me.

"There goes that swag that makes the ladies swoon. The same swag that's made you tons of women's man crush every day," Gail said.

He chuckled, his eyes sweeping over to me. I just raised an eyebrow from my seat across the small room in the studio.

Yeah, bruh, bring it down a notch.

"Nah, I'm all right, but I'm not all that," he said, attempting to sound humble.

Gail laughed again. "Wow, and he's humble. My, my, my."

Okay, this bitch was laying it on a little too thick. I might've been hesitant to pull my clown suit out, but she could still get her ass kicked. Properly.

Damon shook his head. "But in all seriousness, to answer your question, I love what I do, so I don't mind staying busy. Work is really effortless for me, and as far as balancing it with my personal life, my beautiful wife keeps me in check there. She's my muse, my support system, my boss, my baby mama, my everything. Without her, none of what I've been able to accomplish would've been remotely possible. And she runs her own social media management business, too."

"She sounds like Superwoman."

He smiled. "More like Wonder Woman."

There I sat with a big, goofy-ass grin on my face, thinking about all the coochie I was going to give him after we got home, during naptime of course.

"Awww, and I hear *Nick and Dame* is based on your relationship with her? You've known each other since elementary school?"

Damon nodded. "Yep. I met my soul mate in second grade."

"Sounds like a beautiful love story."

"It is, in an unconventional way."

The interview continued for another twenty minutes before it ended and we were freed up to leave. I was glad, because I could tell Junior was getting restless and about to turn it out. This was one of the things I still disliked, him working so much and so hard, but I recognized that he enjoyed it, and he made every effort to spend as much time with his family as he could, to the point of insisting I attend every interview and event within reason with him. He even worked from home most days with Karyn's approval and was an awesome father, not to mention the best husband and provider I could ask for.

"Wanna trade?" he asked, as he leaned in to kiss me while standing our son on the floor.

"Yes!" I quickly handed a sleeping Jason to him and grabbed Junior's hand. "Thank you."

He kissed Jason's forehead as he put him on his shoulder. A tiny replica of Damon, Jason was a little taller and heavier than his fraternal twin brother, and when he slept, his dead weight was almost too much for me to handle.

"You ready for this trip?" Damon asked, as we left the studio.

"Can't wait!"

"All right, let's hit it, baby."

*****

"There they are!" Daddy gushed, rushing toward us. Although he took the time to hug me and Damon, I knew he was referring to Junior and Jason, who were his "little buddies" along with Little Zo and Renee's youngest baby boy, Clarence.

Renee appeared in the living room with a grin on her face, her huge belly announcing her presence first. Another boy. I swear, Zo *kept* her ass pregnant! "Hey, you two! I can't believe you left that big house in LA to come see us," she said.

"Aw, now, it's still a tent compared to the Higgs estate," Damon said, as he pulled her into a hug.

Renee gave him a smirk. "Whatever. So, how was your flight?"

"Good," I answered, as I hugged her and rubbed her stomach.

"Well, we're all in the kitchen, tryna let Daddy have his quality time with his boys."

We followed her into the kitchen, where Zo, Angie, Ryan, and their little bundle of joy all sat around the table. I bum-rushed Angie, snatching Little Ryan from her. He was definitely appropriately named with his little Ryan-looking self.

I smiled down at him. "Oh, he's getting so big! He's like two months now, right?"

Angie nodded. "Yep. He'll be on 'little buddy' status with Daddy in a minute. You know how Daddy does it."

I nodded. Daddy was a trip with his grandsons. As I sat beside Angie and nuzzled the baby's little neck, I asked Ryan, "She still refusing to give you more babies?"

Ryan gave me a smirk, then looked at his wife. "Yeah, your sister is petty as hell."

Angie's neck snapped toward her husband. "Petty?! I gained fifty damn pounds! I'm still struggling to get rid of twenty-five of them, my feet swelled up, my nose was gigantic, and all I wanted to do was screw and eat all the time. No, sir. I'm done."

Ryan tilted his head to the side. "So, you didn't like the screwing part? That's what you're telling me?"

Angie rolled her eyes.

I laughed. "I feel you, Angie. I'm glad I had a two-for-one, and hell, Renee is having enough kids for all three of us."

"Yeah, but this is it. I'm too old to keep popping babies out. Zo's getting a vasectomy," said Renee.

Silence from Zo.

"Right, Zo?" Renee urged.

"Uh..."

"We agreed, baby!"

"I know, but..."

Renee threw her hands up and fell into a chair. "Fine! I'm getting my tubes tied, then."

"No, I told you I don't want you getting cut on," Zo insisted.

"I'ma get on the pill, then."

"They could cause blood clots," Zo said.

"Well, we gotta do something! I'll get on the shot."

"Hell-no to that, too. I read somewhere where that can make you dry and not wanna fuck. Screw that."

"A hysterectomy," Renee countered.

"Shit, no!"

"It's *my* body, Zo."

"Since when?"

She sighed. "Condoms."

Zo raised an eyebrow. "You're allergic."

"Maybe not. We can try to be sure."

"Nope."

Renee blew out a frustrated breath. "Weren't you the one who said we were done having kids after Little Zo?"

"And weren't you the one who said you'd have another baby in a heartbeat? Shit, I'm just giving you what you want."

"Well, three is enough, so...no more sex, since we can't agree on a method of birth control."

Zo stared at her for a second, then gave her a smirk. "Yeah, right."

She glared at him. "I cannot stand your ass sometimes."

"I know. But you love me."

"And?"

I chuckled. Those two had this same argument the last time we were home. I knew there would be no end to it.

Glancing toward the counter at the food in foil pans I'd smelled upon entering the kitchen, I asked, "You cooked, Angie?"

She nodded. "Yep. All his favorites. Glad we decided to do this here. I was able to heat everything up at the same time since Zo and Renee have two ovens."

"Table already set?" I queried.

"Mama's setting it now," Renee answered.

"I can't believe none of those boys have come running in here," Angie observed.

"They love their granddaddy," said Renee.

"Humph, and he sure loves them," I added.

We laughed and talked, got caught up on each other's lives, and thirty minutes later, Mama summoned everyone to the dining room. We took our seats, and after Mama lit the candles on the cake, we began singing happy birthday to my daddy, who sat at the head of the table.

When he started crying, Zo asked, "What's wrong, Pops?"

⤷ Daddy smiled as the tears continued to race down his face. He looked around the table where he was surrounded by his family—his daughters, sons-in-law, grandsons, and his wife—and he said, "Nothing, son. Everything is right. Everything is just right."

And it was.

It really was.

38

Damon

About seventeen months earlier...

"You can do it, baby! Can't you? I think you can! Shit! I gotta calm down! You ain't even pushing ye—what the fuck is that?!" I grabbed my head and tried to control my breathing. "What are you doing to her?!"

The doctor stopped in her tracks, holding some long plastic hook-looking thing in her hand. "I'm going to break her bag of waters."

"Her what?! She got—Nick, you got a bag of waters?! Where? What the hell is a bag of waters?!"

"She's breaking my water, baby. Damon, you gotta calm down. You're making me nervous as hell right now," Nicky said. She was lying there like this was some normal shit. She was past her due date, and they had induced her labor. This shit was really happening. She was about to have a baby, *my* baby. Two babies!

Two!

Shit!

I stood there and watched the clear liquid gush from between Nicky's legs onto the towel underneath her.

"Oooooh, fuck!" I yelled.

Shit just got real.

The doctor shook her head.

"Dame, you wanna wait in the lobby?" Nicky asked calmly.

Hell, yeah! "Nah, why?"

"Because you seem to be losing your damn mind up in here."

I am! "I'm good, baby. I wanna be here for you."

The doctor left, and I took the seat next to the bed, stuck my thumb in my mouth, and started nibbling on it.

"Dame?"

I looked over at Nicky. "Yeah, baby?" I replied, thumb still in my mouth.

"Are you sure you're okay?"

I snatched my thumb from my mouth and nodded my head. "Yeah. I guess I just didn't know what to expect. I read all that stuff you gave me, but damn. This is crazy. They up in here breaking bags of water and shit. The doctor keeps sticking her hand up you every other minute. I mean, the fuck?"

"If you can't handle it, I won't be mad. I know it's a lot."

That's a damn lie. If I leave this room, I'll never live it down.

"No. You're always there for me. I'ma be here for you. I can take it. You okay? You hurting?"

"Yeah, the contractions hurt, but not that bad. I've wanted this for a long time; I can handle it. You call our families?"

"Yeah, everyone's on their way."

She sighed. "Good."

She jerked a little and at the same time, the machine that was supposed to be monitoring the babies' heartbeats made a loud sound.

I jumped up. "What is it?! What was that?! Why you looking like that?! Shit! What's happening?!"

"Nothing. One or both of them kicked…really hard."

"Oh…"

"Damon—"

I fell back in my seat, started bouncing my knee and gnawing on my other thumbnail. "I'm good, Nick. I'm good."

"Okay…"

After six hours of me damn near shitting on myself, it was finally time for Nicky to push. I stood there and held her hand. She had requested a mirror be placed overhead so she could see the babies as she pushed them out, which meant I could see it, too.

I. Could. See. It. Too.

Got. Damn.

That was something I was definitely not ready for.

"Come on, baby!" I yelled, as she strained, her face tight as she groaned with each push. "You can do it!" I coached, my knees knocking against each other. I had no doubt she'd make it like a trooper. I wasn't so sure about myself, though.

Junior was the first to be born. I managed to hold it together even when I saw his hairy little head begin to poke out. I watched the doctor pull on him, finally tugging him from Nicky's body. That's when I felt the tears on my face. I bent over to kiss her, was in the middle of thanking her when I felt my knees give completely out on me and my big ass hit the floor.

Yeah, I fucking fainted.

I didn't get to witness Jason's delivery, because I was *still* knocked out. And I looked dazed in all the pictures of me holding them right after they were born.

Ryan and Zo ragged on my ass for a year for passing out. But whatever. It was still one of the happiest days of my life, second only to that day in the second grade when I first met Nicole Strickland. Nothing will ever beat that.

I loved that crazy-ass woman, the mother of my sons—forever. And ever…

And ever.

Thank you sooooo much for reading the Strickland Sisters series! I loved writing these stories and spending time with these characters. Shoot, I actually miss them!

I appreciate the overwhelming support from readers, and hope you will enjoy my next project. Stay tuned!

XOXO,

Alex

A southern girl at heart, Alexandria House has an affinity for a good banana pudding, Neo Soul music, and tall black men in suits. When this fashionista is not shopping, she's writing steamy stories about real black love.

Connect with Alexandria!
Email: msalexhouse@gmail.com
Website: http://www.msalexhouse.com/
Newsletter: http://eepurl.com/cOUVg5
Blog: http://msalexhouse.blogspot.com/
Facebook: Alexandria House
Instagram: @msalexhouse
Twitter: @mzalexhouse

Also by Alexandria House:

The Strickland Sisters Series:

Stay with Me

Believe in Me

The Love After Series:

Higher Love

Made to Love

Real Love

Made in the USA
Columbia, SC
27 December 2024